Dreamers

(Dreamers Series – Book 1)

By Neutralus

Dreamers
Dreamers Series Book 1

First Edition

Paperback ISBN: 978-1-7369684-0-6
Ebook ISBN: 978-1-7369684-1-3
Hardcover ISBN: 978-1-7369684-2-0

Published by McKenzie Quinn Publishing, LLC
Requests to publish work from this book should be sent
to: tqueen@mckenziequinnpublishing.com
Editor Stephanie Mojica -
info@gettheirattentionnow.com

Cover Design by Diana Savu
Facebook/Instagram: Devdiaart
Contact me: devdia.art@gmail.com

www.mckenziequinnpublishing.com

To all the dreamers.

Contents

Prologue 1

Chapter 1 – Dreamers..13

Chapter 2 – Late Arrival.......................................25

Chapter 3 – Trouble in Paradise 35

Chapter 4 – Round Two...45

Chapter 5 – Recharging 63

Chapter 6 – The Heist 73

Chapter 7 – Breaking & Entering 81

Chapter 8 – Free Falling.....................................105

Chapter 9 – Dazed and Confused 123

Chapter 10 – Arrival...133

Chapter 11 – The Game.......................................151

Chapter 12 – School's Out...................................165

Chapter 13 – To Boldly Go...................................187

Chapter 14 – Rising into the Black 205

Chapter 15 – Undiscovered Country 227

Chapter 16 – A Beautiful World 253

Chapter 17 – The Hunt Begins 271

Chapter 18 – School's in Session 281

Chapter 19 – Enemy at the Gates......................307

Chapter 20 – The Turning Point 325

Chapter 21 – Interrogation 345

Chapter 22 – A Change in Tempo....................................359

Chapter 23 – Invasion 371

Chapter 24 – Rescue 385

Chapter 25 – A New Beginning..417

Chapter 26 – Checkmate...433

Also by Neutralus...442

About the Author..443

Acknowledgments

I'd like to acknowledge my wife, who believed
in me and made this book a reality.

I'd like to thank all my beta readers for their
help, thoughtful advice, and entertaining sarcastic
comments.

PROLOGUE

I couldn't help but wonder what the world would be like if I were alive. Not that I was some vampire or zombie like those so often mentioned in cheesy teen novels. I still drew breath, my blood still flowed, and I still thought and dreamed.

I was just an ordinary human man living in a world where I didn't exist, at least not to the rest of the world.

The rainstorm battering against my office window pulled me back from my self-reflection. My attention focused on the autumn-colored trees displaying proudly in the park below me. The trees of Central Park in New York City paraded orange, brown, and red leaves as they contrasted with the deep green fields of grass surrounding it. The park represented the only haven for nature in a city frequented by joggers, writers, explorers, and of course the occasional criminal. The park's serene beauty stood out like a beacon in the city, surrounded and oppressed by the stone and metal goliaths providing apartments and corporate headquarters for various companies.

New York City during the fall was my favorite time of the year. The cool air blowing in from the north collided with the heat already present in the area, creating a downpour of rain that washed the current year's dirt off the city. In doing so, it prepared the city for preservation by the cold winter weather sheltering Earth in dazzling white snow and hard unforgiving ice. The preservation would wait for the coming spring as it ushered in a new year. The cycle continued year to year as Mother Nature played her part in renewing the world that humanity called home.

My office occupied a small space on the thirty-sixth floor of a skyscraper nestled against the park. The building housed hundreds of businesses that took up single spaces like mine or in a few cases several floors. Incom Investments and Logistics stenciled on the door identified my business. The space limitations required me to share a secretary with half a dozen other offices to complete the illusion of commerce.

On paper, Incom was a small startup investment firm specializing in penny stock trades. It made barely enough to afford this office and provide a modest income for its single owner/employee to survive on. Any calls to the office by new or present investors were automatically routed to a random customer service representative. The representatives were buried among hundreds of other people answering questions about everything from available apartments to new cell phone service that was located only God knows where. The low volume of investments and revenue generated through Incom didn't even register on the Security and Exchange Commission's radar…and with the company itself not on the stock exchange, it was easily ignored. However, the true work at Incom by its sole employee and owner was for investments far larger. The office represented the nerve center of a vast empire hidden from government scrutiny while providing the vast majority of my wealth.

I first became interested in investing after my father opened up a bank account for me with five hundred dollars when I first started high school. He saw it as a stepping-stone to my future and instructed me to make it grow.

I imagine his original intention was for me to get a job after school while slowly building it up to help pay for a college education. I inherited strong analytical skills and acuity for economics from my parents, allowing me to parlay the small investment into a more substantial sum as time progressed.

In my junior year, while away at a young entrepreneur's symposium, my parents' house caught fire and burned to the ground.

The police reported that my parents died from smoke inhalation before emergency services even arrived.

The arson investigators speculated the fire originated from a simple electrical short in one of the outlets, though the police continued their investigation until they ruled arson out. The building material burned hot enough to leave only a few skeletal remains of my mother and father. I remember sitting in my hotel room crying as I watched the news broadcast with a thousand thoughts going through my mind. I couldn't bring myself to believe that this was truly happening. My anguish was rudely interrupted by a startling revelation; the newscaster stated that I had died in the house as well. Though the newscaster's error was confusing, it lacked significance compared to the loss of my parents. The shock and pain that I felt from my parents' deaths caused me to shut down inside, a necessary defensive measure to help protect what little sanity I had left.

If you have suffered a loss like this, you'll understand why a person craves isolation. To feel like I would make it through this, I needed time to process the pain and sorrow that I felt. Through all of my misery, it didn't even dawn on me to inform the police that I was still alive.

After several months of living in hotels and wallowing in misery, I began to move on. I wasn't sure what I wanted to do with my life; the life that I once had just seemed so hollow now. I hadn't been in school since the fire, I had no home, no immediate family, and I wasn't really interested in living with some aunt or uncle whom I barely knew.

As far as the world was concerned, I was dead…so no one was looking for me. I had an opportunity to just start over, to create a future for myself of my own design.

Ultimately, I didn't know what I wanted and I wasn't entirely sure where I was going, just that I would need money to get there. I transferred the money I had left in my bank account from my old life to a dummy corporation account I created (which became Incom) and then I closed out that last remnant of my past. The person I was no longer existed and the pain I endured helped provide the focus for the future before me.

Through Incom, I was able to open up several new bank accounts in various countries throughout the world. I wanted to find my success but still remain dead to the world, so I knew I would have to learn ways to hide any success I achieved. I invested my money over the next decade, shifting it from one investment to the next depending on the status of the stock market. As time passed my fortunes multiplied exponentially, requiring me to push the money farther and farther away and divide it up into hundreds of accounts.

Each of the accounts was listed under different names of either people or businesses that existed only on paper.

Taxes were paid to the appropriate federal, state, and local governments so the banks didn't see anything amiss and I could avoid the scrutiny of the various government taxation bodies.

By the time I was twenty-seven, I began purchasing small businesses and investing in natural resources all over the world. I branched out into food production, mining, energy, and water resources, purchasing smaller operations that were seen by the larger corporations as inconsequential. Each acquisition was made from a separate account and a separate entity, so none of them could be linked together. None of them were publicly traded, so the financial statements about any business success or failure remained internal. I restructured each one remotely through email, phone calls, and faxes. I visited each business I acquired only once to deliver instructions from the "owner" and place someone in charge. None of the executives or employees identified me as anything other than a messenger and I was quickly forgotten.

I absorbed several insurance companies and provided insurance to all my employees to cover all their healthcare needs at no cost to them. Combining this with better pay, equipment, and benefits than my competitors increased the productivity of all my employees and guaranteed each company's success. I utilized a portion of each business' profit to help offset the healthcare costs until I started buying into the pharmaceuticals and healthcare industry. I purchased medical clinics and hospitals in whatever city or country housed one of my businesses and encouraged the employees to utilize these facilities for care.

To offset the high cost of healthcare workers, I contracted with graduate students and those recently out of medical school and put them to work at lower wages while supplementing their pay with tuition reimbursement. After a few years when their contract had been fulfilled, they would be hired on for somewhat higher pay or a new graduate would be transferred in to take their place. Each business was molded to encourage the employees to value what they had as well as the work they were doing. Only those truly bent on becoming wealthy moved on, while those who cared about the job they performed and the company they worked for stayed behind.

As my businesses grew in success, they were quickly noticed by other companies in the same industry. Though my businesses were still small by comparison, the larger companies noticed them and attempted to buy them up to enhance the value of their own businesses. Much like a larger fish eating a smaller one, offers were made and some outright strong-arm tactics were used to purchase, manipulate, or coerce the smaller business that I owned into the fold. Just as the mouth of the large fish began to open to swallow its smaller prey, the little fish turned around and became a shark.

A small company with fewer assets would then absorb a much larger company in comparison with a sudden influx of capital. The maneuver would be so quick in most cases that the executives would come in the next week and see me standing in their conference room with their new instructions. Publicly traded companies were easier to absorb because all I had to do was buy up a controlling amount of stock. Any stock that was still outstanding after I acquired them was eventually bought up and the company was removed from whatever country's stock exchange it was a part of. This tactic was done so the company managers only had to answer to their invisible boss and not to random stock investors.

When a large business was obtained, few changes would be made initially to maintain the illusion that what just happened didn't really happen. A small press release would be posted in a local paper stating that the larger company had merged with a smaller one. The legal documents required for such a merger would be completed, the administrative fees and taxes were paid to the appropriate governments, and the whole event would soon be forgotten.

Administrative robots were unconcerned with who absorbed what as long as it was legal and they could tax it.

At thirty-eight years old, I stood in a small office on the thirty-sixth floor facing Central Park in the fall. I was the sole owner of 12,107 businesses around the globe and a shareholder to countless others. I had become the single largest business owner on the planet. My wealth surpassed the combined wealth of all the other recorded billionaires by a significant margin, except no one was aware that I even existed. My purchases and acquisitions made me the sole owner of almost every type of business invented. The methods I put in place to isolate each business purchase allowed me to obtain monopolies in several key areas, violating commerce laws across the planet. I always figured that until the companies responsible for the monopolies were identified, there wouldn't be much risk of government intervention.

As I stared at the park outside my office window, the cell phone in my pocket started vibrating from an incoming call and caught me by surprise. I reached into my pocket, pulled out my cell phone, and answered it.

"Yes?"

I waited patiently for a second so the person on the other line could respond.

A male voice with a British accent said, "The kids are on the move!"

"All right," I said. "We'll leave in an hour. Get the jet ready."

"Yes, sir!" was the response before the call disconnected.

I returned the phone to my pocket and then continued to look out into the park, thinking to myself about these kids. If I was wrong about them and the potential threat they posed, the empire I had constructed could end. I had made the mistake of realizing too late that they were persistent enough not to stop until they found the truth. I just hoped they were prepared for the truth when they finally found it.

CHAPTER 1 – DREAMERS

SOUTHERN CALIFORNIA, MARINA
KYLE BISHOP

"Kyle, wait up!"

I turned around and noticed my best friend Phillip running in my direction. Phillip Jennings and I had been best friends before either of us could even remember. Both of our parents lived next door to each other in cookie-cutter houses stamped out in the mid-1980s. We both lived in southern Oregon by the coast, crushed between the warm weather of the south and the icy overcast of the north. Both of us were serving life sentences in suburbia and we both had a paper-clipped photo of ourselves hanging from the dashboard of every police cruiser in town.

Not that either of us broke the law…intentionally, but if some prank or mischief had taken place, law enforcement normally just started with us. I was born and raised in this small town and it was the only life I knew. I made A's in school and I didn't even have to bother trying. I spent my free time finding any activity or in some cases mischief to take up the hours and stave off the boredom. While in kindergarten, Phillip and I began our mischief by shaking down the boys for lunch money while avoiding the girls for fear of being infected by cooties. I was a homegrown white American; Phillip, on the other hand, was Chinese or was at least born to parents who were. At 5'10", he was slender and just as active in his life as I was, which was necessary if he expected to keep up with me. His dark-colored almond-shaped eyes and year-round tan all but guaranteed him second glances from the girls at school.

Phillip's parents adopted him from mainland China just after he was born, so he had no idea who his real parents were. His adoptive parents loved him fiercely and instilled in him a love of engines. His father was an automotive engineer who designed and built the future of automobiles, as he described it. Phillip's engineering skills often came in handy as we occasionally flexed the local laws.

A few months back, we attached an addition to the roof of the police chief's car. The chief didn't notice until later the Mickey Mouse ears that were lying flush on top of his roof the day after he returned with his family from Disney World. Well, he hadn't noticed them until they popped upright while he chased a speeding car down Main Street. Instead of the normal police warble, his siren whistled Mickey Mouse's "Steamboat Willie" that was hard-wired into his PA system. I remember standing just down the street from where the chief normally staked out speeders, laughing so hard with Phillip as his car blew by. We weren't the only ones laughing and pointing that day, but we were singled out immediately by the fuzz.

"Hey Phillip, are you ready?" I asked.

He looked me directly in the eyes, as though he wanted me to believe his answer and expected me not to, "Yeah, I'm good. Where are the others?"

I answered quickly, "Simon called and said he was on his way and should be here in a few. I haven't heard from Alex and I'm not sure if she hasn't changed her mind."

Phillip smirked at me like he knew something I didn't. "She'll be here, just give her some time."

I looked at Phillip to share what I was thinking, "You know she is probably confessing everything to her father as we speak, and we should be preparing ourselves to be carted off to jail any minute now?"

Phillip couldn't help but laugh at my statement, but he couldn't deny that the possibility existed.

Once he got his laughing under control he responded, "Are you still harping over the Mickey incident? That's history, man!"

I'm sure Phillip could see the shocked and betrayed look on my face, "What do you mean history? It was two months ago and she sold us out to the cops!"

"She didn't sell us out to the cops; she just told her father as any good daughter would do! You have got to let it go, man!"

Phillip put his hand on my shoulder as he said this.

I looked at him and just really wanted to punch him, "Her father is the police chief, the freaking king of cops. If it wasn't for her, we wouldn't have spent two weeks picking up trash around town."

Phillip fought to keep a smile off his face, knowing it would upset me more.

He settled for looking towards the ground and shaking his head back and forth. "Hey, I thought we got off lightly, if it wasn't for her little sister thinking her dad was her personal hero for turning his squad car into Mickey Mouse just for her, we might not have gotten off with a slap on the wrist."

I put my thumb and index finger up to the bridge of my nose, trying to rub the newly arrived headache away. After a minute of cooling down, I said, "That's not the point; she shouldn't have told on us to begin with. When we started this little adventure of ours, we became a team, or a family, or whatever you want to call it. The point is because of our mutual interests we should be looking out for each other, not digging a knife out of our back."

Off to the right by the Marina steps, there was clapping. We both looked over and saw Simon sitting on the top step doing an exaggerated clap.

The smile only came off his face when he spoke.

"Such drama, and here I thought I would have to pirate an episode of Battlestar Galactica to get this type of entertainment."

I looked at him and deadpanned, "Bite me!"

Simon started laughing. As Simon stood up, I couldn't help but compare him to a meth addict. Simon Weiss wasn't incredibly tall, but he was incredibly thin. He had a type of thinness that compelled a person to check his teeth for signs of meth use, as well as feel guilty for eating around him. Any muscle he may have had on his small frame was well hidden by the baggy clothes he constantly wore.

Of course, Simon had never done drugs in his life, but it was difficult not to stereotype him. He wore round Harry Potter glasses and had light brown hair that was starting to thin. Simon had a love for all things electronic, from cell phones to computers. He would tear apart anything and everything electronic to determine how it worked and what he could do to make it better. He got ahold of my cell phone when we had first met and upgraded the service plan that came with the phone to something unlimited.

My unlimited plan didn't seem to cost me anything, as my carrier stopped charging for my phone. My mother contacted the cell phone company to determine why my usage wasn't showing up. After several weeks of phone calls, she finally gave up and just accepted the inevitable. I've been waiting for the FCC to show up at my doorstep to demand the phone from me and slap me with a nice hefty fine.

Simon had a genius quality to everything he did but surprisingly, it rarely went to his head. His unlikely loyalty to our group was also in contrast, considering he was so shy and didn't make friends easily.

"Did you have any problems with your parents?" I asked Simon as I tried to gauge his willingness to go on this little adventure.

All of us had told our parents the same story, that we had scheduled a week's vacation on the beaches of Southern California before our summer ended and we returned to school for our senior year. I had turned eighteen a few weeks ago, but Phillip and Alex were still seventeen and Simon was still sixteen for another month as he had skipped two grades…which was why he was also coming up on his senior year.

Simon forged documents that showed we had reservations at a small hotel in Southern California and had already ordered and stored all the necessary summer vacation items that most teenagers accumulate during a trip such as receipts, T-shirts, and posters. He was thorough as our group went about its mischief.

With a grin on his face he responded, "Nah, my parents are cool with it. I think they are just psyched that I actually have a life outside of my room, much less actual friends to hang out with."

Simon then looked at Phillip and said, "I hacked into the Marina website and scheduled a cleaning for your uncle's boat, so the dock people don't wig out if they realize it is missing."

Our planned trip was taking us about five hundred miles off the California coast to a non-existent island that required the use of a boat. Thankfully, Phillip's uncle had a fishing boat in the marina that suited our needs just fine.

Phillip said, "Wow, Simon, I'm impressed."

Phillip looked back at me and continued, "Whoever heard of a nerd that was capable of accidentally being cool?"

I started laughing and Simon retaliated, "Whoever heard of a Chinese guy named Phillip?"

Phillip's grin spread across his face as he fought off a laugh and attempted to feel slighted, "That's just harsh, man. Where's the love?"

I looked at them both and said with no small amount of sarcasm, "If you guys want to find a room, we can reschedule this for tomorrow."

Simon and Phillip looked at each other and said in unison, "Noooo!" and we all started laughing.

We paced near the docks for about half an hour waiting on Alex until I finally had enough.

"That's it! Let's go."

My statement startled both Phillip and Simon, but Simon was the first to state the obvious, "But Alex isn't here, are we leaving without her?"

Before Simon could finish his question, I had already turned my back on them and started walking to the boat. We had to get out of here before the sun finished coming up and someone noticed us hanging out where we shouldn't be.

Both Phillip and Simon jogged to catch up with me as my eyes fell upon Phillip's uncle's fishing boat. If you could even call it a fishing boat; it was twenty-two feet long with an actual physical walking area of about eight feet in the back. The rest of the outside of the boat was made up of a shell that looked like it melted over two-thirds of the boat as a strong wind blew the melted plastic back towards the aft section. A tiny six-inch rail which appeared to be more for looks than actual safety lined the front section of the boat. How anyone could actually fish off of this boat without wrapping the fishing pole or its line around an antenna was anyone's guess. The cabin contained the wheel, throttle, radio, and GPS system to navigate with and doubled as the main living space. The boat was decked out with enough electronics that it could autopilot itself to a destination and all you would have to do is dock. Painted on the keel was the boat's name, "Sweet and Saucy."

All three of us stared at the boat, especially its name.

Phillip interjected as way of an explanation, "What can I say? My uncle is crazy!"

He shrugged and walked onto the boat first, with me and Simon taking up the rear.

Dreamers

CHAPTER 2 – LATE ARRIVAL

SOUTHERN CALIFORNIA, MARINA KYLE BISHOP

After Phillip and Simon moved towards the boat's controls, I began looking around the cabin to verify whether we had enough food and supplies to make the trip. According to Phillip, his uncle normally kept the boat pretty well stocked and ready to go whenever he was in the "fishing" mood as he called it. The cabin contained a small bed on the starboard (or right side) and a small kitchenette on the port (or left side) containing a portable fridge and prep counter with a coffee maker secured to it. Hanging overhead was a built-in microwave. I pulled up the seat cushions that comprised the remainder of the outside ring of the cabin and discovered basic gear such as two life preservers, flares, and a small inflatable raft.

Downstairs there was a smaller area containing a decent- sized ice chest, probably for any fish his uncle managed to catch and not scare away with the boat. The cabin also contained the engine compartment, which was kind of sweet. Everything on the boat appeared modern and impeccably clean. I made a mental note to keep any trash we generated, so anything eaten or used could be replaced and put back before his uncle noticed anything was missing. The engine started up while I was in the compartment, so I returned to the main cabin to witness our departure. When I made it up the stairs, I saw Phillip at the controls with a wide grin on his face like Christmas had come early for him.

He looked at me and asked, "Mind disembarking and untying the moor lines, so we can get underway?"

I nodded and a small smile crept up on the corners of my mouth as I headed to the starboard side of the boat to release the mooring lines.

After releasing the aft line and tying off the rope so it didn't dangle everywhere, I moved to the fore or the front of the boat to release the other line. As I knelt to untie the line from the mooring cleat, I heard footsteps on the pier running towards us. For a brief second, I thought that a dock worker had caught us and was running to stop us from taking off with a boat. But when I looked up, I saw an extremely attractive young woman running my way. Alex had finally arrived to grace us with her presence, and I could feel another headache coming on.

Alex, aka Alexi Masters, was the bane of my existence. She was a 5'5" blonde perfectionist with startling green eyes and a slender frame that was well-toned from an active lifestyle. She was attractive enough if you went for the stereotypical blonde look that's always been so common on the East Coast, but it was her eyes that set her apart from the rest. It was hard for students at my school not to notice her or occasionally sneer at her, depending on who you were. School had become the outlet for her perfection and teenage stardom, as she was the student body president and a shoo-in for valedictorian in our senior year. The last part was only possible because Simon had gotten a "C" in health class during his freshman year and, from what he said, had no intentions of retaking it.

Alex's parents thought she could do no wrong, and they were probably right. The fact that her father was the sheriff of our little slice of Americana just made me despise her more. Like any guy who first gazed upon her, I had thought I was in love. As time passed it seemed the distance between us grew, but it never lessened my desire to be near her.

At first blush, a guy would want to classify her as the standard bimbo, but that classification came to a sudden face plant after you actually talked to her. Though I believe she played her looks for all they were worth, which allowed people to underestimate her. Underneath it all was a sharp, analytical mind at work.

Alex was the first to identify the strange anomalies in the financial markets that eventually led to us ending up on this boat. She had identified some pre-ordained stock crashes anticipated by investment firms that ended up not crashing as badly as originally predicted. Adding to that fact, she had located news articles reporting on corporate takeovers that were publicly announced and then were later hushed up and put on the back burner. All the little things began adding up and she was the first to stumble onto a pattern between them and bring it to Simon's attention. Alex asked Simon to run a more in-depth search on the internet for other possible hits from even further back. When Simon's search was completed, he brought the results to my attention first before mentioning them to Alex.

Alex leapt onto the boat as though she had just hurdled across a water chasm to catch a runaway ferry…even though we hadn't pulled away from the dock yet.

"You weren't going to wait for me?" she asked as she glared at me while trying to catch her breath.

I finished tying off the last line and got up to walk back to the cabin. I looked at her and said, "You're late!" as I walked inside.

She walked in right behind me, noticed Phillip and Simon, and stated quite brazenly, "I'm not late; my period was just last week!"

I could feel the blood rushing to my face and was sure I turned several shades of red. Phillip and Simon completely lost it and laughed so hard I thought I saw tears as Phillip leaned over the wheel, banging his fist on the console. I had to bite my tongue until I could taste blood in order to stave off the sarcastic response that was at the front of my mind. I gave everyone a minute to calm down. Alex took the time to put a tight control on the smile that threatened the lines on her beautiful face.

I looked at Phillip and said, "Get us out of here!"

Phillip couldn't stop smiling at me and Alex. Then he turned around and replied, "Aye, aye, Captain" as he increased the throttle and eased us away from the docks.

A little over an hour into the trip, I sat on the forecastle located on the top front of the ship and watched the sun climb into the sky. Today was turning out to be beautiful with clear skies and blue as far as the eye could see. I couldn't help but feel free as I cast myself out into the world with no one to answer to. My friends trusted me enough to see them through this until we could find the answers we were looking for. Even though this whole mess started with Alex badgering Simon into doing an internet search for her, I couldn't help but plunge into the adventure of it.

My thoughts drifted to my mom at home alone. It bothered me a little knowing that I had lied to her, but even more that she would be there by herself.

I'm sure I drove her to wit's end with the constant trouble I got myself into, but she never seemed short on patience for me. I always felt overprotective of her, as we only had each other in the world. I barely even knew my dad. I just remember him leaving us when I was very young. My mother had gotten pregnant with me as a teenager and was kicked out of her parents' house just after finishing high school…with no support and me, not even a year old, to look after. All in all, she did pretty well by herself. The house was the only place I remembered living in. No matter how rough things got, my mother always worked hard and made ends meet. She worked full time at a daycare near our apartment and then tutored middle school kids in the evening in math, English, or whatever subject they were struggling with for some extra money.

During the summer, I took on a few odd jobs wherever I could find them to help out with my clothes, school activities, and get an old beat-up

Nissan truck. Thankfully Phillip was able to tune it up for me and we were able to replace a few parts through the local junkyard to save money. For his help, I gave him a ride every day our freshman year to school or wherever he needed to go, though we hung out with each other so much we were often going to the same places anyway.

I think I got my strength from my mother in that she didn't let anything slow her down. I smiled as I thought about her while enjoying the warmth of the sun on my face.

I heard someone walking across the deck behind me, so I turned around and saw Simon heading my way. Simon had a grin on his face like he was having the time of his life. I was glad he was enjoying himself. I wasn't sure how Simon would handle the water, and it appeared the sun was already trying to convert him to a lobster. With his nerd title firmly in place, I wrongly assumed he would be spending this trip puking his guts out over the side. Simon sat down next to me and started playing on the Nintendo DS that he had brought along, thumbing away at whatever game he had going.

"The trip will take about twenty-seven hours to get to the island at our current velocity," Simon remarked without looking up from his handheld.

I calculated the time in my head, realizing that we would arrive the next day sometime around eight or nine a.m., provided we didn't get lost or sunk in a typhoon. The timing worked out great, as it was early enough not to draw too much attention and late enough that we would have sufficient light to scout the island before figuring out how to get ashore. After a minute Simon stopped pecking on his handheld and turned his head to look at me, squinting his eyes to block out the sunlight that threatened to blind him.

"Do you think we'll find anything there?"

I thought about the information we had collected to date.

"Perhaps. At the very least, I think we will find another piece of the puzzle. You dug up the data. I know you wouldn't have come along with us if you didn't see a connection."

Simon thought about this for a second, running all the data through his head for the zillionth time.

After a minute or two of silence, Simon finally said, "I don't think I would have broken into that factory with you and Phillip if I wasn't sure. I just wanted to know that I wasn't the only one who felt certain."

We both heard a gasp behind us, causing Simon to turn around to look. I didn't have to turn around to know who it was. Alex didn't know about our little break-in operation. I knew if we had told her she would have run straight to daddy and buried the knife in my back again.

Simon greeted her, but she seemed to ignore Simon's greeting as I figured she was preoccupied by staring a hole into the back of my head.

CHAPTER 3 – TROUBLE IN PARADISE

OFF THE SOUTHERN CALIFORNIA COAST
ALEXI MASTERS

Simon took a moment to look back and forth between me and Kyle, his eyebrows raised and his lips squeezed together as if he were saying "Ewww" to himself.

"I'm going to go and make sure Phillip isn't steering us to Japan!"

Simon looked between us again, noticing the rage in my face and the uncaring slump of Kyle's shoulders.

"Right!" Kyle exclaimed as he walked back to the cabin, staying as far from me as possible without falling off the boat.

I continued to look at the back of Kyle's head in the full belief that I could make it explode. Kyle turned his body around enough to peer directly at me. Kyle Bishop was 6'2" and was one of the taller guys in school as well as one of the few kids at school that I was forced to look up at when talking to. It irritated me that he always looked so smug, as though his whole life was going just as he planned. Kyle always wore a long-sleeve pullover shirt that hugged his torso with the arms pushed halfway up his forearms. The shirt pressed against his back, outlined the indentation of his spine, and emphasized that his body was a stranger to fat. His sleeves couldn't hide the well-toned and tanned muscles that caused most of his friends to swoon when he was within visual range. His sandy brown hair was always unkempt, but that only magnified his soft smoky brown eyes that smoldered naturally. I had met his mother and he definitely didn't get his eyes from her. To her, Kyle looked like a cross between Chris Hemsworth and Brad Pitt with a type of body that you expected to see modeling underwear.

Kyle's good looks didn't sway my opinion of him. Kyle was a user. He used people and discarded them, especially the girls at school. Most of his male friends were blind to his behavior or simply chose to ignore it...like Phillip and Simon.

All throughout high school, Kyle had been the center of attention and had dated dozens of girls, none of which lasted more than a week. Near the end of our junior year, my best friend Megan accepted Kyle's invitation to the school dance. Apparently, he made such an impression on her that she fell in love with him...or so she felt. Even though I warned her about his week-long romances, Megan thought she was the one to break the curse. A week later she got dumped by the ingrate. The first few months after Kyle dumped her, she would burst into tears at random times whenever he was near. This required me to really play the best friend role by comforting and supporting her through the withdrawals.

The day after the breakup, I went over to Megan's house because she wasn't in class that Monday morning. She answered the door with her face puffy and red, mascara staining her cheeks, and still wearing last night's pajamas. It took half a box of tissues and a whole package of Oreos before I was finally able to get some details. On Sunday morning, Kyle came over to her house and ended their relationship. Megan told me that he didn't want to get into a long-term relationship with her and didn't want to mislead her in any way. She talked about how much of a gentleman he was and even defended him any time I started to attack him. I could only assume that he was really good at charming helpless girls into thinking that he meant no harm. Well, I wasn't fooled for a second.

Kyle never stayed in a relationship for more than a week for as long as he had been at school. I even assumed he was gay and was just putting on a show for the other guys, so no one would guess. That turned out to be false, as I had never seen him even remotely interested in the same sex. The guy "friends" he had, he just hung out with at events and played sports with…but he never looked at any other guys that certain way. I knew almost everyone in school saw him as a decent guy, but I just couldn't help but hate his guts. So, I stood there staring at his smoky brown eyes as they smoldered back at me and prepared myself to go to war with Kyle Bishop.

Kyle turned around and faced me with his arms hanging at his sides. By his stance and demeanor, I could tell he was observant enough to know that I was pissed at him about what I had overheard. Growing up with a father who was the police chief bred healthy respect for the laws and the need to enforce them. I wasn't any different and followed all the rules — from the simple rules around the house to the state and federal laws that everyone had to abide by — because they were there to protect people. Well, Kyle just felt he was above it all.

I walked towards him near the front edge of the boat, just as a big, stupid grin started to plaster his face. I could tell he knew why I was angry and realized there was nothing I could do to change it. I could feel my face heat up from how mad he was making me.

I finally stepped up in front of Kyle and before he could even say a word, my hands shot up and pushed him hard against his chest...pushing him off balance. As he took a step back to regain his balance, his heel caught on the six-inch deck railing...preventing him from correcting himself. I could see the look of shock on his face, that I'm sure matched my own for what I had just done, as he fell over the side. When his body hit the water, my right hand came up to cover my mouth as a laughing bark burst out and I struggled to contain myself as a triumphant grin spread across my face.

After a second, I realized the engine on the boat shut off just as he had hit the water. I figured Phillip had probably seen him falling overboard and reacted to shut the engine off as quickly as possible. Kyle's head popped up out of the water and he began to slowly fall back as the boat continued to drift forward. I walked to the rear of the boat and climbed down onto the rear cabin deck to watch him as he floated away. I noticed as we slowly moved forward that he didn't appear to be drowning and seemed to be capable of treading water.

Phillip came up behind me and stood at my right as I heard Simon call, "Man overboard!"

Simon turned around and went back into the cabin as Kyle began to swim towards the rear of the boat. I couldn't stop the giggling fit I was having, nor remove the smile that I failed to hide behind my hand while Phillip kept looking over at me and then back to Kyle as Kyle swam closer.

"What happened?" Phillip asked me as I stood there laughing and not helping in the least.

I looked at Phillip and saw the confused look on his face and I couldn't stop laughing long enough to answer his question. Phillip clutched the back-deck railing for support and extended a hand to Kyle to help him climb back into the boat. Just then, Simon came back out from the cabin with an orange fluorescent life-saver doughnut. After seeing Kyle climbing into the boat, he sheepishly realized he was a little late for a rescue.

Kyle immediately started stalking towards me as I backed up to the wall next to the cabin. His approach couldn't be confused with walking, as it appeared he was stalking prey that just happened to be me. I could see the anger on his face as he sloshed ocean water across the deck with him. I managed to stop giggling by the time he reached me and stood less than a foot from me, staring into my eyes. I felt fear start to build up inside of me as I attempted to smother the smile on my lips. My fear was competing with the excitement building up at the same time from having his smoldering eyes burning into me that closely and I found it difficult to breathe. I saw water beads falling from his face and onto his shirt, and I could swear that most of the water on him was turning to steam.

As we stared at each other, both refusing to back down, Kyle raised his right hand as though he contemplated strangulation. I could see his fingers slightly flexing as though anticipating his next move. My heart raced to the point where I could hear it in my ears and I wondered if the sound was betraying me to my hunter. The fingers on his hand kept flexing in and out slightly. I could see from his lips that he wanted to say something and was trying hard to fight it back. Being this close, I noticed his face was sculpted to perfection and enhanced further by the sheen of water still in place. It should be against the law to look so good and act like an ass.

After what felt like an eternity, though in reality it probably was only a minute or two, Kyle let out a low growl that caused his chest to rumble. The unexpected sound surprised me, and my eyes opened wide in response. He put his hand back down to his side and walked through the cabin door to my right. As the tension eased in the air around me, I relaxed enough to exhale the breath that I didn't realize I had been holding. I was slightly disappointed to have him leave, but then I realized that Round One of the war with Kyle had gone to me and I was thrilled.

I looked over to where Phillip and Simon were standing by the aft ladder. Simon was grinning, happy he got a ringside seat to the main event. On the other hand, Phillip looked at me with irritation bordering on anger…so I figured he wasn't too happy with me for almost killing his friend. Phillip walked past me into the cabin, doing his best to ignore me, as Simon followed closely behind. I decided to stay out on the deck and give Kyle a chance to change and cool off. Poking the bear had been fun, but I wasn't foolish enough not to realize that it also felt extremely dangerous.

Dreamers

CHAPTER 4 – ROUND TWO

OFF THE SOUTHERN CALIFORNIA COAST
KYLE BISHOP

As Simon walked away after Alex gasped behind us, I sat there thinking about Alex and what she had overheard. I knew she would be upset about us breaking into the plant, but I just didn't see any way to confirm our information or dig up any new clues. When I first decided that we needed to take things a step further, Simon asked if we were going to invite Alex along. I immediately shot down the idea, because I knew she would immediately run to daddy. The spoiled princess that she was prevented her from breaking the rules. However, I admit that I was a bit curious to learn if she was more upset at me for breaking the rules or for not inviting her along. The corners of my mouth turned upwards thinking about that.

I looked over my shoulder at Alex and saw her flushed cheeks and her eyes that burned into me. Yeah, she was pissed. I turned my head and shoulders back around and stood up to approach this problem head-on. Something about her being upset at me left mixed emotions stirring inside of me. It upset me that she felt that way, but I also saw it as a challenge to fight against…or maybe for, I wasn't sure. Either way, I was interested to see what she would say regarding the matter. I always pictured Alex as a lobbyist fighting to save whales, hug a tree, or petition to save the ozone. Pretty much anything where conflict was available and she could take the moral high ground during the attack.

When Alex stepped towards me, I couldn't help but let the smirk from earlier creep back onto my face. Her hands shot out and pushed against my chest, with my surprise only coming from how strong she was. I didn't expect a young woman who acted so girly to have so much strength. When she pushed me, I fell backward and felt the railing of the deck pressing on one of my calves. My momentum pushed me over the edge. I felt more surprise than anger at that moment as I waited for the water to come up and meet me. I prepared myself in the second I had before crashing into the water. I took a deep breath and felt the water slam into my back and shoulders, almost knocking the wind out of me. During the few moments I was underwater, I saw the bottom of the boat going by me. Then I spotted froth from the propellers churning the water, leaving oxygen bubbles in its wake. I swam a few feet away from the boat, so I wouldn't get sucked into the boat's propellers, and then kicked my way to the surface to begin treading water. As the boat slowly drifted away, I looked at the back of the boat and saw Alex looking at me with her hand covering her mouth as she was laughing.

The anger inside of me started building as I thought about what she had just done. Though she had a right to be angry for what I had done, it hardly justified pushing me off the boat. I mean, she could have killed me. I could have broken my neck or been paralyzed. Ok, maybe the chances were slim…but she still shouldn't have done it.

As I saw the boat stop drifting, I started swimming towards the aft ladder to climb back on board. I spent the time in the water thinking about how much I wanted to throw Alex into the ocean. Phillip reached out a hand and helped me into the boat, as Simon stood behind him just smiling like an idiot with a life-saver doughnut in his hand. Yeah, I thought that was a lot of help.

Once I heaved my last soaking wet foot onto the deck, my eyes immediately zeroed in on Alex. She was standing a few feet from the cabin door with her hand still over her mouth, laughing away and failing miserably at trying to control it. I slowly walked towards her one step at a time, causing her to take a few steps back until her back brushed against the wall and she realized there was nowhere left for her to run. I felt like a predator stalking its prey, and I was ready to kill. As I closed in, within an arm's reach of her, I stared into her eyes with the thoughts of what she did running through my head. I replayed the image of throwing her into the sea over and over in my mind, and fought the urge to choke the life out of her. I was pretty confident that Phillip and Simon would vouch for my innocence if Alex came up missing. I kept getting distracted by her eyes and the beautiful skin on her face, which forced me to relive the previous moment repeatedly so I could continue to hate her.

I raised my left hand as my fingers clenched in the shape of a vise. I wanted so badly to toss her into the ocean, but I just couldn't do it. When it came to the conflict between us over these past few years, I always felt I had to struggle to hate her. No matter how much she drove me crazy and as stuck up as she was, I just couldn't harm someone out of anger…especially her.

To save myself from doing something stupid, I turned away from Alex and walked into the cabin to find some dry clothes. Ignoring the water that fell from me, I walked over to one of the cabin seats that my backpack was on. I rummaged through my bag and pulled out a change of underwear, a pair of faded cargo shorts, and a clean shirt. I pulled out a bottle of sunscreen and shoved it into one of the shorts pockets. Then, I climbed down into the engine room to change clothes.

After I changed, I climbed back up into the cabin with my wet clothes in hand. I saw Phillip at the controls getting us back underway again and

Simon was sitting on one of the cabin seats plugging away at his DS.

"You ok?" Phillip asked.

I thought briefly about the incident and how much I still wanted to strangle Alex.

I told him I was fine, as I was determined to choke down my frustration as well as the soreness in my muscles from the unexpected dip.

Phillip looked at me like he was trying to determine if I was being truthful.

It didn't take him long to shift gears and ask, "What the heck happened? You were lucky. I saw you go over the side and was able to get the engine shut off before you ended up as a mixed drink."

I could tell Phillip was upset about the incident and I wasn't very happy about it either. We had been friends as far back as I could remember and when one of us was in trouble, we both were. We spent so much time at each other's houses that both of our parents just accepted each of us as an additional son they never had. We were two brothers in spirit, if not in blood.

I looked over and saw Simon watching both of us, but keeping silent to let us work it out.

As I turned back to face Phillip, I said, "I just had a run-in with the ice princess. I'll deal with it!"

It looked as though Phillip was going to let the matter drop, at least for now.

"We are about twenty-four hours out provided nothing happens. Simon mentioned that this boat can auto-drive itself, but I'd feel safer if at least one of us were at the controls at all time."

I nodded my head in agreement.

"I'll take the third shift."

I looked over at Simon, "Wake me up when you feel like you're going to nod off."

I didn't wait for Simon to answer as I exited the cabin looking to confront Alex.

I heard Simon commenting quietly behind me, "Those two should just get a room and get it over with."

Phillip told Simon to shut up and I could hear Simon laughing in response as I walked out of the range to overhear anything further.

When I walked outside to the aft deck, I didn't see Alex anywhere. With so few spaces to hide on this boat, it was obvious she was up on the deck from where she had pushed me off. I hung my wet clothes from some hooks on the outside cabin wall to dry off, then turned to the ladder and started to climb up onto the forward deck to have a chat with Alex. As my head raised high enough to see onto the deck, I noticed Alex lying down in the same spot in which I had been sitting and she appeared to be sleeping. I saw her straw-blonde hair fanned out behind her head across the deck and the curves of her face as the sun highlighted certain spots and shaded others. It was moments like this when her attitude wasn't in play that she truly shined and her beauty was just magnificent.

I shook my head quickly to shake off those thoughts and considered heading back down the ladder to avoid waking her. My conscience raged inside of me for a moment, until I realized that if she slept there the sun would burn her to a crisp by the time she woke up. Though I felt I was owed some vengeance for her pushing me overboard, I couldn't bring myself to be so petty to her. So, I steeled myself as I finished climbing up onto the deck and sat next to her.

As I sat to her right, I saw her chest moving in and out as she breathed. She was dressed in a pair of designer jeans and a tank top, with a pair of diamond studs glinting from the bottom of her ears. When she first came onboard I hadn't even noticed what she was wearing, as it was often difficult to take my eyes off of her face. I caught myself staring at her full lips and wondering how soft they would be. I had an internal war with myself over my feelings for her, and I growled again at the frustration she caused. Part of me wanted to push her over the side and sail away, and the other half of me wanted to do everything I could to protect her. She had always been such a contradiction to me in school. Like every other guy, I noticed her when she first showed up and her dad became the new sheriff. A person would have to be dead not to notice the day she first walked into school. Just her presence caused so much drama; The tension in the school was so thick the first day you could cut it with a knife. Momost of it was the result of almost every guy who craved her attention competing against the girls who were jealous of the attention she drew.

Out of a sheer survival instinct the popular girls immediately flocked around her, so they could be important and accepted by association. Within a day of Alex arriving at school, the guys around me started flirting with her to see if she was interested.

Some of the braver guys outright asked her out for a date.

I remember her glancing at me that first day as a horde of other students surrounded her, as though she singled me out from everyone else. When her gaze fell upon me, I felt a warm feeling growing in my chest and causing the rest of my limbs to start buzzing. From that look, I thought maybe she was interested in me. I figured I stood as good a chance as any of these other guys and thought about asking her out.

But after Alex's first week at school, that notion was quickly crushed when I found out she had accepted one of her previous offers for a date.

As the months passed I heard that she had gone out with several other guys, but none of them appeared to last more than two days. According to the gossip network at school, her overprotective sheriff father pretty much crushed anyone's hope for a long-term relationship.

As our first three years in high school passed, I ran into her often during school functions or out on the town. She became increasingly hostile towards me and I never figured out why. Our aggression towards each other peaked after the

Mickey incident when she sacrificed us up to her dad for punishment.

Bringing my mind back to the present day, I pulled the bottle of sunscreen out of my pocket and began applying it to any exposed skin. After I was done, I lightly pushed Alex's shoulder to nudge her awake and saw her eyes open slowly and look over at me. I was unsure if Alex snored while sleeping, but I questioned whether she had been asleep.

I held out the bottle to her, "Put some of this on before you burn up out here."

Alex sat up without looking away from me and carefully grabbed the bottle from me. She looked at the label of the bottle for about a minute, like she couldn't believe I could be nice and give her something without dire consequences attached. She squeezed some of the lotion onto her left hand and set the bottle down. She rubbed both of her hands together and began applying the lotion just as I had done.

Alex asked, "Did you get the location of the island when you broke into the office Simon mentioned?"

I paused for a second, unsure how much I should tell her.

Ah, what the heck, I thought.

"That's right," I said defensively, daring her to open that can of worms.

I saw the thoughts running through her head as she analyzed the situation. I knew her moral compass always interfered with her decision-making. It upset me that she always ran straight to the law to defend her decisions and actions. In my opinion, Alex refused to be flexible even when it was necessary to achieve a goal.

"Tell me what happened!" she demanded.

I looked at her and raised my eyebrows.

I could see that she expected me to obey without question, like all the other sycophants who followed her around at school.

After seeing my expression, she reluctantly added, "Please."

Alex slowly breathed in and out, waiting patiently for me to answer her.

After a second, I turned and faced forward and began telling her about that night.

"All right, you remember back when this started and you first went to Simon to research a connection between different businesses as well as the last-minute rescue of the pending stock crash?"

She nodded, but didn't say anything.

I continued, "After Simon told me about the search, he convinced me that what happened shouldn't have naturally happened. The stock market should have crashed, maybe not heavily, but there should have been a significant drop in stock value."

Alex interrupted, "I thought it was strange that the market could recover so quickly, but what I found odd was that the analyst had clammed up after the fact and even the news wasn't reporting anything on it. It was as though everyone was trying to forget it happened."

I nodded at her observation as I continued, "Apparently you and Simon agreed on that part and when he told me about it, I couldn't let it rest."

Alex pressed her lips together tightly like she was trying to bite back a sarcastic response, but she let it go.

I continued, "I asked Simon to do another search, but this time to look for any local companies that may be connected."

I took a breath.

"He couldn't find any companies that directly affected that market save, but he was able to identify several local companies that were attached to them…either directly or indirectly."

Alex jumped in.

"How certain was he that the companies were related?"

I smirked, as I was always impressed with Alex's analytical mind. She worked problems out in her head as much as me; she just preferred more information before she acted. I would act compulsively based on a gut feeling. More often than not I was right, but often my decisions led to what she saw as irresponsible actions. I hesitated to answer her question, knowing that she would hardly be receptive to my response.

Before I could answer, her cheeks flushed with anger and she blurted, "How could you break into a business when he wasn't even certain? You could have been arrested."

She had already guessed the right answer to her first question.

"No, he wasn't certain," I replied. "The only commonality he could find between the businesses is that all of them were functioning internally the same way."

Surprise appeared on Alex's face as her mouth opened and closed like she was going to say something, but couldn't decide what.

She retorted, "A lot of businesses run the same; it's called a successful business model and…"

I held up my hand to get her to stop talking for a second.

"Look, he found a textile factory in Portland that matched up and on a *hunch* I decided to go check it out to see if it was connected and see if I could find another piece to this puzzle!"

"Ohhhhh, you had a 'hunch'!"

Alex was pulling out all her sarcasm now as she flexed her index and middle finger on each hand into a quotation as she said the word "hunch."

Her voice got louder as she said, "That's just great, risk going to jail, possibly getting shot by some weekend rent-a-cop all because you had a 'hunch'."

Without even pausing for a breath, she continued berating me.

"It's that reckless attitude that keeps getting you in trouble with the law!"

My face heated up as my anger began to boil.

"No, my reckless attitude didn't get me caught, it was the fact that someone I trusted turned me in to Daddy and stabbed me in the back!"

Alex leaned back in shock as though I had slapped her in the face, and I saw moisture gathering around her eyes from the hurt.

All of a sudden, we heard banging on the deck we were sitting on and we both realized that we were yelling loud enough for Phillip and Simon to hear our conversation.

"Shut up out there, I'm trying to take a nap!" Simon yelled through the door of the cabin behind us.

Alex looked embarrassed, turned her torso and head away from me, and discreetly used her left hand to wipe her eyes.

I sighed. I didn't want to hurt Alex and it was apparent that my mouth had run away from me.

I looked down at the deck, "Sorry, I...I didn't mean what I said."

I looked up into her eyes and saw how red they were.

"Yes, you did!" she whispered.

I couldn't dispute her words. I turned away from her gaze as I thought about those three words.

Dreamers

CHAPTER 5 – RECHARGING

PACIFIC OCEAN
ALEXI MASTERS

After Phillip and Simon followed Kyle into the cabin, I leaned against the outside cabin wall to force myself to relax. The battle of emotions between Kyle and I were intense. I felt the fear and excitement build up in me as he climbed up on the deck and stalked towards me. I felt a bit like a trapped animal and the hunter had just arrived. I kept breathing in and out slowly, trying unsuccessfully to calm myself down. I couldn't help but smile as I remembered the look on Kyle's face when I pushed him overboard.

I turned to my left and climbed up onto the top deck where the incident began. I walked over to where Kyle had been standing and replayed the images in my mind, trying to remember everything and pull what details I could from the scene.

I pictured everything from the moment my head raised high enough to see him sitting in this spot talking to Simon and remembered the movements played out by him and me. When I arrived at the moment where he turned his head and shoulders to face me, I knew how much I was drawn to his eyes. I blushed at the recognition, but then I saw something I hadn't noticed before. Kyle had a small smile on his face, and I could tell it was because he was happy. Was he happy to see me or was he happy that he knew I was going to be irritated with what I had overheard?

I had always been good at picking apart a situation to examine it from as many angles as possible. It was one of the traits my dad identified in me when I was a little girl and he encouraged me by giving me more puzzles than dolls to play with. At the end of each puzzle, whether I had solved it or not, was always a prize like a toy or some candy as my reward for trying.

Truth be told, it wasn't the puzzle or the reward that I enjoyed about the games. It was the time I got to spend with my father learning from him and feeling the love and pride he felt for me. Because of that, I always tried to make him proud of me by doing the right thing. I grew up a daddy's girl and I loved every moment I spent with him.

I loved my parents fiercely, but my dad was definitely Number One in my life. I made sure my room was always clean, my grades were always good, and every decision I made was to make him proud. The day I told on Kyle and Phillip for the prank they pulled on my father was the toughest decision of my life. I felt guilty for telling on them, especially Kyle, but I didn't want to let my father down. Though I had hid it well, I didn't like hurting Kyle the way I did. I remembered back to the day I first saw him at my new high school. He looked at me and I looked at him before any others. When our eyes met for the first time, I felt an electric charge between us. I felt goose bumps rising up on my arms from that look. It scared me because of the feelings it caused, so I looked away. Every time I passed Kyle in school or out in town and our eyes locked again, I always felt that electric charge. Lately, that look had only been matched by the loathing I saw in his eyes after he found out I turned him in.

I really didn't understand why it was that big of a deal; it was only a stupid prank. Considering the embarrassment Kyle caused my father, I thought he and Phillip got off rather light. But after seeing the look in Kyle's eyes, I felt my heart break. The change it caused pushed all the emotions inside of me further to the surface, where I couldn't ignore them. I was saddened by what I had done to him, but at the same time I was angry with him for how he treated other girls... how he had treated my best friend. Though I would never admit it to anyone but myself, I was mostly angry that he had never asked me out. I knew if he had, I probably would have just been another one of his one-week wonders. I doubt I would have had the strength to say no to him, even knowing that. But he never asked.

I finally sat down on the deck where Kyle had once sat and tried to organize my feelings for him to where they made sense. Thinking of Kyle brought out anger, loathing, joy, fear, excitement, and hope inside of me. No matter how much I tried to organize these feelings, they just didn't make any sense. I stretched myself onto the deck and in the sun. I felt the heat of the sun above me as I closed my eyes, and felt the heat beneath me from the aluminum of the boat. I concentrated on my breathing, fearing the time when Kyle would come back on deck.

After I rested there for several minutes, I heard talking from the cabin below me. I couldn't make out anything more than muffled conversation through the deck, but I could tell that there were three distinct voices. I knew Kyle would be up here soon, and I was both excited and scared of what he might do. After I heard someone walk out onto the back deck, I closed my eyes tight and pretended to be sleeping. I wasn't sure if it was Kyle, but I considered it a likely scenario. I didn't know if I was just a coward for not wanting to face him and the argument that I knew we would have or if I was afraid he would roll me off the deck in retaliation for earlier. The excitement built up inside me and I couldn't wait to find out.

I heard the sound of Kyle climbing up the ladder and then standing on the deck. By the lack of sound, I figured he was standing by the ladder and hadn't closed the distance between us.

What was he waiting for?

Was he wrestling with the decision?

How hard can it be to decide a course of action?

I mean seriously, talk about keeping a girl waiting.

Then I heard Kyle start walking towards me. It was only about ten feet from the ladder to me, so it didn't take him long to stop just to the right of my head.

I thought, Oh my God, is he going to kick me?

I quickly banished the thought. Kyle wouldn't kick me. In the three years we had been in school together, I'd never seen Kyle lift a hand against anyone.

Relax…breathe, I told myself.

Kyle sat down next to me, but didn't say anything.

I became more frantic, and my thoughts were chaotic from one moment to the next. I was afraid to open my eyes and look up at him, but he wasn't saying anything. What was he waiting for, horns to pop out of my head?

Then I pictured myself lying on the deck with him sitting next to me and staring down at me, and it finally dawned. My heart was pounding in my chest loud enough that I was sure Kyle could hear it and it was getting harder to breathe. Here I was lying on the deck next to Kyle, asleep like Sleeping Beauty. That's just great!

Was he going to kiss me?

Did I want him to kiss me?

What the heck was I thinking?

Of course, I wanted him to kiss me. I mean, what sane girl would not want Kyle to kiss them?

My hormones shifted long enough for my brain to play a part and I remembered his one-week wonders, which cleared my head up enough to decide. If he kissed me, I would slap him.

I heard Kyle rustling around next to me, but I didn't know what he was doing. So, I decided to wait to see if he would make the first move.

After a minute, the smell of lotion washed over me and I had no idea why. I couldn't help but wonder what he was doing...and then it dawned on me that he was putting on lotion. Probably sunscreen, I mean we were in the Pacific Ocean and the sun was bright that day. So, Kyle must have been putting lotion on himself...on his arms, his legs, his handsome face.

Grr, get a hold of yourself, I thought.

Kyle poked my arm. I opened my eyes and looked at him. The sun glinted off of the right side of his face and for a brief moment he looked like an angel. After he handed me the plastic bottle and I verified it was in fact sunscreen, I squeezed out some lotion and applied it to my arms, face, and neck.

After I was done, I asked how he had learned about this island we were heading to. It didn't take long for our conversation to turn into a heated argument that apparently got loud enough to warrant a response from the peanut gallery below.

As I turned away from Kyle with tears forming in my eyes from what he had said, I couldn't help but feel angry with him and angry with myself for turning him in. He was right, I did turn him in…but he didn't fully understand why I had to do it. I wiped the tears from my eyes, embarrassed that he might see them. It caught me by surprise when he apologized for what he said, causing me to turn back around and look into his eyes. Once I looked at him I didn't believe for a second that he was sorry about what he said, but he was sorry about something and I couldn't latch onto exactly what.

Embracing the anger I felt towards him for his harsh words, I told him that he'd meant what he said. He couldn't seem to refute my statement, so the silence between us grew at that moment and neither of us dared to break it.

Dreamers

CHAPTER 6 – THE HEIST

PACIFIC OCEAN
KYLE BISHOP

We didn't talk to each other for several minutes, allowing the silence to grow. What Alex said was true and I felt the hurt inside of me because of it. I said something to intentionally hurt her, and I did it on purpose. At the time, I felt she had betrayed me when she turned Phillip and me in to her dad. I knew she was just being Alex, following the rules, and I figured she probably had a close relationship with her father. I knew overall the incident was minor, but betrayal had always been something next to impossible for me to forgive. It had been that way since my father left for no reason when I was a kid, walking out on me and my mom. He had made vows to her and then betrayed them.

But was what Alex did the same?

Should I have held her to the same standard?

I'm not sure she meant to cause harm, but surely she had to realize what would happen when she told her father.

Regardless of what she did, I still felt miserable for what I said. I let my anger get in the way and allowed it to blind me. I knew I should probably beg to take back what I said, but I just couldn't bring myself to act that way. I never wanted to hurt her, but I guess with us it was inevitable. I sighed and just focused on my breathing for a minute to make sure I was calm.

I could tell that Alex wasn't going to start the conversation again, so I decided to continue where I had left off.

"Well...umm...anyways, I had decided that in order to get more information, we needed to have a look into one of the companies' systems. Simon was able to locate a textile company in Portland called Synthtex that seemed large enough and likely enough of a target."

Alex looked at me again and I could tell she was also trying to bury her anger and focus on what I was saying to siphon out any details.

Seeing that she hadn't raised a question yet, I decided to continue, "By itself, the company wasn't large enough to affect the overall textile industry or the market. But as I mentioned earlier, the company had the same organization as the larger corporate businesses that were able to affect change in the market."

Alex looked at me and pursed her lips. I could tell she was still dissatisfied with my hunch, but she didn't say anything and allowed me to continue.

"I asked Simon..."

Before I could finish my sentence, Alex interrupted with a question.

"Who's the CEO, and are they publicly traded?"

I shook my head, "No, they aren't publicly traded. That was the first thing I checked. The company appears to be too small. The CEO is some guy named Ralph Winthrop. Apparently, he's always owned the company."

I looked at Alex to see if she had any other questions. Alex chewed on her bottom lip and her eyes glanced away from me. I could tell her brain was trying to figure something out, so I decided to give her a minute. Startled, she looked up at me as if she had figured something out.

Her accusing eyes bored into me as she said, "There was something else, wasn't there? Some other piece of information you had that made you decide on this company."

I felt warmth inside of me when she said that. I always felt that her mind was an amazing gift in how she approached the world. Though no sane guy could deny how beautiful she was, it was her mind that truly made her spectacular.

"You are correct, there was something else. Simon was able to hack into the company's server and copy their financial records."

Alex inhaled from this statement. I didn't want to mention it earlier, because I knew she would hate the fact that it was illegal and that I had allowed it.

Before she blew off the handle again, I said, "What Simon and I found is that nine years back there was a significant influx of cash into the CEO's personal account."

Alex's eyes opened wide.

"Also, the ownership listing in the owner's equity section no longer carried his name."

"Whose name was on it?" Alex asked.

"There wasn't anyone listed, and the financials from that date forward only show a general account name for the capital investment."

Alex sat there and chewed on that morsel of information. I wanted to see if she would come up with the same conclusion I had drawn.

After a moment she asked her next follow-up question, "Were there any press releases around that time regarding that change?"

I shook my head no and waited.

After less than ten seconds she didn't disappoint when she proclaimed, "Someone bought them out!"

A smile spread across my face, as I was proud that she had figured out the same thing I had. I must admit I did feel a smidgeon of annoyance that she had figured it out faster than me.

I confirmed her suspicions with my own, "That's what I concluded as well."

Alex got a confused look on her face, and I could tell something was bothering her.

"What?" I demanded.

Alex looked at me, "But Simon mentioned that you broke into their office earlier."

She was trying to work it out in her head, "If you had him hack into their server, then why did you have to break into their office? What were you hoping to find?"

Last weekend, Phillip, Simon, and I had broken into Synthtex to go through the CEO's office and hack into his personal computer.

I looked at Alex, expecting the answer to be obvious…but either she hadn't guessed it or wanted to hear it from me.

"We wanted to learn the 'who' in our questions."

Alex bit down on the tip of her thumb as she appeared lost in thought again.

I interrupted her thinking, "We didn't find the specifics of the 'who' while we were there, just that our trail led us to this island we're heading to. When we're there, I'm hoping to learn the 'who' and the 'why'."

Alex sat up straighter, like she was preparing herself for the answers we hoped to find when we finally arrived.

"Tell me everything that happened that night and don't leave out any details."

Again, my eyebrows rose up at her command. Man, she can be bossy, but who knew bossy could be so sexy?

Alex rolled her eyes at my response and reluctantly added, "Please."

Dreamers

CHAPTER 7 – BREAKING & ENTERING

PACIFIC OCEAN
KYLE BISHOP

Simon climbed up onto the deck and sat down next to me and Alex.

"What's going on?" he said as he looked back and forth between Alex and me.

I looked over at Simon, noticing that he had also changed into some shorts and a shirt with Ms. Pac Man on it chasing a pellet and the words "Eat Me!" below it. As pale as Simon was for spending most of his waking hours in his room, I figured the sun was going to turn him into a burned match. I picked up the bottle of sunscreen and handed it over. Simon began to squeeze some of the lotion into his hand and waited for an answer from one of us.

"Alex wants to know about last weekend," I said.

Simon looked up and said, "Ahhh."

He quickly added, "That was fun, let's not do that again."

He looked at me and asked, "So, are you telling the story or am I?"

He grinned.

I looked at him and could tell I wouldn't like his version and the accuracy would be questionable.

"I thought you were taking a nap?" I replied.

"I wasn't sleeping; I just said that to annoy you both," he said with a smile.

Alex slapped Simon's shoulder playfully, causing him to flinch and pull up his other hand to cover his shoulder.

He put on his best wounded look, "Alex, violence is never the answer. Think happy thoughts!"

Alex looked like she wanted to hit him again; instead, she went with, "I'm sure the violence I want to inflict will make me happy."

An evil grin spread across Alex's face as she said this and the color in Simon's face drained. I laughed out loud at their banter and couldn't get enough of the shocked expression on Simon's face. I don't think either of us had ever heard her say anything that would be considered "improper" for a lady. I think I found it so funny because of the way she responded.

Simon looked like he was trying to figure out how to respond and kept looking back and forth between us. He gestured at me, "Go ahead, Kyle, let's hear the tale. Don't worry, I'll be here to fill in all the difficult bits and remind you of my daring heroics."

My eyes rolled at that remark, but I wanted to get this out of the way. I needed Alex to get past this, so we could focus on the island tomorrow.

I took a deep breath and let it out, "All right."

I began to explain to Alex how we met up that night at Phillip's house before heading out. We figured it would take us several hours to get there, get in, and get out before anyone was aware of our presence. Being a Saturday, we were going to pull an all-nighter as we had to drive up to Portland. All three of us lived in the same neighborhood and we just had to cut through a few yards to get to each other's houses. Phillip's room was decorated with wall posters representing his favorite bands and one of Seattle's running backs. To my surprise it was cleaner than my room, with a twin bed shoved into a corner, a discount store dresser that looked ready for the dump, and a worktable presently occupied with a small engine that was only half assembled.

Displayed on the bookshelves were the occasional paperback and a horde of trophies, plaques, and ribbons showing various standings in a multitude of sports and activities we both had participated in. Most of them were exact copies of what was in my own room. I think both of us only used such things to take up space because to us, all of those activities were just fun things we enjoyed doing and we were rewarded for doing it well. The only high-quality object in the room was the plush Berber carpet beneath our feet that his parents had installed earlier in the year.

Phillip's parents never had any kids of their own, which was why they had adopted him. Because of this, they encouraged him in any activity or project he had a mind for. Any time not spent working was occupied with dinners and games at either their house or one of their friends, with the weekends reserved for church and some quiet time. Surprisingly they were both laid back, but it was his father who got Phillip interested in engineering. Phillip's dad began rebuilding a half-destroyed 2008 Chevy Charger that he had picked up at the junkyard when Phillip was twelve. Phillip started working on it in his spare time and, of course, he got hooked. It wasn't until four years later when they were closing to finishing it that Phillip's dad gave it to Phillip as a sixteenth birthday present. Since then, Phillip had reupholstered the inside, got a new paint job, and it now looked like new.

Simon was lying on Phillip's bed with his legs dangling over the side punching away at his DS, while Phillip and I put our gear into a gym bag. We knew this was breaking and entering and we would most likely end up in jail if caught. Though Phillip's parents would be disappointed in him if that happened, my mom would probably kill me quickly…if I was lucky. Simon's parents, on the other hand, would probably die of shock that their kid did something spontaneous in his life, even if it did require a bond to get out of jail.

We packed three dark-colored pullover hoodies, three flashlights with red light filters, and an assortment of granola bars to hold us over.

Simon was bringing along a laptop and a small bag of electronics to assist with bypassing security and gaining access to the CEO's office. I got a copy of the building's plans from the county office, so we could identify which office was most likely the correct one.

Once we gathered our gear, we left Phillip's room on the way to the garage via the kitchen. Phillip took a moment to tell his parents goodbye while Simon and I walked through the kitchen and out into the garage. Simon climbed into the back seat and I took shotgun.

After about a minute, Phillip came out and closed the garage door behind him. He climbed into the driver's seat and cranked up the 2008 Dodge Charger's 425-horsepower engine. He clicked the automatic garage door opener attached to his visor and pulled out into the road as we made our way to Portland.

An hour and a half later, we arrived in Portland at the Synthtex plant. My research into Synthtex identified it as a textile manufacturer of the synthetic material used in clothing. They combined hemp and synthetic fibers to manufacture the rolls of fabric used to make stain-resistant and anti-wrinkle clothing. Their website advertised it as being the next best thing since individually wrapped sliced cheese. How a website could describe something so boring in such an exciting way is a credit to their advertising department.

The company itself was located in a manufacturer's business park surrounded by other factories that produced car parts, magazines, and chemicals. The million-square-foot plant was built about a dozen years ago and was two stories high with built-in loading docks and a rent-a-cop at the main gate. Security was supplied by the business park's owner and offered at a respectable rate to the various tenant businesses.

We sat in the parking lot of the plant directly across the street from Synthtex. Synthtex was a day manufacturer, so there weren't any cars parked in their lot. To avoid standing out we parked in their neighbor's lot, which appeared to have round-the-clock shifts. So, there were plenty of cars on this side to blend in with. Phillip parked in the closest available spot to our target while staying between two light poles and the dark gap created from their poor placement. We looked over the place for about half an hour to get a sense of any patrols. From the back seat, I began to hear the theme music from *Mission Impossible* playing over Simon's laptop speakers. Phillip and I turned our heads to look at Simon in the back seat as a grin appeared on Phillip's face.

Before Phillip or I could comment, Simon looked up at us.

"What?" he said, as he shrugged his shoulders and then looked back down at his laptop.

I turned in my seat to look back at the plant. I figured Simon needed help occupying his time, so I asked, "What's the best way in, Simon?"

Simon cut off the theme music and started typing on his laptop in search of the answer.

"The best way in is through one of the side doors that goes directly into the executives' entrance. Unfortunately, we will need a key card to pass through."

I looked at the door he was referring to and could see a small light bulb above the door with the keycard scanner to the left of the door.

Not liking that option, I asked, "Can't you hack into their system like you did before and get us access?"

I could see Simon shaking his head from the reflection in the front windshield.

"Synthtex's system doesn't control the security for the building. It's controlled by the security firm that was contracted by the business park. I could hack into their system, but we would still need a swipe card and a terminal to program it at."

Simon breathed in and then exhaled before continuing, "The only way I can think of is the docks. The loading dock doors are motorized to open and close. They can be manually opened as long as they haven't been locked out for the night."

Simon looked at Phillip and me with concern on his face, "We'd have to get lucky!"

I thought about what other options we had, and they were less appealing.

I replied, "All right, let's do this. In and out!"

I picked up the gym bag at my feet and opened it up. I pulled out the hoodies and passed two to Phillip and Simon. I knew hoodies were kind of cliché, but we weren't exactly commandos here. I gave one flashlight to Phillip and kept the other.

Simon would be between us and already had enough to carry. After we pulled the black hoodies over our shirts, I could tell that we looked like three guys ready to knock off a 7-Eleven. Hopefully no one would walk out into this parking lot to see us as we were coming and going. I occasionally saw a camera here and there attached to some of the light poles, but none appeared to be aimed towards us.

We all got out of the car and crouched low near the front end of the charger, trying to stay inside the darker shadows. None of us were exactly trained for espionage or stealth beyond the occasional paintball battles Phillip and I had participated in. We stuck to the shadows and worked our way across the street and to the right of the building where the loading docks were located. As I saw from the car, there were several trailers already pulled up to a few of the docks waiting to be filled or emptied. Accessing any of those doors would be impossible, as the trailers were pressed against the door seals and not even Simon would be able to squeeze through. We split the remaining doors between us to check them all as fast as possible. The first one I ran up to was in a set of three squeezed between two trailers. Simon and

Phillip headed around the trailer to check doors further down.

I grabbed the handle and attempted to push it up, but it didn't budge. The aluminum doors made stress noises as I attempted to move them, and I cringed because the noise sounded incredibly loud. I looked around to see if I could hear anyone coming. After a few seconds, I moved to the next door and attempted the same thing, but with a little less force. Again, it was locked and I had one more try before going to check on the others. The third dock door was partially lifted as though a truck had incorrectly backed up into it, causing the left side of the door to sit about two inches off the ground unlike the right half. I hoped the third time would be the charm, so I grabbed the door handle and pushed upwards. Mistakenly I used too much force again, but beyond the offensive noise the door made it didn't budge. Swearing, I turned to my right and ducked underneath the trailer I was up against to cross over to the other side where Simon and Phillip were.

When I reached the other side, I came up behind Simon who had his back to me. Simon was keeping an eye out for Phillip and I knew if I called out to him or tapped him on the shoulder, he would probably jump out of his skin and possibly call out. Grinning to myself, I stalked up behind him and in a quick move wrapped my left arm around his left arm and chest and put my right hand over his mouth to prevent him from calling out. I felt Simon jerk and tense up as I grabbed him, but considering I was larger than him he couldn't break free.

I put my mouth up near his left ear, "Simon, it's me!"

I immediately felt him relax and I let him go. Simon turned on me and the lenses on his round glasses magnified the size of his eyes, displaying the shock on his face. I was pretty sure Simon would need to change his underwear after we left.

"What did you do that for?" he berated me.

After his eyes got a little smaller, he said through gritted teeth, "You gave me a heart attack!"

I looked at Simon, realized he wasn't exactly commando material, and lightly chastised him for his poor observational skills.

"Pay better attention next time." I told him.

Simon gave me an annoyed look, "I was trying to keep an eye out for Phillip."

I looked around for a second to make sure no one was around and saw Phillip heading back towards us.

"Don't worry about Phillip, worry about everyone else around here…like security."

I could tell Simon was about to respond in his normal sarcastic defense, when Phillip jogged up and said "Hey!"

Simon jumped again as he turned around to face Phillip.

Phillip looked at Simon's reaction, "Jumpy much?" as Phillip pinched his eyes and lips together and shook his head side to side as though he was answering for Simon in a mocking way.

I quietly laughed and half-heartedly tried to restore some order to myself. After Simon had calmed down, I asked if they had any luck finding a way in. Simon shook his head and Phillip said no. Both could see from the disappointed look on my face that I had struck out as well.

I asked Simon, "What other options do we have?"

Simon was thinking for a moment and I saw his eyes go from left to right, as if he were trying to visualize the place.

He looked up at me and said deadpan, "The front door!"

"No way," was Phillip's reply to that suggestion. "There's no way we could get past the guard unseen."

I remembered that there was one rent-a-cop stationed next to a turnstile that led into the front door. I tried to think of possible ways to distract him or draw him off, but I was sure that he would just call for assistance and make it worse on us. Phillip and Simon both looked at me for the answer and watched me trying to puzzle through it. I recalled the schematics of the building we had obtained and tried to visualize each access point to see if Simon had overlooked any option. The building had the front door, one admin door for the executives to come and go, the dock doors (which we had ruled out), and a bunch of fire safety doors that only opened from the inside and were rigged with fire alarms. Our options didn't look very good.

And then it came to me, "Skylights!"

Both Phillip and Simon looked at me like I had lost my mind and were probably wondering why random meaningless words were coming out of my mouth.

I could tell they didn't understand, so I explained, "There are access ports on top of every factory for carbon dioxide exhaust."

Simon raised his right hand up and away from his body; his hand was at face level with a finger pointing up like he was in a classroom and wanted permission to ask a question. He put it back down, but raised it again like he was trying to find fault with my suggestion.

Phillip broke the silence, "How do you know the exhaust ports aren't locked and more importantly how do we get down from the room to the ground floor without dropping twenty-something feet?"

Simon finally broke out of his internal debate and answered for me.

"Most are automated and can be manually opened if necessary."

Before Phillip could butt in, Simon continued, "It's doubtful they are locked, because how many people would think to break in from the roof? And last, there is a catwalk underneath that area which is probably used by maintenance to get onto the roof to work on the air conditioner."

I gave Phillip a minute to find any holes in this approach, as he had as much at stake as the rest of us.

"If this was a possible choice, then why didn't you mention it earlier?" Phillip asked Simon.

Simon shrugged before answering, "Because how many people would think to break in from the roof?"

Phillip looked back at me, "How are we going to get up there?"

I looked past Phillip and Simon in the direction from which Phillip had come and gestured for them to follow me. We walked quickly over to the right side of the dock where it was even darker, which was perfect. We came upon a cardboard compacter attached to the plant for the crushing and recycling of any cardboard used, spotting a few compressed bundles already loaded onto pallets.

I climbed to the top of the compactor and then gazed at the roof to judge what distance remained. I could see that the distance was still too far, but I noticed that the trailer parked next to it was a few feet higher. I jumped the small distance onto the top of the trailer and looked again. The roof edge still appeared to be nine to ten feet higher, but definitely more doable. I looked down at Phillip and Simon and gestured for them to climb up. Phillip began climbing up the compactor, but Simon just looked up at me like I had lost my mind.

In a shaky whisper, Simon spoke up, "I don't think this is a very good idea."

I could tell Simon was nervous and figured he was probably afraid of heights. I considered leaving him there to watch our exit, but then I realized I needed him to hack into the CEO's personal computer. My computer skills were too limited to ensure our success.

"We'll be fine, Simon. Phillip and I will be right here beside you and we'll take it one step at a time."

As Phillip completed his climb and jumped onto the trailer with me, I noticed Simon looking around. He'd probably just realized if he stayed behind that he would be out here by himself and likely didn't relish the thought. He turned to the compacter and began to climb up.

I walked over to the wall and gestured Phillip over, "Phillip, give me a boost!"

Phillip looked over at me then up at the remaining wall. He figured out what I was referring to, stood next to the wall, and laced the fingers of his hands together to make a stirrup for me to climb onto. I turned and saw Simon jump onto the trailer without any issues. I quickly moved forward towards Phillip, trying to pick up a little speed, stepped up into his cupped hands with my left foot, and leapt up. Phillip pulled up at the same time, trying to increase my momentum and get me up the last few feet. The distance wasn't as far as I expected and I came to a stop, with my hands grabbing the edge of the roof at chest level. I easily pulled myself over the remainder of the way and onto the roof. I took a moment to look around the roof and saw plastic sheets covering the roof, several exhaust ports, and two air conditioners. I turned back to the ledge and leaned over the side, stretching out my arm to help the next one up. Simon waited for Phillip to give him a boost. When Phillip noticed me leaning over with a hand out, he turned to Simon and signaled for him to go ahead. I saw that Simon still looked nervous, but I was confident that he could do this. Simon repeated the steps I took to boost himself onto the roof, but I could tell when he stepped into Phillip's hands that he wouldn't be able to jump up as much.

Regardless of Simon's ability, the simple boost of Phillip holding him up and attempting to raise him higher was sufficient for me to grab onto Simon's forearm and pull him up to the roof. Simon was light enough that I was able to easily pull him over and he flopped onto the roof like a dead fish. Seeing that he was fine, I turned back to assist Phillip up. Phillip backed up about the same distance as the rest of us and did a quick running leap to reach out for my hand. I grasped his forearm before he impacted the wall with a slight exhale of breath escaping. Though Phillip was heavier than Simon, he was able to pull himself up onto the roof with my assistance. Once we were all up top, I decided to give us a second to catch our breath before proceeding.

After the brief rest, I stood up and walked towards the center of the roof. I remembered from the schematics that the catwalk ran underneath the center of the building from one end to the other. When I approached the central skylight, I saw a square faded yellow plastic covering that was about four feet in size. The color of the plastic looked like the whole building had smoked a pack of cigarettes every day during its life and the skylight was also stained with this brackish yellow color. I saw the hinges attached to the skylight and figured out which end opened. I grabbed underneath the lip of the skylight with my fingertips and pulled up. At first it appeared locked and wouldn't budge, but then it jerked loose and my hand flung up...almost hitting Phillip in the face. I hadn't noticed that Phillip had walked up behind me, as I was too focused on the skylight.

I looked down into the hole and noticed a small metal ladder going down about six feet to the metal catwalk. I didn't see any alarm strips around the skylight, so I was pretty sure I hadn't set anything off...though I wasn't completely sure if I was right. I looked past Phillip and saw Simon sitting where he landed, with his back against the roof lip. I signaled for Simon to head over, so we could go inside.

"I'm going first," Phillip said as he stepped past me to climb down the ladder.

I let him go and made sure Simon caught up. I wanted him between us at all times, so we could keep him out of trouble. Simon arrived next to me and leaned over to look into the skylight access. All that could be seen below the catwalk was darkness with occasional glints coming off the metal of whatever machinery the manufacturer used. Simon saw Phillip climbing down the ladder to the catwalk and I could tell that he noticed the darkness below him.

"No way...no way!" Simon backed away from the skylight with his hands in front of him, as though he was pushing himself away from the edge.

I stepped towards him, trying to reassure him with my confidence.

"Simon, you can do this."

He crossed his arms, put his hands in his armpits, and just kept shaking his head no.

"Simon!" I said louder than I wanted to.

Simon looked at me. His eyes had gotten large again behind his glasses, but at least I had gotten his attention.

I tried to calm him down, "Simon, I know you're not a fan of heights. But we have to do this."

I kept my voice calm and firm in what Phillip referred to as my command voice.

"Phillip is already on the catwalk waiting on us."

Simon turned his head away from me and I could tell he was trying to fight his demons. I knew Simon had the strength to overcome his fear, but sometimes a person's mind just needs something else to focus on. I let my anger build up inside of me; I knew that I would need it to sound remotely convincing. In the best menacing tone I could manage, I looked directly at Simon and called his name. Simon's head swiveled back to look at me and I stared directly into his eyes, focusing all the anger I could find inside of me into that look. I'm unsure if the look came across as menacing or stupid, but either way I had his attention.

"Get down that ladder...now!" I stated matter of factly, leaving no room for discussion.

I heard my heartbeat thumping in my ears and waited through a few of those beats before Simon moved back toward the skylight. He didn't look eager to go, but reluctantly did as he was told. I knew I couldn't force him down there, but I needed him too much to not try to convince him.

Simon turned around, so he could climb down onto the ladder rung, and slowly lowered himself down. I watched him as he took each rung slowly until his feet finally touched the catwalk. It was my turn, so I started to climb down as well. I left the skylight open, so we could leave the same way, and continued down the ladder.

When I was about three rungs from the ground, I heard what sounded like a metal pole shearing away from another piece of metal behind me. I turned my head quickly and saw Phillip falling back and going over the edge. I didn't know how it happened, but the railing pole where Phillip was standing just wasn't there anymore. Time felt like it slowed down and each fraction of a second felt like a minute. I jumped the last few rungs down and landed heavily onto the catwalk. I rushed to grab Phillip before he fell, but I knew I was too far away to reach him in time. Just as his upper torso came even with the floor of the catwalk, I prayed he would be able to reach out and grab a handhold…but I knew that he wasn't going to make it. Phillip was falling to his death.

Dreamers

CHAPTER 8 – FREE FALLING

PACIFIC OCEAN
KYLE BISHOP

As Phillip's hand passed the catwalk floor, I noticed Simon collapse on the floor and reach out. I dived onto the floor to Simon's right side, with half of my body hanging off of the catwalk. I didn't see Phillip as he was falling and confusion set in when I tried to figure out where he was. During that brief second, I couldn't see him anywhere and felt he had already passed into the darkness below.

Then Phillip came swinging into view from under the catwalk, dangling from Simon's outstretched hand. I couldn't believe it. My heart was racing, I was so scared. Simon had caught

Phillip and now was swinging back and forth from his momentum.

"I can't hold him!" Simon cried.

I looked at Simon and realized that my pencil-thin friend was holding up someone twice his size. His face was covered in sweat and was bright red from the exertion. I blinked myself out of my momentary shock, reached down, and grabbed Phillip around the back of his forearm. Once I got a good grip, I began pulling both of us up onto the catwalk. Simon held on, even though I knew he was exhausted. I had to give it to him; he held firm and reacted fast regardless of his fear of heights. I always liked Simon for the odd personality he brought to our little group, but I was never more thankful for him as a friend than at that moment.

When Phillip was finally on the catwalk with only his feet and calves still over the side, we all lay down to try to calm our racing hearts and regain some composure.

Phillip looked at me and with all seriousness said, "For a second there, I thought I was dead!"

I couldn't help but laugh from my giddiness at the close call and responded, "Die on your own time! You're working for me right now."

Phillip and Simon started laughing and I let the tension go myself. I didn't care if anyone was around to hear us; it just felt good to be alive. After taking a short break to regain our sanity, I stood up and offered a hand to Phillip to help him to his feet. Phillip accepted my offer, stood up, and then turned around to offer the same to Simon. When Simon had regained his footing, Phillip hugged him fiercely and pounded on his back with his palm. I heard Phillip whisper his thanks. Simon appeared surprised by Phillip's reaction, but quickly returned the embrace. I'm sure Phillip would agree with my thoughts that Simon had earned his way into the best friends' category of our relationship.

After the bro moment passed, I decided it was time we continued on. Now that I think about it, I don't remember hearing the metal bar that detached from the catwalk ever hitting the ground. Something like that was bound to make enough noise to wake the dead. Seeing Phillip plunge to what I thought would be his death was enough distraction to allow me to ignore everything else around me. I chastised myself for having such poor situational awareness and promised myself I would work on improving it.

We needed to start moving, so I motioned for the others to move, "Let's hurry up; there's no telling if someone heard all the noise we made."

Phillip and Simon looked at me and then looked at the spot where Phillip fell. Simon leaned over, which surprised me, to see if he could see where the pole had gone…but it was too dark below to see anything. Simon looked back up, waiting for me to take the lead. With Phillip falling over the side and Simon going to his rescue, our order on the catwalk had changed. Simon was now in front of Phillip and me.

"Are you going?" Simon asked me.

I looked at Simon, noticing his eager expression to get moving, and said, "I would, but you are in the way."

Simon looked between me and Phillip, looked behind him at the way we had to go, and realized he was in the lead. I heard Simon swear as the eager expression left his face.

"I still think this is a bad idea," Simon mumbled to himself.

I could hardly disagree with Simon after the recent events, but I didn't want to leave until we had gotten what we came for. Simon turned around and slowly started to baby step his way across the catwalk. We had about half the plant to cross on this catwalk and there should have been a ladder leading down the wall near the front, provided the plans were still accurate. Simon didn't look happy about leading our group and I saw him fight to grab hold of the railing for support, knowing that the railing wasn't reliable.

After the day and a half that it had taken us to walk across the catwalk to the ladder, our senior citizen moment had finally passed. I couldn't blame Simon for taking it slow, considering his lack of love for heights and Phillip's heroic brush with death. I think Simon was eager to get his feet on solid ground, as it didn't even take any coaxing to get him onto the ladder to go down. Before he could start his descent, I told Simon to be careful and to test each rung before putting his full weight on it. Simon was about halfway down, so Phillip started his climb down and I worked my way up against the ladder as I waited for my turn. After Phillip made it about halfway down, I head down and made it to the concrete floor of the plant without further incident. Simon and Phillip were both waiting for me when I arrived.

I motioned for them to follow me as I headed in the direction of the administration department. Phillip and I turned on our flashlights to help guide us, but kept them aimed at the floor to limit anyone else from easily spotting us. I didn't want to dwell on the catwalk incident and didn't want Simon to stress over the fact that we would have to leave the same way. The ladder we came down was just to the right of the admin area and only required us to walk about twenty to thirty feet before we reached the outer edge of the department. A set of double doors stood open and I spotted a receptionist desk inside with a faint glowing light shining off of it. As the three of us entered the reception area, I could see the reception desk in front of us more clearly. To the left against a wall was a coffee table, covered with a few magazines, in front of several cushioned chairs. To the right of the reception desk was a small crystal waterfall decoration that put off a soft light in the room, while the water made trickling noises as it impacted the little stones at the base. The room also contained several large filing cabinets as well as the standard generic corporate art prints that were hanging on the wall. The room reminded me of the reception area at the school office and the chairs I often sat in before being ushered in to see the principal.

To the left of the desk was a hallway leading further in and I knew that the office we were looking for was at the very end. I walked down the hallway about twenty feet, turned ninety degrees to the right, and proceeded to the end of the hallway. After I reached the end of the hallway, we stood outside of the CEO's office which had a small name plaque next to the door identifying it as his. I doubted there were alarms inside of the building, so I opened the door and looked into the office. I quickly swept the flashlight across the room to make sure no one was in there and nothing felt out of the ordinary. Through a quick glance, I identified an office desk with one chair behind it and two in front of it with a few work items and papers on the desk. To the left of the desk was a PC case with wires leading up to the monitor mounted on the corner of the desk. The wall behind the desk contained several plaques and picture frames containing what appeared to be licenses and diplomas, probably from the CEO's college and other educational institutions. I also noticed at least two pieces of corporate art hanging on the walls and a small filing cabinet along the right wall. There weren't any windows in the room which surprised me, until I remembered that I didn't see any windows on the outside of the building when we were scoping out the place.

I pulled my head back out of the room and looked at Phillip.

"Keep an eye out here while Simon and I have a look around."

Phillip nodded his head and walked towards the reception area to keep an eye on the plant floor. I motioned Simon into the office and pointed at the computer monitor on the CEO's desk. Simon walked over immediately, sat in the chair behind the desk and began typing on the keyboard. As he started typing the monitor lit up and cast a glow in the office, making it easier to look around. I went to the filing cabinet first and started going through the files there, while Simon stayed busy hacking into the computer.

The filing cabinet was a small two-drawer model, which didn't take long to go through. From what I could determine by going quickly through the files, it held a few contracts, a couple of employee records, and some invoices. The company dealt with large rolls of fabric that required extended forklifts to load them on and off of the trailers. I looked through the contracts first as I thought they would be the most helpful, but the few that were there appeared to be in a negotiation phase and showed several letters back and forth haggling on prices. I put those back, passed over the employee records as unimportant and started going through the invoices. The invoices appeared to be for large orders of fabric to be transported to the nearest docks. What bothered me is that the invoices looked like any other invoices you would expect to see from this type of business, but I couldn't figure out why they were here and not filed in another office.

I started at the beginning and slowly read each of the invoices, looking to see if I could see some type of code or pattern to the script. I wished Alex was here to help. I didn't know of anyone who could identify patterns better.

When I reached the third one, the shipment transit and delivery address caught my attention. I flipped back to the first two and noticed the same instructions, flipped through the rest in the stack and noticed that they had all been all delivered in the same way over the past decade. What was strange about it was that the fabric was being taken to a dock on the West Coast to board a ship for delivery in New York, which was on the East Coast.

Why someone would use such an out-of-the-way delivery system confused me. Transport to New York by ship from the West Coast required the ship to travel through the Panama Canal or further south around the tip of South America. Both methods were more expensive and time consuming then shipping the rolls via truck, train, or airplane. I pulled one of the first invoices out of the cabinet and closed the cabinet.

I walked over to Simon, as he was still pecking away on the keyboard, and said, "Hey, look at this."

Simon grabbed the invoice and started looking it over.

"It's an invoice for fabric, so what?"

I pointed at the invoice in his hand and instructed him to look at the shipping instructions. Simon looked back at the invoice and studied it for a minute or two.

Then he looked back up at me, "That doesn't make any sense."

I could tell he had caught on to what I noticed as odd.

His eyes shifted for a few seconds as he thought it through and then he turned back to the computer, "This invoice appears to have been faxed to the company. I'm going to run a search on all incoming and outgoing faxes and see if we can identify the sender."

I was relieved that Simon had an idea on how to take it further because this information was suspicious, but didn't give us the next step for our search.

Simon spoke up after a minute or so of typing, "I have already searched the CEO's email, the system files, and even the computer's garbage can for deleted files…but couldn't find anything."

Simon kept typing away at the keyboard as he explained this to me.

"I was hoping you had come up with something, because so far I haven't had any luck," I said.

"There!" he exclaimed.

I looked at the information on the monitor, but didn't understand what he was seeing.

The screen just contained a list of numbers separated by periods. After a minute of looking at them, I realized I was looking at a list of IP addresses that were used to identify server locations. With an IP address, Simon should be able to track the origin of the fax. He began typing again, entering codes into the system. I could tell from the previous crash course in computer programming he had given me that he was creating a search string to find the IP address' location. After a minute or two, the computer came back with a return line showing the word <Null> with a set of numbers following it.

Simon blinked in surprise, "Normally, that program would come back with a server name and a city location. It appears the server used wasn't labeled."

I thought about this for a second, felt the plot thickening and asked, "What about the numbers following it?"

Simon looked at them again and responded, "If I had to guess, I would say they were GPS coordinates."

That didn't make any sense to me. Why would a server be that vague?

"You mean longitude and latitude," I said.

I didn't phrase it as a question, but Simon answered anyway.

"Yeah, that's right, but these coordinates put the origin server as somewhere in the Pacific Ocean."

I thought about this for a minute, figured we had enough to go on, and that we needed to get out of here.

"Put everything back the way you found it; it's time to go."

As I walked back to the filing cabinet to return the invoice, I heard loud footsteps in the hallway. I pulled the file cabinet drawer open, shoved the invoice back into its spot and closed the cabinet. Just then, the door burst open.

Phillip ran in slightly winded, "We have to go, right now!"

I didn't bother to ask questions. I saw Simon already heading to the door. The three of us ran back down the hall towards the plant floor. As I neared the reception area, I saw a lot more light than what should have been there. When I crested the corner, I saw that the plant floors' lights were all on and only the admin area was still dark. Phillip pointed in the direction of the main entrance and I saw four security guards had just arrived. One of them immediately spotted us and pointed. I couldn't hear what he was saying to the other guards.

I immediately started running out of the admin office and around the corner to the catwalk ladder and began climbing up with Simon and Phillip behind me. Once I reached the top, I checked to make sure Phillip and Simon were moving quickly as I glanced over at the guards. They had run across the plant floor and were only about twenty feet from the ladder. Simon started coming over the edge onto the catwalk, so I turned and ran as fast as possible down the catwalk, jumped onto the ladder leading to the roof, and began to pull myself up. Once I climbed onto the roof, I saw Simon climbing up the ladder. I waited until he reached the top and pulled him onto the roof with me. Phillip kept looking behind him, which meant the guards were already on the catwalk heading his way. Phillip didn't waste any more time and climbed up to the roof. Once he made it up, I slammed the skylight cover back over the hole to slow the guards down. There was no external lock on it, so I couldn't lock them in, and there was nothing to put over it to weigh it down. So, I just turned back towards where we had climbed onto the roof and ran for dear life with Simon and Phillip on my heels.

I knew that with the guards coming up fast we wouldn't have time for a safe descent from the roof, so I just reacted on instinct and leaped over the roof at the spot I knew the trailer was parked. My aim was dead on, as I impacted in the center of the trailer a few feet from the door. The aluminum of the trailer absorbed some of my impact. I allowed my legs to collapse under me and used my body and shoulders to roll forward to absorb some of my momentum. I stopped in a kneeling position and turned to see Simon in the air right behind me and Phillip just starting his leap off of the roof. I was glad to see that they didn't hesitate in jumping after me, either trusting that I wouldn't get them killed or being just as stupid as I was for trying such a stunt.

Simon impacted on the roof less gracefully than I had and didn't know to bend his legs and roll to burn off his momentum. When he fell, his legs collapsed underneath him and he wasn't able to control his forward velocity or his angle of descent...causing him to roll off the side of the trailer. I was too far away to catch him in time, but I figured falling from a trailer was less serious than from a catwalk about thirty feet in the air. Phillip landed next with more grace and was able to stop himself as I did. He followed me as I dropped from the side of the trailer to the ground, not bothering to climb down the compactor. As I hit the ground, I spotted Simon lying with his back on a compressed bale of cardboard next to the compactor which had broken his fall. Judging by the expression on his face, his landing wasn't all that comfortable and appeared to have knocked the wind out of him.

I grabbed his hand and pulled him none too gently off of the bale and onto his feet as Phillip landed behind me.

"I planned that!" Simon wheezed as we raced back to the car.

I could easily tell he was full of crap, but I wasn't about to stand around and argue the point.

"Of course you did," I replied.

I ran around the plant and across the street to Phillip's car with my two friends close behind me. I glanced back at the roof and saw one guard up there talking into a handheld radio, but no sign of the others. I figured they weren't brave or stupid enough to follow us over the side of the building probably went back the way they came to chase us from the front door.

We all climbed into the Charger. Phillip immediately started the car and peeled out of the parking lot. He got us onto the main road away from the business park and put some distance between us and any pursuit. I wasn't worried about the guards chasing us down once we got in the car and I doubted any of them were close enough to make out our license plate. But they probably called the police. I wanted to be far away from here before they arrived. As we drove away, I thought about what we had found and the coordinates for the fax server. It looked like we were going to have to make another trip, but first we needed more information about the server location.

Dreamers

CHAPTER 9 – DAZED AND CONFUSED

PACIFIC OCEAN
ALEXI MASTERS

I sat on the deck of the ship and listened to Kyle talk about when the broke into Synthtex. Though it upset me that they had willingly broken the law and they could have been arrested if not killed from their stupidity, a small part of me was jealous that Kyle hadn't invited me along...but I knew that Kyle didn't trust me the way he did Simon and Phillip. The fact that I had turned him in before was reason enough for his decision to leave me out. Though I would have tried to talk them out of going, I don't think I would have told on him again. I knew Kyle was reckless at times and figured it was just part of his nature. I just didn't want to see him hurt. Nothing could match the hurt I felt when I saw the disappointment in his eyes after my betrayal. The look in his eyes caused my heart to drop to my feet and it took everything I had not to cry in front of him. When I got back home that day after I saw my dad arresting him and Phillip, I cried into my pillow and stayed there until I exhausted myself enough to fall asleep. The next day, I promised myself that I wouldn't betray his trust again.

Kyle finished up his story by explaining that they determined that the coordinates led to this mysterious island that we were sailing to. I remember him calling me up to let me know what new information they had obtained, but he was vague at the time on how he came across it. After hearing the story, I understood why he didn't tell me. Kyle mentioned that the three of them had decided to use Phillip's uncle's boat to check out the island. I was glad Kyle didn't see the frown on my face through the phone from knowing that they were obviously stealing a boat. I figured it unlikely that Phillip's uncle would have them arrested if he found out. I knew Kyle had only called me to update me on the information they found since I was the first to identify the stock fluctuation, but I felt uneasy letting them go off by themselves. Surprising myself, I asked to come along. The silence on the phone after I made my request was deafening, but I gave him some time to decide. He had no reason to invite me or trust me, but I hoped he would hear my sincerity and not my desperation in my request. After Kyle finally agreed to allow me to come along, I couldn't contain my excitement. I immediately hung up and began packing, even though we wouldn't be leaving until the weekend. I spent the remainder of the week researching boat safety, international maritime law, and whatever information I could glean about our destination.

I looked first at Kyle then over to Simon and couldn't help but feel grateful to him for saving Phillip's life. These three had unknowingly created a comfort zone for me that I had missed when I was away from it. I doubt any of them considered me as a friend and my past behavior had hardly earned me that distinction. But I found comfort being around these three guys who possibly saw me as someone worth being around and not just for my looks. I could only hope the protectiveness I felt for them would one day be reciprocated. Without really thinking about it, I leaned over in Simon's direction, put my arms around him, and gave him a hug and a kiss on his cheek. I could tell he was surprised by my behavior, but it didn't seem to stop a grin from spreading across his face.

"What was that for?"

I looked at him and considered my answer, "That was for saving Phillip's life. Thank you!"

Simon's grin spread from ear to ear. When I let go, I quickly glanced over at Kyle and saw the expression on his face displaying several emotions at once. Did I just make Kyle jealous? I smothered that thought and looked back at Simon. I always felt Simon was really sweet, even in his nerdy ways. It was a shame that most of the girls at school were too self-centered to really notice him. Though he would never turn heads like Kyle and sometimes Phillip did, deep down he was a naturally kind person. I felt he deserved someone wonderful to be his match, and I hoped that one day he would meet her. After concluding that thought, I quickly lashed out and slapped Simon lightly on the back of the head. The slap caught him by surprise again and he reached up and rubbed the back of his head where

I had hit him. His grin disappeared and mock outrage replaced it.

Though I didn't hit him hard, I could tell he was shocked by my actions.

"And what was that for?"

I pointed my index finger up at his face.

"That was for not trying to talk some sense into them and prevent them from doing something so reckless. You should have known better..."

I glanced over at Kyle, who was equally guilty, and I could see the anger building up in him...which made me leave the remainder of what I wanted to say unsaid. Kyle was about the most levelheaded person I'd ever met, even when people were angry at him. The only exception to that rule was when someone attacked anyone he considered a friend...then, all bets were off. I could tell he saw my slap as an attack on Simon's character and he wasn't pleased by it.

Simon stood up, still rubbing the back of his head and probably trying to contain his wounded pride.

"I'm going inside to spot Phillip; it's my turn at the wheel anyways."

Simon walked to the ladder to descend to the lower deck and I turned back to face Kyle. After Simon left, I realized that I was again alone with Kyle. Kyle was staring directly at me with a gaze that felt like he was trying to figure something out about me. I felt my heartbeat picking up in my chest and the heat build up in my cheeks because of that gaze. Even though I could tell he was still angry with me, just being focused on so closely was making it difficult to breathe. Kyle had a dangerous intensity around him that was both exciting and frightening. Though I knew he would never intentionally hurt someone out of malice or spite, the fact that he was capable of such action was worrisome.

"You shouldn't have hit him; it wasn't his fault that Phillip almost fell!"

After regaining my breath from his statement, I couldn't help but immediately fire back, "No, it isn't; it's yours!"

I looked at him accusingly, "Phillip and Simon..."

I inhaled a breath to get this out, trying to fight down the emotional turmoil in me, "...trust you. Both of them would follow you anywhere if you just asked, regardless of how reckless or dangerous it is. That is the level of respect that you command from them. Because of that, they are your responsibility and anything that happens to them will be because of you."

I spat out the last word at Kyle as I finished ranting. I saw his anger change to hurt, but just as quickly get crushed under his control. Grr…he frustrated me sometimes.

I waited for Kyle to explode. I knew it was coming; I had openly challenged him, and I didn't see him as a person who would take that lightly. If wanted to argue it out, then fine; I was game. Kyle turned and faced the front of the boat, looking out at the sea.

"You're right!" Kyle stated so softly that I almost didn't hear him.

But before my brain could process his response, I knee- jerked into a reaction, "What?"

I said it like I wasn't sure I heard him correctly. This had to be a dream; did he just say I was right? I don't think I had ever heard Kyle say something so unselfish, at least not while I was around.

"You're right!" he said louder for my benefit.

I was shocked and didn't know what to say. I blinked several times as my brain tried to process this information and formulate some response. Nothing came to mind.

Kyle continued, "I know they trust me to make the right decisions. But they also look to me to make the tough decisions and accept the consequences of those decisions."

I stared at Kyle watching his lips move as he spoke and stared off into the distance.

"When Phillip almost fell, during the second it took me to understand what had happened, I felt the pain of losing him. After Simon saved him and we pulled him back up and I was lying there on that catwalk, I couldn't help but think of the life he and I have had together. We are brothers in spirit, if not in blood."

Kyle looked at me for a second and then turned back to the approaching sunset. The sun was setting just to the right of us and was just inches from the horizon.

Kyle swallowed more of his pride and continued, "I don't like putting either of them at risk, but at times it is necessary for me to make the hard choices to do what I think is right. And if the decision brings risk, then I can't think of anyone who I'd rather have at my back than them."

At that moment, the sun finally touched the horizon. The moment it did, a bright light was born and looked like it was reflecting from a distant mirror. When the light faded enough for us to comfortably see, the surface of the ocean ignited in flame. The entire surface of the ocean as far as I could see was lit up from the red and orange in the sun, causing the ocean to appear to be on fire. The view was truly magnificent! I wasn't sure if I would see something so wonderful again.

My eyes began to tear up, but the view was just the match that ignited my emotions beyond my control. It was Kyle's words that fueled the blaze. I didn't want to cry in front of Kyle. I didn't want him to see me as weak, as just some girl. I fought the emotional battle within myself, not allowing anything more to show except for the tears building up in my eyes.

Dreamers

CHAPTER 10 – ARRIVAL

PACIFIC OCEAN
KYLE BISHOP

The next morning, I woke up feeling groggy from the last shift. I had been surprised when Alex spotted me at the wheel about two hours before sunrise. I hadn't planned to have her take a shift, but I didn't feel like arguing with her and she was more than capable of steering the boat. With Alex steering in the cabin, I made my way outside to quickly change into some fresh clothes. The ship surprisingly didn't contain a portable shower, so I did without. I couldn't help but think of the talk me Alex and I had last night up on deck.

I walked back into the cabin to put away my dirty laundry and then looked over at Alex standing at the wheel. She was wearing a pair of designer shorts and a button-down blouse, with her hair cascading down her back. I wondered if she would ever wear a frayed T-shirt or a pair of anything with holes in it. Not that it really mattered, as Alex could have made a burlap sack look sexy. It appeared that she had changed into fresh clothes, probably while we were all asleep. Being on a ship with three guys must make it difficult to find alone time.

"How far out are we?" I asked Alex after I completed my appraisal of her.

Alex looked at me as though she were trying to figure the best way to answer the question. I wasn't concerned about any smart-ass replies, as she didn't often stoop to that level.

She finally replied, "We're just a few minutes out. You can actually see the island now ahead of us. You might want to wake up the others."

I couldn't help but feel excited to know that the next step on our journey was moments away. It was time to get moving. I walked over to Phillip, who was sleeping on the seat cushions, and gave his shoulder a slight push. Phillip instantly awoke, as he was a pretty light sleeper.

"What?" he asked.

I looked at Phillip while he tried to rub the sleep out of his eyes, "We're almost there; time to get a move on."

Phillip glanced at Alex at the wheel as I went down to the engine deck to rouse Simon. I climbed down to the engine compartment and saw Simon lying on a blanket near the bulkhead, with a shirt under his head for a pillow. Simon could have slept through a catastrophic event. The engine purring next to him probably just lulled him to sleep. Simon was snoring loud enough to put the engine to shame and I pondered for a brief second if there was a way to harness that type of energy. After a moment I realized it wouldn't matter, as the drool coming out of his mouth would probably short out anything you attached to him. I couldn't help but smile. I lightly nudged his legs with my foot to wake him up. Aside from a few mumbles in his sleep, probably commenting on the inconvenience of my presence, he didn't even move.

"SIMON!" I yelled.

Simon lurched up into a sitting position and looked at me like he couldn't believe I was real. His eyes were wide open and blinking rapidly, as I must have scared the crap out of him. Simon used the shoulder of his shirt to wipe the remaining drool from his mouth.

"We're almost there; get ready," I told him again.

I looked at Simon until I was convinced that he wouldn't just go back to sleep. I then turned around and climbed back up into the main cabin. A few minutes later, Simon climbed up into the cabin after changing into a pair of faded jeans and a faded black T-shirt with a Roswell alien head on the front. I noticed underneath the alien head were the words, "We come in peace!" I laughed out loud and it felt good; the tension from approaching the island was weighing heavily on me and it was good to laugh a little. I saw that Simon was grinning and I commented on his good choice of shirt.

Simon smiled and said, "I was hoping to send a positive message for whomever we meet."

I thought about that for a second myself. I wasn't sure if we would meet someone, but my instinct said that we would find some answers on the island.

Phillip spoke up, "Well, by the looks of that island, I think it is a safe bet that we found out where Gilligan was stranded."

I looked out the bridge window at the island. From the angle at we approached the island, I saw a peak further off to the right. I also noticed a dense concentration of trees just past the shoreline. As we sailed closer, I spotted what appeared to be a dock jutting out from the beach. I pointed at the dock in case the others hadn't seen it. Alex looked where I was pointing and corrected the course of the boat to head towards the dock.

I felt a little uneasiness creep up inside my stomach at seeing the dock. What were the odds that a dock would be available at the side of the island we were approaching?

Phillip walked up to the controls and relieved Alex as he had more experience in docking a boat, though I never asked him if his uncle had let him dock this one. I trusted him to get us in safely, so I went outside and up onto the top deck to be ready to quickly tie us off when we finally docked. As we neared the dock, I spotted a mooring cleat to tie off to and also noticed that there were plastic bumpers on the side of the dock for the boat to rest against. I didn't see anyone, but noticed a faint trail leading from the edge of the dock into the woods.

As we pulled alongside the dock, Phillip cut the engine and allowed the boat to slowly coast into its berth. I looped a rope around the cleat and tied us off. I looked toward the back of the boat and saw Alex tying off the other side, so I jumped off the boat onto the dock.

As I walked towards the shore, I heard Alex and Simon behind me…followed by Phillip after he had secured the cabin. I stood between the dock and the path waiting to see if something was going to happen, just in case we had been spotted.

Phillip walked up beside me and gestured with his head back at the dock.

"Did you notice the wood on the dock is new and the bumpers and cleats don't have any growth on them? Do you think they knew we were coming?"

I admitted to myself that I was wondering the same thing.

Alex spoke up, "We need to be careful!"

I nodded. After taking a single step I froze, as I heard footsteps heading our way. They were loud and rapid as if several people were running. I considered leaving in a hurry, but realized that they would get here before we could get out of range with the boat. We would be unable to avoid a confrontation, so I decided to meet them head-on. Simon backed up a little to stand slightly behind us, but Phillip remained on my right and surprisingly Alex stood to my left. As the running footsteps grew louder I tensed, waiting for the final moment when these people would make themselves known. The tension among the four of us climbed higher the closer they got. Once I knew the footsteps were here, I stared into the opening above the trail and waited for guys with guns to burst forth.

I was surprised when two pale kids propelled themselves out of the woods like angels being ejected from heaven.

I looked down at the two kids, a boy and a girl, as they skidded to a halt several feet in front of us with the girl in the lead. Just as she stopped, she threw both her arms into the air and yelled in a soft pixie voice to declare her victory in the race. The boy stopped next to her and bent over at the waist to grab his knees and try to catch his breath.

"That's not fair; you cheated!" he exclaimed.

She stuck her tongue out at him and started laughing.

I don't know which of the four of us were the most shocked by these two kids, but they weren't what I was expecting for a welcome party. Both the boy and the girl looked to be about six years old and were both dressed in white. Both of them had shock-white hair and very light blue eyes that seemed rather abnormal in this day and age. Their appearance showed that they were related. Both of them sized us up. I couldn't tell if they were considering trying to beat us up or just rob us blind.

Alex was the bravest of us or perhaps she just overcame the shock faster. She stepped toward them and greeted them. The boy looked at the girl for a second or two and the girl burst out laughing again.

I was extremely confused and wondered where these kids came from as well as where their parents were.

Just as I completed that thought a woman's voice yelled from the forest, "When I get a hold of you two, I'm going to skin you both alive!"

Both of the kids stopped laughing and looked shocked and slightly scared as I heard someone else running in our direction from the forest. The two kids ran around us both in opposite directions and hid behind Simon, hoping he would protect them.

Just then a young woman burst out of the forest and into the light. She stopped suddenly and a look of fear overcame her as she stared at us with wide-open eyes. She had brown eyes and long dark hair flowing halfway down her back. Her skin was a soft brown color, which contrasted sharply with the darkness of her hair and eyes. She looked athletic in her build, which probably helped her chase after these other two. I guessed the young woman was about our age and would definitely be classified as extremely beautiful in any part of the world.

I saw Phillip staring at her quite appraisingly and I could hardly blame him for his admiration. Simon looked similarly stupefied, but kept getting distracted by the boy and girl tugging on either arm.

"Who are you?" she asked in a melodic voice.

I heard the fear in her voice, but I also felt the commanding tone. I didn't think we looked that intimidating to others, but something about us seemed to have upset her quite a bit. I stepped forward and introduced myself.

"I'm Kyle, this is Alex, Phillip, and the one in the back is Simon."

She looked first at me and then followed her way to each of our faces as I introduced us. When she looked at Phillip, she quickly looked away and moved to Simon.

"You shouldn't be here," she said. "You need to leave before you get into trouble."

I looked at her and realized she was overcoming her fear pretty fast, but she refused to even look at Phillip. I stored that thought away for later and focused on the situation at hand.

Realizing that no one else was talking I stated, "We came looking for information and we're not leaving until we get it!"

My statement appeared to have startled her, as her body tensed as if she was going to back up, but she changed her mind at the last moment.

The boy leaned out from behind Simon and said, "Cherise, the Administrator sent us to get them and bring them to the beach."

This statement seemed strange to me since we were already on the beach, as we had just come ashore. His statement brought Cherise back to the moment and she realized that both kids were hiding behind us.

"Aiden, Alia...get over here now," she commanded them.

I looked at the two kids. They looked at each other. Alia shrugged. Then both kids both peeled themselves away from Simon and stood beside Cherise. When they were safely at her side, she told them to go back to the beach. Both of the kids sulked for a second. Then, Aiden turned quickly and took off running back into the forest with Alia hot on his heels.

Cherise looked over at us and hesitantly stated, "Well, if the Administrator wants to see you, then follow me. I'll take you to him!"

She reluctantly walked towards the trail opening, but still looked behind her to make sure that we would follow. Alex and then Simon started following her onto the trail. I looked at Phillip, who still had a dazed look. I smacked his shoulder to get his attention and when he looked at me, I reminded him to breathe. I walked after Alex and Simon, while Phillip took up the rear-guard position.

We walked through a dense forest of trees. Only palm trees lined the beach, but deeper in were multiple types of trees that created a wall that wouldn't be easily passed through. The trail before us appeared to be covered in cedar chips and wound through the trees like a snake. I didn't see any other paths diverging from the one we were on…which was barely wide enough for two people to stand side by side, though not comfortably.

Alex spoke up as we were walking to ask Cherise a question, "What's the deal with those two kids?"

Cherise looked back at her and then at the rest of us as if she were confused by the question, "What do you mean?"

Alex tried to clarify her question, "They both appear to be fraternal twins, but I've never seen any with hair or eyes that pale before."

Cherise nodded, "Both of their parents are geneticists."

It didn't take her long for her to realize that her answer didn't help, so she added, "As you may or may not know, most twins have a bond between them that allows one to know if the other one is upset or hurt or makes them able to finish each other's sentences."

I had heard about the connection that some twins had with the other even over great distances, but those two looked a little extreme.

"Their parents genetically modified them during the impregnation process in the hopes of creating a stronger bond than normal. It worked, but it caused a genetic modification to their appearance as a side effect of sorts."

With the exception of Phillip, whom I believe only heard her voice and not what she actually said, the rest of us were shocked by her revelation. Someone had genetically altered the two kids turning them into...I didn't know what. The word "freaks" just sounded rather cruel.

I asked, "Isn't it a little cruel to do that to them?"

Cherise looked back at me with confusion on her face, "Why?"

I tried to clarify what I'd said while hoping I hadn't offended her, "Well, their appearance makes them different from other kids their age. Weren't their parents worried about their children being bullied because of the way they look? I mean, how could they do something like that to them intentionally?"

Cherise started laughing and though it sounded musical, I couldn't help but think she didn't take what I'd said very seriously. I looked at Alex to see if she had figured out what was so funny, but I could tell that she had the same concern I'd raised. Kids these days were merciless when it came to those who looked or acted differently. Though I didn't have a problem with the way they looked, I just didn't understand why their parents did that to them on purpose.

When Cherise finally stopped laughing, she shook her head and said, "Just because you are different doesn't mean that it is bad. Would you care for your own child any less if they were born with a deformity or perhaps born too smart?"

I thought about what she said and quickly decided that she was right.

Before I could comment she continued, "Both of them were born and raised here and are not seen by anyone as different. Yes they may look different than other kids, but they are both just kids themselves and are treated just the same. I understand your concern better now, but you have to understand that it is often parents that ingrain prejudice into their children. If you let a child decide for themselves without the animosity from the parent interfering, then they often just look beyond such petty differences. In a sense it makes them more mature than adults, as they can accept people for who they are and not how they should be. Besides the only thing they have to fear here is me wanting to strangle both of them from time to time."

After she finished talking, I felt like I'd been lectured and scolded by my mom. I understood what she'd said and realized that life didn't exactly move that way in the outside world, even though it should. Sometimes the naïve perspectives are some of the best to embrace, so I could see why in the correct environment both of those kids could be happy.

We finally made it through the dark forest and arrived at another beach. The area almost looked like the oasis you would hope to find if you were ever lost in the desert. The beach itself was more of a small lake with its own waterfall and sand. Surrounding the entire oasis were dense trees like the ones we'd just left. I could make out beach chairs and a tent set up near the water line. Kids of various ages were diving out of the waterfall at the mouth of the lake. Other kids were splashing into the lake a few feet down, attempting forward flips and cannon balls. Several kids sunbathed and others threw several big inflated beach balls. I noticed several young adults about Cherise's age look at us with wary glares as we emerged. I also noticed an older lady chaperoning the kids, though it surprised me that she had one of the balls and was running away from the kids as though the demons of Hell were on her heels.

"The Administrator is over there," Cherise stated, startling me slightly.

I looked back at Cherise and focused on where she was pointing. She was pointing at the tent that took up a small portion of the left side of the lake. The tent was a metallic dark red fabric with no designs or symbols on it that I could see. It appeared that the opening probably faced the lake, as I couldn't see into it from where we were standing.

Cherise looked at all of us again and her gaze lingered on Phillip for just a minute. Then, she raced after her charges to supervise their mischief. I decided that we had gawked long enough, and I was ready for some answers.

Phillip finally spoke, "Wow!"

I looked at him and was sure he hadn't even noticed the lake or waterfall.

"Let's go," I said.

I turned and walked towards the tent, expecting the others to follow behind me.

Dreamers

CHAPTER 11 – THE GAME

THE ISLAND
KYLE BISHOP

As we approached the tent, I noticed that most everyone near or around the lake stopped what they were doing and stared at us. They probably wondered if we were going to attack or kidnap their beloved Administrator. I didn't come for a fight, but I did come for some answers. We had taken a lot of risk by sailing to an unknown situation, but after reviewing it in my mind I still didn't know how we could have been any better prepared.

As I crested the corner of the tent, I smelled cooked food. My suspicions were confirmed, as I saw two tables connected at a ninety-degree angle from each other and taking up a whole corner of the tent. The inside was a little larger than I'd thought, with a table and several empty chairs close to where I stood. The table was plainly set with condiments, silverware, and a few loose pens.

My attention focused on a man standing by one of the tables resting against the back wall of the tent. I couldn't see his face because of his position, but he appeared to be a few inches shorter than me. He wore beige trousers and a white shirt that was probably button down.

The man turned around and I was surprised that he looked younger than I'd expected. I estimated that he was probably in his late thirties or early forties. He was clean shaven with blonde hair and blue eyes. His eyes appeared old to me, as though he had seen too much too quickly in his life. Otherwise he looked rather ordinary, which surprised me greatly. He smiled in a kind way as the rest of my group came around the corner and took in the scene. He was obviously expecting us, which meant that he probably knew everything about us. I would have to be careful around him, as he could probably easily catch us off guard. He put the plate that he was holding back onto the table behind him and walked towards us.

He extended his right hand and said, "Welcome!"

I was reluctant to respond, but I didn't want to appear ungrateful and I felt a need to size him up and figure out where we stood. I grasped his hand and shook it. His grip was firm, but not intentionally strong as though he wanted to start a pissing contest with me.

Once I let go, he looked at Alex and extended his hand.

"It's a pleasure to meet you, Alexi Masters."

Alex let out a small gasp, probably from the shock of being identified. After he shook her hand, he greeted Phillip and then Simon both by name and then looked back at me.

"I have been waiting for you, Kyle Bishop."

I imagine we all felt a little uncomfortable about being so easily identified and he quickly picked up on that. He gestured to the two back tables laden with food.

"Please, help yourself. This breakfast was prepared for your visit."

He looked at the others as they glanced at the food (or in Simon's case, drooled over it) and then back at me.

"I imagine you have a lot of questions, so let's talk while we relax and eat."

He looked at me as though waiting for my approval and the others didn't want to move without me going first. I looked over at my friends and nodded for them to go ahead. Alex and Phillip walked over to the table. Our host walked behind them and picked up his plate to finish making his choices.

Simon walked up to my right shoulder, leaned in, and whispered, "Are you sure it is safe to eat?"

I hadn't considered that he might poison us, but I figured it was extremely unlikely.

I whispered back, "If he wanted to kill us, Simon, I'm sure that he could have done that before we ever made it to the island. Besides, do you think he would kill us in front of so many kids?"

I gestured back at the lake, where almost everyone had returned to their recreation or whatever they had been doing.

Simon shrugged and went forward to help himself. I followed him, but kept a close eye on our host as I didn't trust him. When I got to the table, I noticed it was covered with breakfast foods though surprisingly none of it looked fried. There were eggs in several forms, fruit, some vegetables, and carafes of orange juice as well as some bottled water sitting in a bucket of ice. I took a little of everything and grabbed a bottle of water. The others were already starting to sit at the table and it was apparent that they were sitting on the opposite side of our host, so I joined them there.

I opened the bottle of water and took a swig without taking my eyes off of the guy across the table.

I decided to jump right in, "Well, it's obvious you know who we are..." and I left the remainder of my statement hanging to see if he would pick up on the clue.

He finished eating the bite he'd started and then smiled again.

"On this island, I'm called the Administrator."

Alex and Phillip paused in their eating to pay attention while Simon continued shoveling food into his mouth like he hadn't eaten in a week. The Administrator didn't seem to pay him any mind, so I let my concern for his manners drop.

Not really understanding his cryptic response I replied, "The Administrator? That's it? It sounds rather vague."

He took a moment before answering. I wasn't sure if he had enough foresight to think of his answers before he spoke or was trying to be careful about what he let slip.

The Administrator shrugged his shoulders slightly before answering.

"It serves. I'm sorry I can't offer you a name, as I haven't gone by anything other than the Administrator for some time now."

He paused for a second before continuing.

"Everyone on this island identifies me with that title, so it seemed appropriate and less confusing to continue using it."

We finished up our light breakfast (or in Simon's case, a heavy breakfast) and sipped our drinks. Once the Administrator finished, he surprised me by standing up and taking our plates. I would assume a person in control of an island would have servants or something running around somewhere. He took the plates and put them in an empty bin next to the table and then returned to his seat. I'd had enough hospitality for the moment and wanted some answers, now.

I sat up straight…but before I could start my round of questions, he held up his hand to signal me to stop.

"Kyle, I know you and your friends are bursting with questions, but one more thing before we start the inquisition."

He smiled.

"A game…of sorts."

He picked up a small stack of what appeared to be white, square note cards that were about two inches. He passed one card to each of us and then sat back down and reached for one of the pens on the table.

I spoke up before he could continue.

"Look, we're not here to play games."

I stared at him and he looked back with what looked like thoughtfulness in his eyes. This Administrator seemed like someone who always considered his answers before speaking. I hoped he'd picked up on the fact that I prefer directness over games and such.

He smiled and then answered, "Of course not, you're here for answers. But if you will humor me for a few moments, I will make you a promise."

Alex spoke up, "And what promise would that be?"

I could only imagine she was running worst-case scenarios through her head and was probably expecting a promise to leave with our lives. My gut was telling me that he was hiding something, but I didn't get the feeling that he was particularly dangerous.

The Administrator gestured to the cards in front of us, "If you play the game and do so with one hundred percent honesty, I promise to answer all of your questions with equal honesty."

Alex bit into the carrot that was dangling before us, "Any limitations on the questions we can ask?"

The Administrator thought for a second before responding, "None! But I should warn you not to ask any questions you are not willing to accept the honest answer for."

He paused for a second before finishing.

"Some truths are hard to accept."

Alex leaned back in her chair, trying to fight off the Cheshire Cat grin on her face. I couldn't help but wonder how much he would willingly give away. I didn't know him well enough to determine if he was a liar, but I doubted it. Regardless, I was going to stay on my guard. I had to worry about the safety of my friends and make sure that we got back home.

I nodded.

"All right, we'll play your game."

I picked up a note card and a pen and the others did the same.

The Administrator looked at each of us again and explained, "This game is simple. In a single word, describe yourself."

Simon began writing on his paper.

"To clarify, I'm not asking for a physical description, but a character description," the Administrator interjected. "One word that deep down describes you best."

I saw Simon scratching out whatever he wrote and starting again. The rest of us took a moment to think of our answers. A character trait? I could think of a lot of them and some of them applied to me. Faithful, charismatic, aggressive...I felt each was a part of a whole. But what word would I use to describe that whole? I looked at Alex as she wrote her answer down. I was again amazed by her beauty. Then, the answer popped into my head and I wrote it down. The Administrator also participated in the game and wrote his response on his own card. I was curious to see what he wrote.

The Administrator started folding his card and said, "Once you are done choosing your word, fold the note card in half and stick it in your pocket."

We all put our card in either our shirt or pants pocket. The Administrator put his card in his slacks pocket and I was still curious about his answer.

After we were done, he continued, "We will finish the game just before you leave. For now, since you have shown me patience, it's only fair I extend the same courtesy to you. I believe you had questions for me."

He looked among us and finally settled on me.

Phillip beat me to the first question.

"What is this place?"

The Administrator smiled and stood up.

"That is as good a place as to start as any. Come with me and I'll show you."

We all stood up from the table ready to join the Administrator on a tour of the island. As we exited the tent, I saw many of the kids and young adults stop and stare at us again. When their eyes met the Administrator's, they smiled. It was clear they had affection for him. I figured that if someone else owned the home I lived in, I'd probably be nice to them as well. The Administrator began walking towards the entrance of another path that led back into the woods. As we walked away, I again noticed that the entire lake and waterfall area was enclosed by a dense forest. Though it must have taken years, I was convinced the forest had been grown to provide some level of privacy for the island's occupants.

As we entered the new path, I noticed that it was much wider and more used compared to the one from which we had originally entered. Before my thoughts could wander any further, the Administrator began speaking.

"For a little bit of history, this island is the remnant of an extinct volcano that last erupted about sixty million years ago…or so I have been told."

The Administrator had an easy voice to listen to. His wasn't the most exciting voice I'd ever heard, but the way he spoke seemed to encourage a calm atmosphere. I was still wary about this whole setup, but also satisfied that we could start learning more about what was going on and how it fit into our conspiracy theory.

The Administrator continued his tour.

"I purchased the island from Peru about twelve years ago. The purchase was for sole territorial rights as well as discretion on the purchase itself."

Simon jogged a bit to catch up and get within talking range as he asked, "How much did it cost?"

The Administrator looked back at Simon and smiled before answering, "Just over two billion U.S. dollars."

Simon gasped.

"What discretion did you pay for?" I asked.

The Administrator smiled at me as well, realizing that I wasn't going to let him off that easy.

"My desire to purchase the island was contingent that the details of the sale remain secret and not to be disclosed to the public or any foreign government."

I thought that it must be nice to have so much money to blow on your own personal paradise.

"As far as the world is concerned, this island is still the property of Peru. It would take an official diplomatic inquiry by a foreign country to determine the truth."

I found it interesting that he approached the purchase of this island with all the cloak and dagger stuff included. I wondered what was so important to hide, so I decided to ask…but Alex beat me to it.

"Why hide the sale and your ownership of the island?"

The Administrator thought about this for a few seconds before answering.

"Well, Ms. Masters, you'll be happy to know that nothing on this island violates international laws and, of course, I do enjoy my privacy. But mainly it is to protect what other people may covet."

I could tell that Alex absorbed the information quickly and I decided to let her run with her questions for now.

"What do you have that people may want?"

The Administrator seemed pleased by her question.

"Not people, Ms. Masters, but governments...and I imagine they would want this!"

He pointed ahead to where the trail ended.

CHAPTER 12 – SCHOOL'S OUT

THE ISLAND
ALEXI MASTERS

It blew my mind that we were walking with a man who owned an island. As the Administrator explained about the island we were on, I looked at the others and noticed that both Phillip and Simon were enraptured by what he was saying. Kyle looked curious as well, but I could tell he was being cautious about the situation. Our quick breakfast with the Administrator gave me the impression that we weren't in any immediate danger, but I couldn't wrap my head around the fact that this person encompassed everything we'd been pursuing. He seemed too ordinary for something that felt beyond extraordinary to my senses. As we walked out of the forest, a citadel of crystal rose up in front of me and displayed a level of beauty I had never seen before. A crescent-shaped cliff that appeared to be a part of the funnel of an extinct volcano surrounded several crystal spires as though it were protecting them in its embrace. Time had weathered away the sharp edges of the cliff, while Mother Nature had claimed the rest.

The wall of the volcano was impressive due to its side, but paled in comparison to the structure built into it. Unlike Yosemite Park which displayed the faces of past American presidents, this was something I had never seen before. At the foot of the cliff was a stone base that supported the crystal structure. The structure merged with the cliff in several locations, providing the illusion that the structure was grown instead of man-made. The crystal spires were a work of art that appeared crafted for both beauty and function. A rainbow's worth of colors were represented in the crystal structure, perfectly complementing the green hues reflected from the plant life surrounding it. The walls were sheer crystal interspaced with occasional obsidian pillars. Further up the cliff face, I saw balconies leading into crystal sliding doors. The balcony rails were all crystal with an obsidian railing and the base of them appeared to be solid stone pieces protruding from the cliff face. Several of the balconies were small half circles, providing outdoor access for spacious apartments built inside the cliff. A walkway spanned the entire length of the cliff face, allowing easy access from one side of the cliff to the next. Interspersed along the walkway were small tables and chairs, allowing the residents to enjoy the tropical weather while eating a meal or relaxing. At the halfway point, a stone staircase with crystal railing rose up at about a forty-five-degree angle and continued twenty feet to another long balcony that stretched the remainder of the way and eventually disappeared into the cliff itself.

I saw dozens of people on the walkway moving from one location to another or just sitting at the tables. A waterfall flowed around the spires and down the front of the structure, allowing the water to disappear into the ground through strategically placed fissures. The main entrance was a pair of double crystal doors about two stories high that slid to either side as people approached to go in or out of them. Out front, I spotted a beautifully manicured garden containing a variety of tropical flowers and small trees. Included with the small gardens were benches that were occupied by both kids and adults.

Off to the left, there were several partially enclosed areas with a roof supported by four obsidian pillars. Inside each enclosed area was a classroom setting with students' chairs and desks molded into the ground, requiring each student to kneel down in front of their desk. The chairs were more of a small angled platform to sit against, preventing the student from resting their weight on their legs. Without any back support, the chairs required the user to sit up straight. The tables were attached at an opposite angle from the chairs and contained a built-in electronic interface pad on the entire surface. At the front of one of these classrooms was a dark- haired, European-looking woman gesturing at a holographic display of a double-helix DNA strand. From what I could overhear of the lecture, she was teaching about the fundamentals of genetic coding in the human genome. The lecture material sounded appropriate for any college setting, as it was beyond what was normally covered in high school biology. The surprising part was that her students were kids who looked to be between eight and twelve years old and were paying rapt attention, like she was cluing them in on how the secrets of the universe worked. I shook my head at that, turned, and looked to the right.

Most of my new view consisted of an open grass field surrounded by a cedar wood chip track with several kids of various ages playing soccer in the middle. Around them were others who were exercising or running around the cedar track. It didn't appear like anyone was watching them.

Beyond the field, though barely visible through a few trees, I could make out what appeared to be a greenhouse. The greenhouse was huge and designed with softer edges than the normal blocky glassed-in ones that you would normally see.

I was caught by surprise when Phillip spoke. "Wow!"

I looked at Phillip as he broke the spell of the place. I attempted to collect my thoughts. I couldn't believe that I'd let my guard down for even a second. I shook my head a bit and tried to keep my eyes focused on nothing for more than a second or two.

When I looked over at the Administrator, he had stopped and was facing off to our left to give us a few minutes to absorb the beauty before us.

"Is this a school or something?" I asked the Administrator while the others were still looking around.

He smiled at me and I saw the kindness behind it. I could tell that he was proud of this place and I could hardly blame him. If this building were in any other country, it would be considered a modern wonder of the world. The more time I spent around the Administrator, the harder it was for me to see him as the villain. He displayed a level of kindness not often seen in the world, but I still sensed an underlying sadness in the background.

"Yes and no," he answered. "Follow me and I'll show you what I mean."

He walked through the double transparent doors into the facility. As we walked, he began explaining his answer further.

"When this facility was originally built, it was utilized as a research laboratory. It was made entirely of stone at the time and didn't look anything close to what it does now. The expansion that you see on the outside with the crystal, the walkways, and the school environs were added later as more and more people came to work and live here."

As we walked through the doors, I noticed a significant temperature change from the outside. It was a few degrees cooler and more comfortable than the mild tropical weather outside. The lobby was an open, circular-shaped space pushing up into the spires above it with light flooding in from the outside through the transparent panes. Just inside the entrance, wide paths branched off to the left and right and merged at the completion of a circle on the other side of the room. Small staircases hugged the walls leading up to the three main spires of the citadel. The entrances to those stairs were closed off with what appeared to be some form of energy barrier to prevent any of the residents from gaining easy access.

Along the length of the two main paths were other smaller hallways that led deeper into the sides of the facility. The centerpiece of the room was a large crystal shard in a light pink color. Light pulsed faintly from the crystal as if it were the heart of the facility. Bordering the walkways on either side were various rooms with transparent walls as well as others that I couldn't see into. Those that I could see into were filled with various students and teachers interacting with holographic displays modeling everything from anatomy cross-sections to chemical formulae. Unlike my high school, I didn't see anyone who wasn't paying attention and the material far outstripped the curriculum that I was taught. At random times, kids left the classes they were in to walk to another classroom or go outside.

Floating along the hallways were small robots about the size of grapefruit. They appeared to be gliding to different locations and I figured they were probably used for messages or observation units for whatever passed for security around here. Several of them glided into the elevators at the far side of the room with other occupants going up or down. A few descended over the open center section that was dominated by the large crystal centerpiece. A larger sphere was painted white and had a red cross on it, and people stepped aside as it moved at a faster rate and shot out of the front door that we'd just used. I figured it was some form of medical droid responding to an accident.

The Administrator interrupted my thinking as he continued explaining everything as though he was a tour guide, which I guess he was.

"This floor was originally the main research labs, but as we grew the labs were pushed further down and this was converted to a school. We felt that the students here would progress better in an open environment near the surface and their family quarters. The cliff face outside houses mostly residential apartments that almost everyone in this complex live in. A few apartments spread into other parts of the facility as space became available and the demand was in place."

We approached the railing surrounding the circle containing the pink crystal centerpiece. The centerpiece was larger than I imagined; it went down almost thirty feet and was suspended a couple dozen feet above an open floor below. I saw a bunch of tables with people sitting at them, but I was too far away to make out the purpose. The layout brought to my mind images of the inside of a shopping mall. If they replaced the rooms around us with stores, it would have been almost an exact match. The crystal was held in place by cabling that came out of three sections of the wall on this level and the lower levels. The cabling appeared to connect to the crystal itself, almost as if it were a parasite latching onto a host.

Kyle looked at me with genuine wonder on his face and I knew my own face was betraying the excitement that I felt.

We hadn't been on this island for more than an hour, and already I had more questions than I originally started with.

"Is all this crystal?" I asked as I gestured at the walls and the centerpiece in front of me.

The Administrator nodded and leaned slightly to look over the chasm.

"That's correct. It is a synthetic crystal alloy that is actually quite strong."

I couldn't even fathom what he meant before a voice made me jump out of my skin and away from the railing edge.

The voice sounded majestic and definitely feminine when it said, "That is not exactly correct, Administrator."

Kyle, Simon, and Phillip jumped at the same time I did and looked around for the source.

I noticed the grin on the Administrator's face before he spoke.

"I'd like you to meet AMIE."

I looked back at the crystal that was pulsing.

"AMIE stands for Artificial Modulation Intelligence Emulator and happens to be the brains of our operation here. She is one of our primary researchers. AMIE also maintains the island and watches over its inhabitants."

Artificial intelligence? I couldn't believe it. I had read articles about this technology, but even the supercomputers out there never came close to making this a reality. Even virtual chess players were limited to the programming done by its creator. I just stuck with saying hi, as I couldn't think of anything more intelligent to say.

AMIE responded to my greeting, and it felt a little eerie speaking to a living computer, "Hello, Ms. Masters."

I looked around for audio speakers in the ceiling as well as in the ground, but couldn't find any. I looked at the Administrator.

"Where is the sound coming from?"

Before he could answer, AMIE beat him to it.

"The voice modulations you are hearing originate from the crystal processing unit before you, which is the nerve center of my system. The crystal shell vibrates at multiple frequencies, allowing me to emulate human speech patterns. Also, speaking about me while I am present is considered poor social manners by most civilizations. Please address any questions directly to me."

I felt appropriately chastised for my behavior, but it didn't in any way dampen my excitement about AMIE.

Simon spoke before I could apologize to AMIE.

"So, this huge crystal is your Central Processing Unit?"

I knew that every computer on the planet has a Central Processing Unit or CPU, which acts as the computer's brain and processes the information programmed into it.

The crystal pulsed a few more times before AMIE responded, "That is partially correct. The crystal matrix core allows me to analyze and process information as needed, but also acts as a storage medium for any information that I choose to store. The initial programming I received allows me to monitor all aspects of life on this island and provide assistance as needed to improve the quality of life for those who reside here."

Simon walked up to the railing and leaned over.

"What are these cables for?" he asked.

I could tell that Simon was in his element now. He loved computers more than anyone else I knew and that was why I'd asked him to help with the original financial problem I'd identified.

AMIE didn't seem to mind his questions and sounded pleased that he was addressing her like he would a normal person.

"The cables provide interface to the remaining structure around you and allows me to access the environmental controls. The lights, doors, and temperature are all monitored and adjusted by me as needed. The structure also provides an energy interface similar to modern-day solar paneling and converts heat and sunlight to usable energy for myself and this structure."

Before Simon could get carried away, the Administrator stepped in.

"AMIE serves many roles here and is a valuable member of our community."

AMIE spoke up after the Administrator finished.

"Administrator, please allow me to clarify your earlier statement and how it is in error."

The Administrator smiled as he interrupted her, "Some other time, AMIE. There is a lot to see here and I'm sure our guests would like the full tour. Thank you for your time, AMIE."

AMIE didn't respond after that, which felt rather awkward, but I felt like a kid at Christmas waiting for the next exciting present to open up.

The Administrator turned and began walking around the left side of the circle and the rest of us followed closely behind.

Our tour continued as he began speaking again, "After purchasing this island, I of course had a small research center built here…but only going down the initial three stories. I recruited young researchers from across the globe, many of whom were barely out of high school or the more advanced university or technical schools. I searched for specific people with not only technical skills, but also personalities similar to my own. As time progressed, many of them started families and we have been growing ever since. With the growth of the facility and the number of inhabitants, it was necessary to expand the size of the structure."

I thought back to the game he'd asked us to play earlier where we described ourselves with a single word. Something told me that the game was linked and perhaps he hoped to find the same personality trait in one of us.

We walked up to a large elevator built into the back wall of the complex. The whole elevator, with the exception of the roof and the floor, appeared to be made with the same crystal material as the rest of the facility. There were two smaller elevators on each side of this main one and they appeared to be used more by the residents. As we approached the door, it automatically opened up and we all stepped inside. The area in which you would expect to find the elevator controls contained another holographic display that identified the different floor levels. The Administrator selected the lowest floor and the doors closed in response. The elevator began moving down, but at a slower pace than I had experienced from other elevator rides, and the size of it made it more appropriate for cargo than people.

"What about the older people here?" Phillip spoke up for the first time to ask a question.

I'd been wondering if he'd become mute. More likely he was awed like the rest of us or perhaps his mind was just being occupied by thoughts of a certain girl he was hoping to see again.

The Administrator stood with his hands crossed in front of him as he answered Phillip's question.

"The people here who are my age or older were family members of those I invited. The family members who came along have integrated rather well into our society and often contribute in other ways. Some become cooks, gardeners, security, or engineers and some continue their education and provide research of their own. They are limited only by their own choices and willingness to grow."

As we progressed down the elevator, the first thing we saw was the floor below AMIE…which apparently was a dining hall. There were dozens of people inside picking up food as they served themselves from buffet lines. Others sat at various tables. Some sat alone absorbed in an electronic device, but many of them were in large groups socializing. The elevator passed the floor without stopping as it descended further down into the complex.

The next few floors we passed appeared to be floors dedicated to the research the Administrator had mentioned. I spotted groups of people working in enclosed crystal-walled rooms with various test equipment and holographic displays. Several of the rooms appeared to have some pretty intense debates going on.

I wasn't sure how the Administrator made this tour spiel sound exciting in his almost monotone voice as he explained what we were seeing.

"The first group I recruited was composed of young researchers who'd recently graduated from medical school. I provided them with all the resources they would ever need and tasked them with discovering a cure."

I considered this as the obvious question came to mind.

"What did you ask them to cure?"

The Administrator smiled again and answered, "I left that decision to the group itself, as long as they focused on one. They decided cancer was a good place to begin, so I challenged them to approach it as if it were a newly discovered disease. I found through my own purchases of pharmaceutical companies that the existing research projects were often only half completed and publications often misdirected other researchers."

I thought about what I knew from my limited knowledge of pharmaceuticals and realized that they would profit more by finding treatments and not cures to diseases.

The Administrator understood the dynamic of a profit- driven industry and didn't seem to be driven by it, which was odd considering that he owned several businesses.

"As you all discovered in your sojourn into Synthtex, the companies I own contributed at the beginning in providing funding and materials for the construction and later expansion of this facility."

From our research, we'd found dozens of companies linked to the Administrator. However, those companies seemed incapable of funding a facility like this. It would take the funding level of a small government to bankroll an operation of this size.

We passed through a total of four floors devoted to research and development. Then, we descended into a massive room that shocked me into silence. I could tell that the others were just as amazed at what they saw. The elevator was still descending to the floor of the room, as it was so massive. The entire outer wall was made of glass or that crystal material and displayed an endless view of the ocean on the other side. We were far enough underground to view the outer edge of the island as it touched the ocean. I saw an uncountable number of fish and even a pod of whales floating nearby. Many of the fish were attracted to the lights coming from the facility, tempting the curious among them to swim close enough to see.

As we arrived at what seemed to be the bottom of the citadel, the elevator stopped and allowed us to exit onto the floor. I remembered a trip to Sea World that I'd taken with my family as a child, and I had to admit their underwater aquariums as well as their huge whale tanks had nothing on this place. The floor itself was covered by submersibles and divers in gear waiting to exit through a huge opening in the center of the wall. The opening was its own large self-contained room that was flooding at this moment to equalize the pressure between the divers and the outside ocean. Along the transparent outer walls were worktables, where I assumed further research was being done. Off to the right side and centered between the rooms was a large conference room table with short holographic images displaying from its surface. Our group began walking to this table as we tried to absorb as much of what was going on around us as possible.

As we arrived at the table, I noticed that the holographic display showed a detailed map of the ocean floor surrounding the island. The island was about the size of a cantaloupe in the middle of the table and took up only a fraction of the entire map.

On the display, I saw small icons representing the divers and some larger ones for the submersibles and probably other machinery as it branched out away from the island for miles.

My thoughts were interrupted by the Administrator.

"As you can see by this map, we have both mining and agricultural projects developed already. The mines provide us several rare Earth elements that are more difficult to come by and the farms provide an alternate food source for our community."

I could now make out actual farms in the ground. Above each image was a small label showing what was being grown. It also seemed like there were several closed-in areas, which appeared to be farms for all types of sea life such as fish, lobster, shrimp, crabs, and various others.

I couldn't help but think that this whole facility was truly amazing. I'd always figured that I had a good grasp on life and what it had to offer, but I hadn't realized until now how wrong I was. The Administrator had thrown a wrench into everything that I thought was even possible. Our tour of the facility had demonstrated a multitude of technologies that weren't developed or possibly even thought of in the outside world.

We explored this lower level for over an hour. The size of it spanned about six hundred feet from end to end. After we completed our tour of the bottom level, we loaded back onto the elevator and ascended to the cafeteria floor. Though the entire tour took a few hours, I hadn't noticed the time passing by so quickly; lunchtime had arrived. Walking into the cafeteria, I smelled many food choices in the air and my stomach wasn't the only one that started making rude and demanding noises. I looked at Kyle and I could still see the excitement on his face. He hid it better than the others, but the more time we spent together the easier it was for me to identify his moods. I wondered how he felt about all of this.

CHAPTER 13 – TO BOLDLY GO...

THE ISLAND
KYLE BISHOP

After AMIE finished explaining about itself, I thought back to the movies Phillip and I had watched that included artificial intelligence. My thoughts lingered on *Terminator* and *I, Robot*. Both contained artificial intelligence that wanted to take over or destroy the world. I'd heard of the debates in the scientific community about developing AIs and it bothered me that this one had free rein of the island. I wondered if the Administrator had considered whether this type of technology should be developed or if he was only focused on if he could.

As fascinating as the computer was, I didn't find it as exciting as the rest of the facility and left the excitement over AMIE to Simon. Simon's eyes were so big, they seemed like they were going to pop the lenses out of his glasses. I couldn't help but smile at that thought. I knew computers and electronics were his thing and he got off on this stuff. Phillip appeared to be off in la-la land, as he constantly was looking around at the people and was probably only vaguely aware of the huge talking computer.

As we loaded onto the massive elevator, I glanced over at Alex and noticed the childish wonder on her face. I also noticed again how beautiful she truly was and how just looking at her could take my breath away. As fantastic as everything around me was, spending time with her was what I enjoyed the most. Our time traveling here as well as the verbal sparring matches we consistently got into helped center me into the world. Since the first time I'd noticed her, I felt as though she anchored me down to the world while providing purpose to my life.

The Administrator appeared pleased, though his face wasn't particularly expressive. I could tell he enjoyed providing this tour and was proud of the accomplishments. After just the brief time we had been here, I was unable to fault his pride. Everything around us was taken to a whole new level of extraordinary. The holographic technology alone could make a person a fortune beyond measure, but I got the feeling that the Administrator didn't care much about money anymore. Considering how much money he must have had in order to run this place, I figured whatever wealth he had was probably enough for anyone.

The four floors of labs we passed through were interesting. I noticed in one of the enclosed rooms the metal frame of a car with disassembled engine parts spread all over the room. It surprised me that the people working in the labs weren't all wearing lab coats. Many of them were just wearing blue jeans or slacks and whatever shirt caught their fancy. The work environment was rather laid back and seemed to be more geared towards self-expression and working at their own pace. I couldn't imagine how much all of these techs and scientists cost, but from the level of technology present I felt certain that the Administrator was getting his money's worth.

Finally, we passed the lab floors and had a brief break. I forgot to mention that stone walls surrounded the lift. The lights inside provided enough illumination to see…but the darkness didn't last very long, as we opened up into what I could only describe as the world's largest aquarium.

Phillip and I had done some scuba diving during our summer breaks from school, so I immediately recognized the scuba equipment and even the underwater UAVs or submersibles as some people called them. The entire floor was decked out with every type of underwater gear imaginable. I couldn't decipher the purpose of some of the gear. The view outside of the massive transparent wall revealed that we were hundreds of feet below sea level, which required special equipment to handle the pressure. The wetsuits several of them were climbing into or out of were thinner than I expected…but considering the level of technology at this place, I was hardly surprised.

Phillip and I pressed our hands and faces up against the transparent wall and gazed into the ocean. The scene before us finally seemed to have purged the daydream that Phillip had been in since we entered the place.

I could tell Phillip was excited from his tone of voice as he asked, "Can you believe this place, Kyle?"

Phillip was grinning from ear to ear and I could tell that he was ecstatic about what this place had to offer. Not even the greatest research institutes on Earth could compare with the one before me. It felt as though we had stepped into the future and we were both waiting to wake up.

"I know, right?"

I pointed at several people who were walking across the ocean floor instead of relying on the normal fins for movement.

"Look at them. They somehow managed to counteract the natural buoyancy problem created from the oxygen in our lungs."

Our diving classes had explained how a person's natural body oxygen content caused the human body to float as though it weighed less than the water around it. Salt water was even denser than fresh water and normally made a human float even higher. Since a diver couldn't naturally use the ocean floor for friction to move, they relied on fins attached to their feet like a fish to obtain forward momentum. But the divers we were looking at weren't using fins and were walking on the ocean floor without a care in the world.

After the Administrator showed us a holographic table showing the layout of his projects, we returned to the elevator and ascended to the cafeteria floor. We passed this floor initially, but once we exited onto the open area I noticed that the area was about the size of the aquarium we had just left with AMIE suspended overhead in the middle of the room and extending all the way up to the main floor. The outer walls contained various rooms also enclosed by rock and the crystal material that was used in the rest of the facility. These rooms appeared to be used for either secluded meal areas for some privacy or as entertainment lounges that contained holographic arcades and television sets with channels from various countries. The main buffet area was sectioned and extended about a hundred feet with a large open kitchen behind it, where dozens of people appeared to be preparing meals. The Administrator led us to the starting point to pick up a plate to load some food onto.

The Administrator pointed to various sections of the buffet as he explained its contents.

"Help yourself to whatever you want. There are five main sections, and each section contains different items from different cultures."

I hadn't noticed earlier that the buffet was divided, but I now noticed that I couldn't even identify some of the food. Very little of the food appeared to be fried, but a few items here and there were available.

He gestured at the two sections closest to us.

"Each section will contain several main course choices, sides, and desserts associated with a country's region. You can mix and match at your leisure. The drinks are over on the wall at the end of the buffet and you can sit wherever you like if you want to speak with any of the residents here."

He smiled at us and then walked towards the third section of the buffet line to make his choices. We divided up in groups of two, with Phillip and Simon going off to a section further away while Alex and I stayed behind and looked at the present one. This first section seemed to be devoted to French cuisine, containing pastries and other light dishes. On the right side were various dessert pastries that were going as fast as the cooks could bring them out. Several people moved around us to grab them the moment they were served. Alex grabbed one for her plate, while I just picked up a simple croissant to chew on and added a scoop of fresh fruit salad before moving to the next section. The next section was more to my liking and seemed to contain some old-fashioned American food. The selection was impressive, but I seldom worried about what I ate and just ate something for the energy. I saw lunchmeat and cheese and constructed myself a hasty sandwich while Alex did the same.

"How are you doing, Kyle?" Alex asked as she constructed her masterpiece.

I threw some bread and meat onto my plate and began adding some pickles and onions as I responded, "Fine. And yourself?"

Alex turned her head to briefly look at me and smiled.

"I'm concerned that this place may be more than it seems."

I thought about what we had seen thus far, and I had to agree that it was surreal. I considered her statement on a more specific level, but my gut told me that the Administrator was being upfront. I nodded as I replied, "Perhaps, but I still think that the Administrator is hiding something. What I can't figure out is why do all of this?"

Alex finished up her cold cut creation and we both walked in the direction of the drink stand.

"What do you think he is hiding?" Alex asked.

I thought about her question, but I wasn't entirely sure. "I don't know, my gut is telling me that he's being open with us and I think he is probably just trying not to scare the crap out of us at the same time."

I noticed Alex mulling this over as we arrived at the drink stand. The drink stand offered bottled water and teas of various flavors as well as cold milk and hot tea on tap. I noticed immediately that there was no soda fountain available and the selection of drinks didn't contain one single caffeinated option. I imagined that Simon would be in tears in a few moments once he got done stuffing his plate with God knows what.

Both Alex and I grabbed a bottle of plain water and headed towards the table that the Administrator was already seated at. Next to the Administrator was a well-groomed guy with neatly trimmed light brown hair and a clean-shaven face. He seemed impeccably dressed for a simple lunch and he talked to the Administrator while picking at the salad on his plate.

I caught the last bit of a conversation as we approached and could tell by his accent that he was British.

"Well, they are snooping and it is only a matter of time before we become visible."

He looked up at us as we stopped at the table, but the Administrator continued to chew his food as he waited to see what we would do. The new guy pushed his chair back and stood up. I noticed that he was just slightly taller than me. His face appeared refined, almost regal, and his eyes were a brown that matched his hair.

"Good afternoon, Mr. Bishop, Ms. Masters."

He bowed his head slightly in greeting and extended his hand to Alex first.

"Percival Smythe at your service."

He shook my hand second. His grip was firm, and I could tell he was attempting to put us at ease.

Alex asked, "May we join you?"

Mr. Smythe didn't hesitate and invited us to join the table. The table was circular with six chairs.

The Administrator and Mr. Smythe were sitting side by side, so Alex and I sat together on the opposite side. I felt that now was the perfect time to test the limits of honesty that the Administrator had promised as I focused on this new addition.

"So, what do you do here Mr. Smythe?"

I stabbed into my fruit salad and shoved a piece into my mouth, waiting to see if he would answer.

The Administrator stayed quiet and kept eating the beef and noodles on his plate with a pair of chopsticks. I figured one of the other buffet sections must have contained an Asian menu.

I glanced around quickly and noticed that the people in the cafeteria seemed to spawn from many ethnic groups. I could overhear a lot of different languages in the conversations ranging from Mandarin, Korean, German and some African dialects to name just a few. The people talking to each other weren't from the same country, so it seemed, and I wondered how anyone could understand each other.

I returned my attention back to Mr. Smythe as he started to respond.

"Well, I'm the Head of Security for the Administrator. I manage the security and safety of the residents while they are here or when they are abroad."

I watched the guy, hoping to catch any telltale signs of deception.

"Abroad?" I asked.

Mr. Smythe finished chewing a forkful of salad before he continued.

"Yes, residents here often choose to visit family in other parts of the world or take a vacation as the need arises."

Just then Simon abruptly sat down at one of the empty chairs with a plate piled high enough with food to be mistaken as a volcano project for science class. As much as he ate, I wondered how he managed to stay so thin and pondered whether as a good friend I should recommend that he get checked for a tapeworm. As Simon made his grand entrance, Mr. Smythe began to rise…but the whole episode ended with Simon sitting before Mr. Smythe could get more than partially out of his seat. Mr. Smythe appeared to be formal in his movements, probably due to his British nature, and didn't offer a handshake for fear of extending his hand across the table. He addressed Simon as "Mr. Weiss" before slightly bowing his head and sitting back down. Simon actually tore his eyes away from his plate long enough to look up at Mr. Smythe for the first time.

I figure I would save Simon some effort.

"Simon this is Mr. Smythe, the Head of Security."

Simon smiled at him and then ignored him as he picked up his fork and began stuffing his face. I figured he was content to let the rest of us speak in his place.

"Simon, are you planning to eat that whole thing?" I asked as I gestured at his plate.

Simon had enough food stuffed into his mouth to puff out both his cheeks while he chewed. He partially opened his lips to state that he was and surprisingly didn't spit out any pieces of his already chewed lunch.

"Where's Phillip?" I inquired before he could stuff any more in.

Simon pivoted his head as he continued to chew and looked over at another table behind me and off to his right. He nodded his head in that direction. I turned to look and saw Phillip sitting at another table across from the girl we had met when we arrived. Apparently, he had found his girl…though it looked like she didn't know what to do with the attention. Phillip appeared to be talking excitedly as he gestured with his arms to illustrate whatever story he was telling.

The girl from the beach, Cherise, appeared to be sitting rather rigidly and didn't seem to be in a conversational mood. She kept staring at him like a second head was growing out of his shoulders. I chuckled, but felt bad for Cherise because I imagined Phillip would eventually break past her defenses and get her to relax.

I shook my head and turned back to face Mr. Smythe.

"Do you really think security is necessary for an operation like this?"

Before he could answer, I continued.

"I mean aside from some industrial espionage, I can't imagine any governments being interested in a research institute."

I knew even as I said it that governments would be interested, but I was trying to gauge how Mr. Smythe would respond. Surprisingly, the

Administrator spoke up and I noticed he had finished his lunch as well as Mr. Smythe.

I picked up the sandwich I had made and started eating while listening to the Administrator's response.

"Industrial espionage is the least of my concerns, Kyle. It is in fact governments that concern me most."

I glanced over and saw that Alex had perked up to pay attention as she ate her sandwich between sips of water.

"As you have seen, the technologies we have developed here could be adapted easily for military and intelligence purposes. When governments start learning about this facility, there will be intense pressure placed on all of us to fall into line."

I thought about this for a second and found it difficult to imagine the United States placing any pressure beyond political against the Administrator, but I couldn't figure out why he would care.

Being isolated on this island, I didn't imagine he would care what the Senate or Congress might do, so I asked, "What type of pressure?"

The Administrator sat back in his chair.

"Regardless of the benevolence or moral high ground governments may publicly display, the technology on this island is something they would want to control."

I still didn't understand what he was getting at, so I pushed a little harder as I asked him to elaborate.

"Well, let's take the U.S. Government for example. Do you believe they would want control of this island either militarily or administratively?"

I thought about his question for a second, but Alex answered for us.

"Maybe, but if the public realized that the government was denying you your rights there would be an outcry."

The Administrator fought a slight smile from his face as he answered.

"I'm sure the United States would be able to pursue ownership with minimum knowledge passed onto the public. And if not, political spin would make us out as a national threat requiring them to take action. Also, do you believe their government would want this technology to fall into some other government's hands like Russia or North Korea?"

He tilted his head to the side, waiting for one of us to respond.

Simon must have figured out how to swallow his food, as he surprised me with an answer.

"The computer technology alone would frighten everyone on the planet. The processing and analytical power available to AMIE outmatch anything presently developed in the world."

I looked over at Simon, surprised so much had come out of his mouth. He had dug down about halfway through his plate, but had paused between bites to answer the question.

The Administrator agreed with what Simon had said before continuing.

"Also, Alex, you need to understand that this island stands apart from the rest of the world, so it doesn't fall under the civil or commercial rights that protect others. In essence, we are standing on our own."

Mr. Smythe stood up from the table.

"If you'll excuse me, Administrator, I have duties to perform."

He bowed slightly, picked up his tray, and walked away.

I turned my attention back to the Administrator.

"What happens if a government decides to fight for control of this place?"

I could just imagine the place being raided by Marines or bombed by the Navy.

The expression on his face was ominous.

"The question is not if Kyle, but when. The island is self-sufficient in its basic needs such as power and food. We have other defenses in place if necessary, but I can only hope it never reaches that point."

CHAPTER 14 – RISING INTO THE BLACK

THE ISLAND
KYLE BISHOP

We finished our lunch and turned our trays in at a kitchen window for cleaning. I signaled Phillip as we walked by him to let him know it was time to go. Phillip looked crestfallen to be leaving his date, but I informed him that the Administrator wanted to continue the tour. Cherise actually appeared to be relaxing a little, but was startled when I'd interrupted them to get Phillip's attention. She turned in her tray as she flushed in embarrassment and Phillip immediately followed her like a lost puppy dog. After they said their goodbyes, Phillip finally returned to the group.

"Have a nice lunch?" I asked.

Phillip face spread into a huge grin.

"Can you believe she is studying to become an engineer and she is only sixteen years old? I would have figured her to be at least eighteen."

Alex was smiling and I could tell she was happy that Phillip was apparently in love.

Simon interjected as though he was a concerned friend.

"I think that's jailbait, Phillip, so you might want to keep a hands-off policy in place."

Phillip looked at Simon like he wanted to throttle him for damaging his dream world. As we walked back into the elevator and returned to the main floor, Phillip explained how he had to switch topics about a half a dozen times until he found something that she would actually respond to. Apparently, she had a fascination with engines just like Phillip. When he brought up the rebuilding of his own car she perked up and finally engaged him in conversation. Phillip was surprised by her level of knowledge of engine components and she even talked about some more advanced stuff that went completely over his head. He was just happy to hear her speak and let her continue on as though he understood what she was saying. It was good that

Phillip was happy; I considered him a brother in everything but blood and it was great that he'd found someone to connect with. My only concern was that we would be leaving soon, and he might have a difficult time being away from her. With enough luck, maybe he would at least be able to call her from time to time and develop a long-term relationship.

After we walked out of the entrance to the facility we turned right, skirting in front of the nearest outdoor classroom. The same holographic DNA strand was still displayed...but while a woman had been teaching before, a man had taken her place. I also noticed that the kids appeared to be different than the ones who were there before.

As we curved slightly to our right around a few small trees and a several rock pillars, I saw two other classrooms, each engaged with kids and a teacher. One showed a holographic display of some chemical formulae and the other was some type of half-disassembled machine. I noticed now that the displays were interactive, and the kids often tapped on their small desk at the same time when something changed in the image. The mechanical or engineering class appeared to be constructing the device, as though the kids were learning from a master builder and not an actual teacher.

We approached the edge of the volcanic cliff where it tapered off with the rest of the island. A small tunnel about six feet wide and ten feet tall was cut though the rock itself. The inside rock appeared to have been cut to precision and then melted enough to cover the surface in a solid rock sheet. When we passed through the opening and reached the other side, there was an expansive beach before us that opened to the ocean. I saw more adults than kids relaxing on the beach or swimming in the ocean.

We continued to follow a trail about a third of the way around the crescent cliff face of the extinct volcano. Just a few feet above sea level, we neared a massive opening inside the cliff face itself. Inside appeared to be a large hangar with two planes undergoing cleaning and maintenance. The left one appeared to be a small business jet and was probably the Administrator's main transportation to and from this island. However, the one to the right that we were closer to was the truly impressive one. It was about three times the size of the first one, but painted in several shades of dark gray. The wings spread out only a short distance to the side and appeared to be molded into the structure of the plane itself. The cockpit window was a little more reflective and was the same dark gray color with a hexagonal grid faintly visible on the surface.

We walked through an open doorway into the hangar itself and got a profile view of the aircraft. The size of it completely blocked the standard executive plane behind it. The plane had graceful lines extending from nose to tail, but didn't contain the normal fins you'd see on aircraft. The entire plane closely resembled a Native American arrowhead or perhaps some type of spear point. There was a ramp underneath the rear section of the plane. A man and a woman guided huge pallets of spare parts and consumables food products into the back of the plane as though they were prepping for a cargo run to some other destination.

As the Administrator walked closer to the plane, another ramp just behind the cockpit lowered. It dawned on me now that we were supposed to board this weird plane, but I had no idea where he planned to take us.

I figured I'd better ask now before we went any further.

"Are we going somewhere in that?"

It became obvious that I'd asked the wrong question. Of course, we were going somewhere; I wanted to know where before I boarded. Everyone else stopped only slightly ahead of me with the exception of the Administrator, who didn't stop until he had reached the base of the boarding ramp.

Alex looked at me with the same concern I felt about boarding the plane without knowing where we were going. I looked at the Administrator as he looked back at me; I could tell he was deciding how to best answer the question. I could also tell he was excited about something and trying not to give it away, because the longer I was around him the better I was getting at figuring him out.

The Administrator continued to smile as he answered.

"Just continuing the tour Kyle, the next part I want to show you will require us to take a brief trip in the shuttle."

I looked over at what he called a shuttle, but was still unconvinced about going along. He hadn't done anything that seemed dangerous, but I was starting to get concerned not by what he was showing us but why. He was sharing everything he had helped create and develop. I worried that he wouldn't let us just walk away with that knowledge. He had kept the secret of this place from the rest of the world and now he was sharing his secrets with a group of kids.

The Administrator watched me and waited for me to decide how to proceed, knowing the others in my group wouldn't move unless I went first.

The Administrator decided that I had taken long enough and said, "The fear of the unknown can be terrifying to confront; we each just have to find the courage to face it."

He turned and walked up the ramp and into the shuttle, while the rest of us stayed outside trying to figure out if we were willing to go along for the ride. Phillip and Simon huddled up with Alex and me to discuss it.

Alex seemed as nervous as I was as she spoke.

"I'm not sure about this, Kyle."

I looked into Alex's eyes. I could tell she was a little scared, but willing to stand by me in whatever decision I made. You would think that boarding a plane wouldn't require this much thought...but my gut was telling me something big was coming and once we crossed the line, there would be no going back. I could tell that Alex was thinking the same thing I was; it scared me at times how closely our thought patterns matched.

Phillip looked eager to go, but he also looked unsure that his decision was correct and hoped that I would ultimately decide.

Phillip realized that I expected him to voice his opinion.

"We've come this far!"

The simple statement was quite true. We had come far since this journey had begun and it would be a shame to end it now. I looked at Simon and noticed that he was taking this discussion seriously.

"Well, Simon, what do you think? Should we go or should we stay?" I asked.

Simon looked at each of us and appeared to feel a little uncomfortable being the center of attention.

Simon shrugged at me before answering.

"We'll follow you in whatever you decide, Kyle…but personally I can't wait to see what he wants to show us next. I say we follow the White Rabbit to Wonderland."

Alex interjected, "He's right, Kyle. It's your call."

I looked at Alex and I could tell it had been a struggle for her to say that. She didn't strike me as the follower type, but in this she was giving me the steering wheel. I gestured at the boarding ramp.

"All right! Let's find out what he wants to show us next."

All three of them brightened up. Phillip and Simon appeared relieved that I wasn't going to bring an end to this adventure just yet.

As we walked towards the ramp I said, "Whatever we find and learn, we do it together."

Alex nodded, agreeing with my statement.

Simon decided to melt the tension as he raised his hand above his head like he was wielding an imaginary sword, "All for one and one for all!"

Everyone broke out laughing at his stupid display, but the release was what we all needed. I shook my head as I led our group up the ramp and onto the shuttle.

The inside of the shuttle was spacious, with six rows of seats and six seats per row split down the middle. Three seats were on each side, split by a center walkway slightly smaller than a narrow hallway. There were two doors at the back of the cabin, one clearly labeled as the restroom. The other was made of some serious metal with a small glass window at face level, so I assumed the other side contained the cargo they were loading. I got the impression this shuttle wasn't designed for commercial transport, as the space wasn't used as efficiently as most commercial aircraft. I looked toward the front of the plane and expected to see a galley or a wall with a door leading to the cockpit. Instead, I saw an open cockpit with a pilot and a co-pilot leaning back in a chair that sunk into the floor of the shuttle. Only their shoulders and heads were above floor level, as they leaned back against the seats head rest at a forty-five-degree angle. The cockpit window was as grayed out as it appeared on the outside and in front of it was a curved holographic display showing the area outside and in front of the shuttle. The display also had quite a bit of data scrolling by. The co-pilot and occasionally the pilot interacted with the display to shift data around as needed. Now I was intrigued.

Instead of going to a seat, Phillip and I walked forward to get a closer look at the cockpit. I saw only a few gauges and switches in the cockpit. The majority of it was made up of holographic displays and controls, some showing status readings of the engine, a structural layout of the shuttle itself, and various other views. The pilot was a guy who looked just a few years older than me. He had beach-blonde hair from what I could see of the top of his head. A few inches in front of his face was a small curved display that was barely visible from my angle. It was probably better seen if you were directly in front of the display. He tapped several commands into a holographic keypad that appeared near his left hand when he moved it. I noticed that the co-pilot was a young Asian girl. She appeared even younger than Simon from what little I could make out about her. She had her own displays that she was working on. It looked like she was rechecking the same things as the pilot was, but appeared unsure of what she was doing.

"Better lash yourself down, mates," the pilot said in an British accent. "We're getting ready to take off."

Phillip grabbed my arm to pull me back to the cabin seats. I pondered what it would be like to fly one of these shuttles as I followed Phillip.

I noticed the Administrator sitting in the aisle seat on the right side of the aircraft with Alex in a window seat in the same section. Phillip sat by

Simon on the left side of the plane, leaving the other aisle seat between the Administrator and Alex open. I could always go back to the second or third row to sit, but that would look a little antisocial. So, I took the seat next to Alex and the Administrator and buckled myself in. I looked to the right and noticed the window was about twice the size of a normal airline window, but it was still just as thick. I noticed the window had a faint hexadecimal grid on it like the one on the cockpit window. Now that I thought about it, I didn't remember seeing any windows on the shuttle outside.

I gave up trying to figure that mystery out and looked back at the cockpit. I saw the boarding ramp lift up and fold into the shuttle and simultaneously heard another ramp in the rear of the plane seal itself shut. I looked at the huge holographic display in front of the flight crew and finally realized that there wasn't a runway outside.

My eyes got big in my head as I looked at the Administrator. He smirked.

"I was wondering when you would notice."

The others heard his statement, but hadn't figured out what it meant. I figured he was trying to get some type of reaction out of me, but I wasn't going to give him the satisfaction. I forced myself to relax as I placed my hands and arms on the armrest and leaned back to enjoy the ride. The shuttle's engine powered up and I felt it build speed as the plane vibrated. Though the power was increasing, the shuttle hadn't moved an inch from where it was parked. I felt the landing gear underneath us retract, causing a slight movement in the shuttle, and we still weren't moving.

The others leaned back to prepare for the g-forces of take-off and it took a moment before Phillip called out.

"Uh...Kyle...There's no runway, dude!"

Both Alex and Simon figured it out at that moment and I saw the panic on Alex's face. Just then, the whole shuttle accelerated forward and shot out of the mouth of the hangar. I expected a runway to magically appear, or perhaps some force field would generate one, but the shuttle seemed to have enough power to quickly push it forward and up into the atmosphere.

The acceleration only created a small amount of g-forces, enough for us to realize that the shuttle was in fact moving, but it eased up as our speed evened out. From what I could see of the display from here, it took less than sixty seconds to accelerate to over six hundred miles per hour. The shuttle appeared to be at about a forty-five-degree angle in order to gain altitude. The initial burst out of the hangar caused Alex to grab my right hand and apply a death grip to it. I could tell that she was freaking out and wondered if she was afraid of flying. I hadn't noticed any hesitancy with her boarding the shuttle, so I figured it was probably the abrupt exit sans a runway that was freaking her out. Beyond her pushing me over the side of the boat I had never actually touched Alex, including holding her hand. I noticed her skin was incredibly soft, even as it turned red from the tenseness of her grip. I had always imagined what it would be like to hold and touch her hand and I must admit that I wasn't disappointed. I wished the Administrator had developed a way to freeze time, as this would be one moment I wouldn't mind preserving forever.

I turned my head to face the front and focus on the cockpit crew again to pass the time while watching the holographic controls they adjusted during the flight. After about another minute, I glanced to my left just past the Administrator and noticed Simon. He was glancing outside, at the cockpit, at us, and then back over and over.

Something was agitating him about the flight, and I wanted him to tell me what.

"What is it, Simon?"

Simon looked at me with real panic in his eyes. The color of his skin was actually paler, if that was even possible.

"Kyle, I think something is wrong. At the angle and velocity that we are traveling, we are going to breach the outer reaches of our atmosphere in less than a minute."

I looked over at the cockpit display and saw we were still traveling in excess of six hundred miles per hour and our angle hadn't changed. I couldn't calculate the ascent like Simon did, as I wasn't that good at math, but I trusted what he'd said.

"Administrator?" I queried.

He responded with unnatural calm, "I'm sure the pilots know what they are doing, Simon."

I glanced at Simon and he didn't seem reassured. Phillip didn't look much better. Alex appeared to have calmed down a little, but she still hadn't released her grip on my hand…which I didn't mind at all. I sat back and forced myself to relax and wait for whatever was going to happen.

I glanced at the window and noticed that the blue sky was darkening awfully fast until the last bit of blue finally disappeared. The first thing I noticed was individual strands of Alex's hair starting to rise slowly upward in defiance of gravity. That's when it dawned on me that we had actually traveled past Earth's atmosphere and into space. The minimal vibration coming from the shuttle reduced even further and fell into the background. Our arms and the rest of Alex's hair also started to float, which caused our hand holding to come to a disappointing end. Even though we were obviously in space and that alone should have freaked us all out, everyone including Simon had massive smiles plastered on our faces.

The Administrator looked at me with a grin on his face.

"Go ahead, Kyle. Take it for a spin!"

I knew what the Administrator was giving me permission for and I wasn't about to argue or waste the once-in-a-lifetime chance. I unbuckled my seatbelt, causing my whole body to rise into the air with a slight spin to the right. I saw the most beautiful smile on Alex's face as she also unbuckled herself and rose to join me. I looked at Simon and Phillip and they both had also seized this moment, though Simon refused to release his hold on his seat's headrest.

I couldn't help but laugh at what we were experiencing. I didn't know of any kid at school who hadn't once dreamed of being an astronaut and floating in space. I looked over just as Alex slightly pushed off from her window, misjudging the amount of push she needed to move. She accelerated and collided with me as I instinctively wrapped my arms around her to try to stop her momentum. Though I got to hold her in my arms, it was naive of me to think that I could slow her momentum when I wasn't anchored to anything. The angle she collided with me at caused both of us to start spinning as though we were dancing with each other on a ballroom floor.

Alex realized what she had done and held on to me out of fear of falling, not realizing that she wouldn't fall. She looked up and saw me staring into her eyes. As far as I was concerned, nothing else in the universe existed. It felt strange and truly wonderful to be in a world where the only thing I was touching was this beautiful girl before me. I couldn't imagine a more perfect time to do something I had only dreamed about. I closed the distance between our lips to the point where I could feel her breath on my face. I could tell that she knew what I was going to do, and I saw in her face that she wouldn't try to stop me. Her breathing was soft, but it picked up the closer I came to kissing her. At that most perfect moment, a hand grabbed my upper arm to stop our movement and almost caused me to let go of Alex.

Phillip had stopped our errant flight, but I could have killed him for his poor timing. Alex blinked, turned her head to look away from me, and her skin was flushed a soft pink color. She pushed away from me and headed back in the direction of her seat, but her aim took her slightly forward instead.

The Administrator smiled at our enjoyment, but brought it to an end.

"Thank you, Captain. You can ease them down now."

I glanced at the Administrator and then at the pilot. He was slowly pushing a holographic icon upwards. I felt myself get heavier as the ground rose to meet me. As I neared the ground I moved my right foot forward towards the floor in order to right myself to the ship's orientation, so I didn't end up falling on my face. Simon and Phillip hadn't strayed from an arm's reach of their seats, so they fell right back into them with me in the open aisle in front of them. I looked at Alex and noticed she was balancing herself on the floor and leaning into the wall of the shuttle. After gravity returned to normal, Alex returned to her seat, buckled in, and turned to face the window. She wouldn't meet my gaze and I wanted to apologize or something for the way I had acted.

Just then, Alex's left hand pressed into the wall next to the window as something outside had caught her attention.

"Unbelievable!" she exclaimed.

I walked quickly over to her and looked past her head and out the window she was looking through. I heard Phillip and Simon behind me rushing to a window in front of our row to look out. What I saw was huge; it appeared at least a thousand feet or more wide and about half as tall from the sideview we were getting. Outside the window dominating our view was a space station.

Alex was right; it was unbelievable. The shuttle turned up to give us a better view of the topmost portion of the station. I realized that the station looked like a child's spinning top that had spun for too long and now the whole thing had started flattening, with the sides moving further out. Throughout the entire structure, pieces were missing where construction was still underway.

Protruding from one side of it was a long extension that robbed it of its symmetry. I couldn't fathom the purpose for the extension. The station wasn't spinning to generate gravity like you see in science fiction movies. It was perfectly stationary, with the lower half facing the glow of the Earth off beneath us. The top center section, which looked like a flattened cookie, contained a circumference of glass around it...which I assumed was probably the nerve center of the place. The shuttle didn't curve around to see the other side of the station, but I imagined it looked much like this half and I had to admit that I was impressed.

On the surface of the station, I noticed some people as well as strange spider-like robots that were continuing the unfinished construction process. The people were dressed in form-fitting white suits with slightly bulkier helmets, but the visors didn't appear to be see-through...at least from this side. They walked alongside the station as though they were taking a stroll without any need for propulsion or a lanyard system to prevent them from floating away. The robotic spiders moved at a quicker pace, helping the other workers with welding as well as other tasks — both mundane and complex.

Even though the station was still being worked on, the immense size of it was staggering. From the outside, it appeared large enough to comfortably house thousands of people. I looked closer and noticed that several sections weren't lit up, at least internally. It was possible they hadn't completed building those sections or perhaps no one was occupying them. I shook my head in amazement as I continued to take it all in.

Dreamers

CHAPTER 15 – UNDISCOVERED COUNTRY

SOL STATION
ALEXI MASTERS

After I returned to my seat from the unexpected spacewalk, I couldn't stop thinking about the kiss that Kyle and I almost shared. I didn't want to kiss Kyle; I wanted to hate him, and I did for what he did to my best friend and so many others at school. But at the same time, my body betrayed me; I wanted him to kiss me. I kept trying to think of something else, anything else to get that moment out of my mind. I gave up hope of ever purging the memory and decided to just look outside the window and the empty blackness of space and hide in my shame. I turned my head to the window, but my eyes were still focused down…lost in thought. I shook my head slightly to banish the memory and looked up, hoping to see what Earth looked like from this high up. At first glance, I saw a large structure and not Earth; I forgot for a brief second that I was in space. It dawned on me quickly what I was looking at and I could only describe it in one word, "Unbelievable!"

My eyes were glued to the structure before me. The space station was massive and took up the entire field of view outside of the window. The outer ring of the station appeared to be nine to ten stories high with the same crystal windows that were on the citadel. Just to our right were large hangar bays with shuttles similar to the one we were in as well as people walking around inside. The opening to the hangars was tinted deep red, almost as if it were covered in clear plastic wrap. Surrounding the opening were various lights flashing at a steady pulse, and I figured we were probably heading to one of these. I heard Kyle as he came up behind me to look out the window. When he was near me, the memory of our earlier moment quickly returned. As he let out his initial gasp at what he saw, his warm breath hit the left side of my neck and sent chills down my body. I closed my eyes briefly and attempted to put Kyle out of my mind again. My success in that endeavor was rather limited.

The pilot flew the shuttle up over the lip of the outer ring, allowing us a better view of the top half of the station. Though the station was still under construction, the sight was no less breathtaking. The top half actually flattened out, with a small flat dome occupying the center of the structure while being surrounded by windows. There was a dip between the center structure and the outer ring separating the two, but the center structure also stood on top of a small rise and rested a few dozen feet higher than the remainder of the station. The shuttle curved back down and to the left, flying towards the hangars I'd noticed earlier. The pilot deftly maneuvered the shuttle, so the front was directly lined up with the center of the red field before us. I could see past the red energy field outside the cockpit window and watched as several people ran across the hangar floor. Being this close to the station, our window views became very limited. So, Kyle and the others returned to their seats — slightly easing the tension built up inside of me.

The pilot glided the shuttle through the red field, landing gracefully in the middle of the hangar. Once the shuttle settled in place, the pilot and the co-pilot began methodically shutting down different systems via their holographic controls as the hum of the shuttle's engine died off. The boarding ramp opened and outside light shone into the shuttle after about a minute, signaling to us that it was safe to depart.

The pilot spoke up for the first time since the flight had begun, "Welcome to Sol Station!"

I unbuckled my seatbelt and stood up slowly, still unsure if the gravity was real. After experiencing a zero-gravity environment, I was a bit disappointed that it wasn't present anymore. The Administrator had already unbuckled his seatbelt and went up to the cockpit to thank the pilots. I glanced at Kyle and noticed he was staring at me with the same hunger I was trying so desperately to crush inside of myself. The awkwardness of the situation prompted me to get moving; I was unsure of the protocol for leaving, so I simply walked to the ramp opening and proceeded down the ramp. Once I reached the bottom of the ramp, I waited a few seconds for the others to join me.

Simon was the next one down the ramp and walked over to stand on my right side.

"This is just awesome! Did you imagine you would be walking on a space station when you woke up this morning, Alex?"

I smiled at Simon. His interruption was a welcome break from the thoughts going through my mind at that moment. I thought about what he said for a second. I'd never imagined that I would actually travel into space, much less stand aboard a space station.

I'd always liked Simon. He approached everything as if he were a child seeing it for the first time and the wonder that it created. But in this case, I fully understood him…as the child in me had also been let loose in this strange and exciting world.

I linked my arm through Simon's before answering, "Nope, but I wouldn't have wanted to miss this for anything."

Simon bumped his shoulder against mine and continued smiling as we looked around. The hangar itself was about four times larger than the one in which we'd started our journey. The shuttle sat in the middle of the hangar, dwarfed by the sheer size of the space it inhabited. Several people wearing blue and gray two-piece outfits walked up behind the shuttle and boarded the cargo ramp. The rest of the passengers came down the ramp behind Simon and me. As each of them reached the bottom of the ramp, they stopped for a moment to take in the view. The Administrator was the only exception, as he walked out in front of us and then turned to face us.

Simon pointed over at the red field and asked, "Is that a force field of some kind?"

"In its simplest term, that is correct, Simon. The field isn't actually projecting energy to a wide area. Instead, the energy is actually being transmitted from one location to the next…creating a molecule tight net over the opening. In this case, the sides of the opening are transmitting the energy to the opposite side. Kind of like a laser beam. Well, sort of. The energy still exists, even when the shuttle passed through it, but was no longer visible inside of the cabin. The technical side of it is well beyond my understanding. I leave most of the technical explaining to the engineers."

The Administrator smiled as he admitted that he wasn't an expert in everything.

He held up his left hand, gesturing at the door to the hangar, "Shall we?"

The Administrator guided us out of the hangar and into a long hallway with people walking back and forth. The floor was a dark gray color, while the walls were a rugged blue with tracks of light embedded into the left and right side. The ceiling was white with a bright glow coming from the center section, causing the passageway to be well lit and eliminating any possibilities of a shadow. About every fifty feet or so, the corridor was sectioned with a small wall break sticking out on both sides. I was unsure if these partitions were merely decorative or served a purpose. There weren't any doors between the sections, so I was unsure how they would block a section off in case of an accident. All along the corridor were various doors that all looked similar, with nameplates across the center of them identifying various residences or workshops. As we walked along the corridor, I noticed that the people also appeared to represent almost every nation on the planet and all of them appeared under the age of thirty. What surprised me most was the occasional kid even younger than us running or walking by from time to time.

"Construction for the station started a few years after the island facility began producing technological advancements."

The Administrator began his tour spiel again. As he explained about the station, the others and I just walked behind him and gawked at what we saw.

"To clarify what I stated earlier, the researchers below were encouraged to pursue any subject they desired. One of those groups first proposed to me the development of our own space station for scientific research and eventual exploration. I didn't wish to approach the issue in the same manner as other space agencies around the world had, so I challenged them to be creative. The first hurdle they overcame was the design and development of the shuttle we rode up on…or one very similar, I should say. The team presented a graphical representation on paper of the station they had in mind. After several weeks of redesign and adjustment, we settled on the design you see now. This design is very basic, but allows additional room for expansion at a later date, a few of which are under way as we speak."

The Administrator spoke in a calm voice, as though he were describing a small office that was being built and not something of this magnitude.

"I scrapped the initial recommendation to shuttle engineers into space to begin construction of the station. The danger to inexperienced people floating around space was too much of a risk that early on."

I could just imagine people like us who had never stepped off of Earth being transported up, shoved out of the airlock and expected to work efficiently. Without the proper training, anyone sent up would have found it extremely difficult to work in a zero-gravity environment while possibly getting dislodged to free float in space.

We turned right towards the center of the station and passed more labs, a break room, and even a cafeteria with several people inside sitting down to eat.

"How big is this station?" I couldn't help but ask as the amount of people I saw going by far outnumbered what I saw on the island.

The Administrator didn't mind the interruption and answered, "There are over five thousand rooms aboard the station that range from small security offices, labs of various sizes, apartments from four to seven hundred square feet, service areas such as that cafeteria back there, and a greenhouse."

My jaw dropped, as I couldn't believe the size of this place. The international space station could probably squeeze into the corridor we just walked through if it was laid out straight.

The Administrator continued his spiel, "The other two areas are engineering — which takes up most of the lower section of the station — and the bridge, which is in the topmost center section which you probably noticed on our flight in."

The corridor we were walking through led to the center of the station as it opened up into a circular walkway similar to the one in the center of the citadel down below. The crystal in the center of this section was larger than AMIE and was tinted a soft baby blue rather than AMIE's pink. The outer ring branched off into four sections going to the four corners of the station, which included the one we were presently on. Each section of the outer ring wall contained three elevators, which appeared constantly in use by the station's residents.

Phillip spoke up, "You must be really rich if you can afford to pay for all of this as well as all of these people."

The Administrator paused next to the large blue crystal and turned to face us while leaning against the railing.

The Administrator looked at Phillip to answer his question, "As you and your friends here have partially discovered, I am quite wealthy. A large amount of funds were poured into the initial development of this station and the island below. The resources required to build something of this magnitude are extensive, but well worth it in my opinion. As for the people I employ here and on the island, that was simple enough to manage; I don't pay them."

That shocked all of us and we all looked at the Administrator as though he had just lied to us, but I could tell he was being completely serious. Phillip's mouth opened and then closed like he wanted to respond, but wasn't exactly sure what to say.

Kyle was the first of us to recover, "What do you mean you don't pay them? How do they live?"

Kyle gestured at the people around us. I could see that all of them appeared happy or content to be here.

The Administrator considered this for a second before responding, "Being paid to live normally encompasses both needs and wants. Needs are things human beings require and often include things such as rent, electricity, food, and transportation. Both on the island below as well as in this station, these things are provided to everyone as they need them. A person shouldn't have to work in order to simply live. The other side of that are wants. Wants are the things we desire to improve our quality of life and are often obtained for entertainment or self-importance. The desire to have something that someone else doesn't."

I thought about what he was saying. Though his description was rather generic, it did hit upon the main points of the subject. The needs in my life had always been provided by my parents, requiring them to work every day. My father had often spoiled me with money to buy beautiful clothes, with the occasional vacation thrown in.

The Administrator continued his analysis, "Wants are normally defined by advertising on television manipulating you as to why you had to have something that you really didn't need. Peer pressure normally takes care of the rest, turning your wants into a very basic need…at least on a subconscious level. I found that a decrease in outside stimuli, such as television, significantly reduced the desire for such frivolous things."

Now that he had mentioned it, I remembered seeing only one large television in one of the side break rooms next to the cafeteria on the island. I'd figured that most people probably had a television in their rooms to watch as they desired.

"Then, why do people work?" Phillip spoke up, breaking me out of my train of thought.

The Administrator smiled as he leaned into the railing and crossed his arms in front of him. "As a species it is in our nature, at least for most of us, to keep busy. When work isn't available, then people often rely on entertainment to occupy their time. Though we have plenty of entertainment choices available, many here choose to devote their time to their work."

Phillip didn't seem very convinced by this answer, but continued listening.

"Imagine having a job that you've dreamed of having all your life, and it was yours before any other."

I fought off a smirk and couldn't help but think that I'd wanted to be an astronaut when I grew up, but I decided to hold that thought to myself.

The Administrator gave Phillip a moment to consider what he had said before continuing.

"People here do the jobs they choose to do and because of this, they self-motivate to educate and improve themselves as well as find ways to further develop their field for future generations."

I looked over and saw Simon shaking his head.

"You can't tell me that someone grows up hoping to be a garbage man or a maid," Simon said.

The Administrator smiled, which was the only feature I had noticed that really made his face stand out. You could tell when he smiled that it wasn't forced; he generally enjoyed what he did.

The Administrator nodded at Simon, "You're quite right. As a requirement, each person here is to devote at least four hours of their week to a less-appealing profession. This allows the necessary duties to be completed and provides a brief change in social atmosphere that many people are sorely lacking. At first, there was resistance to this course of action and several thought they should be excluded due to their contributions to the community through research and development. However, I refused to allow any exceptions. As time has passed, many of them have seen the benefit of this method."

As he described this, I couldn't help but think of the book *Host* by my favorite author Stephanie Meyer that contained alien souls that often shared such duties on the world they'd acquired. I quickly dismissed the thought of checking the Administrator's neck for a scar.

Simon pointed to the large crystal behind the Administrator, "Is this another artificial intelligence like AMIE?"

The Administrator turned his head back to glance at the crystal then back at the group.

"No, this crystal processor was actually the first success in our new computer technology advancements and we decided to have it manage the near-infinite calculations required to run the station. This one doesn't have the same processing power as AMIE, but it serves the purpose. We had to modify one of our shuttles to transport the crystal up here during construction and had to sheath it in a special transport container to survive the rigors of space."

Simon looked a little disappointed by the fact that AMIE didn't have a brother, but he appeared to get over it quickly enough. We followed the Administrator into the elevator, and I noticed it also operated with a holographic control panel. The elevator whisked us upwards until we arrived at the nerve center of the station, the control room.

As we exited the elevator, I noticed the control room was a complete circle with two levels. The outer part that we arrived in was the lowest, with the outer walls around it being transparent with a faint hexagonal grid across them and an endless view of space. The outer windows doubled as displays and scrolled various data or images across all of them. The lower section we occupied was divided into four sub-sections or pits with various consoles being manned by crew members that appeared to be ages sixteen to thirty. Each person wore the same type of two-piece outfit with a collar that came to a slight V-cut at the neck. Everyone's suit was a dark gray color with a lighter beige offset and none of them appeared to have any form of rank insignia that I could make out. The younger kids sat side by side with an older person at all times. The center and highest level of the control room contained four control panels, one on each side stretching about a meter wide with an operator working behind them. In the center of the room stood a beautiful woman who appeared to be in her early thirties with porcelain ebony skin and long black hair. Her build was athletic, and she wore a dark gray and blue suit similar in cut to the other operators around her. Surrounding her were four separate holographic displays directly behind each of the four panel operators. All four displays were within an arm's reach of her as long as she stood in the absolute center.

We followed the Administrator up to the topmost section and stood between two of the panels, facing the lady in the center. She was busy tapping and dragging icons on one of the holographic displays, but then stopped and walked in front of the Administrator. As she left her circle, the four displays disappeared and she smiled as she shook the Administrator's hand.

The lady spoke in a strange accent that I couldn't place, giving her words a very musical tone, "Good afternoon, Administrator."

She looked at us before continuing, "Giving a tour, I see."

She smiled at us, and her teeth were so white in contrast to her skin that she could probably pass for an angel if the need ever arose.

Thankfully, the Administrator took the lead for the introductions.

"Lera, I'd like to introduce my guests."

He pointed out each of us as we shook hands with her. Her skin was incredibly soft to the touch and her smile was a contagious disease that all of us were catching.

After we had all been introduced, Lera spoke again, "It's a pleasure to have you all here. You are more than welcome to look around, but I would request that you not touch anything."

She mildly scolded us like we had entered a shop with priceless antiques on display, but I didn't imagine that any of us would have a problem following her directions.

My curiosity caught up with me, "Excuse me, I don't mean to be rude, but might I ask where you are from? Your accent is very beautiful."

She smiled even more if that were even possible and like normal, the Administrator stayed out of our conversation.

Lera was stunning in a regal sort of way as she answered, "You are not being rude. In this station, there are so many of us from different countries that we are all learning to understand each other. I am from Nigeria and was at one time a simple schoolteacher there until I was recruited by the Administrator here. Now, I have been tasked with running this station."

She paused and glared at the Administrator and her tone became slightly harsher.

"At least until the Administrator gets off his ass and finds my replacement."

She glared at the Administrator as his skin flushed a little from embarrassment at her statement. At the same time, I heard a muffled cough somewhere behind me.

The Administrator was saved by Phillip putting his own foot in his mouth, "By any chance, do you have a daughter named Cherise?"

Lera's smile immediately died. She stared daggers at Phillip and started eyeing him from head to toe as though she contemplated skinning him alive. Phillip actually took a slight step back from her and Kyle and Simon tried to contain their laughter.

She pointed a finger directly at Phillip's face.

"You stay away from my daughter or I'll eject you from an airlock!"

Phillip's eyes widened and he visibly paled at her statement.

The Administrator walked up and placed his right hand on her left shoulder and turned her slightly to face him.

"Be nice, Lera. The young man didn't mean anything by it."

Phillip stammered an apology, but wouldn't step any closer to Lera for fear of losing a limb.

I figured a distraction was in order, "Lera, what happened to the four screens that surrounded you?"

Lera continued to stare at Phillip for a few seconds, then finally looked at me.

"Step over here and I will show you."

Lera stepped back into the center of the room and the four holographic displays lit up again. Standing closer, I spotted writing and images…but they were all backwards as I was seeing them from the other side.

She gestured at the displays as she spoke.

"The four displays provide summaries of the four surrounding consoles manned by the operators around you. The four displays encompass system communications, engineering, navigation, and station maintenance."

Lera pointed from screen to screen as she described each display respectively.

Kyle walked up to stand at my left shoulder. His closeness surprised me a little, but I buried the feelings that were trying to surface.

I had to take my mind off of Kyle and I was thankful when he asked a question, "Would you mind explaining each of those a little? I mean this is a space station, so I don't see how navigation is important unless this station moves."

Kyle looked from Lera to the Administrator and back, "Does it?"

Lera smiled.

"You are quite correct, Mr. Bishop…and, no, the station does not move. The station is in an extremely high stationary orbit directly above the island you just flew in from. The altitude is one of the station's protective measures from being noticed by the governments or the curious below."

I could tell Lera enjoyed educating us on the systems, probably due to her prior employment. I found it amazing that a teacher in what was considered a Third World country was in charge of what amounted to be the largest and most advanced space station ever made. I could tell that she was an extremely educated woman. As the director of the station, she'd been provided a very rare opportunity and held her own with so much responsibility. I wondered if I had what it took to be in her shoes and perform even half as well.

She continued speaking and I had to remind myself to pay attention as though I was in school.

"System communications covers any and all communications in our solar system."

I blanched and stared at her like she had grown a third eyeball.

I guessed she'd noticed our expressions or had seen the same reaction before because she spoke before we could ask any more questions, "There is more to this world than what you have imagined so far!"

Lera looked among the four of us and then turned back to the communications display. She pointed to the operator behind the panel.

"The operators actually handle the truly important communications and prioritize its importance depending on the situation. They will then either route the call, as it were, to the correct party or forward it to me as the station director. Those you see in the section of pit in front of the operator are the sub-operators managing communications from the planet's surface to the station as well as any internal station comm traffic. They also get the more tedious task of sorting through ground traffic to identify any mention of our little operation."

From the way she was explaining it, the operator and the crew below (numbering about thirty in total) were managing or monitoring the communications for the entire planet and beyond.

She moved on to the next panel.

"Engineering covers the manufacturing, maintenance, and monitoring of any facilities or vehicles being built as well as those presently in use, such as the shuttle you flew up on. They are also tasked with resource management in relation to those duties."

I didn't fully understand what this encompassed, but it sounded like they would be responsible if a moon base or something needed to be built.

Lera rotated another quarter turn and faced the navigation screen.

"Navigation covers any and all traffic in the system, including shuttles and navigational hazards such as asteroids and the trash left over from previous attempts at space exploration. Also, navigation monitors all satellites presently in orbit over Earth as well as tracks and monitors the International Space Station or ISS as it is often called."

She turned to the final holographic display and tapped a button, which caused an image of the station to appear on the display.

"And lastly, there is station maintenance. This display provides any and all relevant data on the condition and operation of the station, including gravity, environmental controls, personnel tracking, and station defenses. All four systems are aided by the station's computer core in the calculation or routing of information."

"Excuse me!" I blurted before thinking about how rude it was to interrupt.

If Lera minded the interruption, she didn't show it and turned to face me.

"You track everyone in this station?" I asked.

She smiled, glanced at the Administrator, and then back at me.

"That is correct. Every living soul in this station as well as on the island below is tracked as to their whereabouts and health at all times."

I'd heard discussions about such things and the privacy issues that concerned most people.

"What about their privacy?"

Lera looked at me as though she was thinking of the best way to respond. She walked through the holographic display, causing all four displays to blink off. Then, she walked up to me and placed her hand on my arm.

"It is my responsibility as the director of this station, and ultimately the Administrator's responsibility, to ensure the safety and health of all the people who have been placed in our care. Concern for privacy is only raised in our world when someone has something to hide or trust in those who lead has been lost."

She let go of my arm, looked at Kyle, and then back at me.

"The way of life that we are building at this moment is one of trust and respect for each other and for the Administrator. There is no guarantee that such ideals will last forever in everyone who becomes part of this world, but it is my hope that it will last as long as we keep faith in each other."

CHAPTER 16 – A BEAUTIFUL WORLD

SOL STATION
KYLE BISHOP

Alex stared at Lera as she talked about ideals and faith and I saw the fight going on behind her eyes. I knew that all four of us had experienced the selfishness and pettiness in others along with the good qualities that made us human. I couldn't imagine a society that engendered ideals such as trust and respect, helping each other out for the betterment of everyone. But I couldn't deny what I had seen today on the island and in the station. Though the people in both locations would barely add up to the population of a small town and made up such a small minority of the human race, they'd created a dream world, in which anyone looking in to their world would see as naïve, but anyone looking out would see it as the way life should be. Human beings consistently dream about different worlds and ways to live life; these are portrayed in movies, games, books, and even our very dreams while we sleep. Some of those worlds display the horror of which we as a species have been capable of committing. In other worlds, we have seen the beauty that can be created when we choose to do so.

I could tell that the Administrator was just as enraptured by what Lera was saying. It was obvious from the expression on his face that even if just this once, he had found victory. The Administrator noticed me staring at him. We looked at each other, as though we were communicating with each other.

The look lasted only for a moment, but it felt much longer. The Administrator turned back to Lera.

"Thank you, Lera, for your time. I have a little more I want to show our guests before we depart."

The Administrator's statement caused a brief silent pause in the group before Lera spoke up.

"Of course!"

She looked among the four of us.

"It has been a pleasure, and you kids remember to mind yourselves while you are aboard."

Lera looked at Phillip when she said this, and I saw Phillip physically gulp again. The Administrator turned around and began leaving the way we had come in. I walked past Phillip and slapped him on the shoulder, startling him. As we all walked out of the control room, the Administrator steered us back to the elevator and we went to a lower level.

When the elevator door opened, a jungle opened up before us. I saw a path made of small stones that trailed away from the elevator; the path was surrounded by a massive greenhouse of plants, flowers, and vegetables of about every type I could imagine. There were people of all ages pruning or harvesting.

The Administrator started walking along the path, expecting us to keep up.

"The greenhouse takes up an entire level of the station from one side to the other."

The entire group looked around at the various plants. Hidden within the foliage of the various plants, I spotted the occasional small bird and various insects fluttering around. The ceiling and walls had lights blazing out with no rhyme or reason to the design. Overhead at various locations, I saw a small mist being sprayed into the room to provide water to all the life growing around us.

Though he was walking slowly, the Administrator didn't stop as he explained.

"The greenhouse provides some support to our air system and prevents the station's air from going stagnant as well as providing both fresh food and plant life for the residents."

As we walked along the path, I couldn't help but reach out and pull a handful of red grapes from a vine entwined and hanging from a support bracket in the ceiling. I popped them into my mouth and bit down. The juice inside the few grapes exploded in my mouth, causing some to squirt out of my mouth before I could close it all the way. The grapes were sweet and juicy and tasted better than anything my mom had gotten at the store.

I mumbled while I chewed and pointed at my mouth, "Sorry, these are really good."

The others grabbed a grape or two and tried them, as though they didn't believe I was being honest. All of them were nodding and smiling…including junk food lover Simon, who I'd always figured would end up dead if he ate fresh food. The Administrator just smiled and continued walking along the path, still expecting all of us to keep up. As we came around the corner of some dense foliage, we walked into an open park-like area covered in grass and small stone benches. All of it was very impressive, but it still paled in comparison to the view.

Apparently, we had walked to the outer edge of the station and before us was a huge glass window with those faint octagons outlined in it. Beyond it was a view that was unmatched by anything I had ever imagined. The beautiful blue Earth was before us in all her majesty, with the clouds rolling across the surface and the different continents. I walked to the window to get a better view. The others went off to different parts of the glass to take in the view. I heard the Administrator sit down at one of the benches behind us.

Because of our location and stationary orbit, I could make out the state of Hawaii and most of the United States as well as a good portion of Asia. At this distance, it all seemed beautiful. For a moment, I couldn't imagine a world that wasn't at peace. I couldn't hear anyone nearby and the glass didn't reflect anything, including me, to show if anyone was nearby. For a brief moment, I thought I'd been left behind. I looked to my left and saw Phillip and Simon watching Earth below us; Simon was still stuffing his face with more of the local food. The Administrator sat behind him and took in the view as well; I assumed that any time he could manage for a break must be wonderful.

I didn't see Alex anywhere, so I looked to my right. Alex stood next to me a few inches from the glass and I saw tears building up in her eyes. As I looked at her, I remembered when I saw her on that first day of school that now seemed so long ago. I was wrong about my earlier thought. There was something more beautiful than the planet below me. I realized that the more time I spent with Alex, the more I would forget about all the negative baggage from our past.

Regardless of the view out the window, I couldn't tear my eyes away from Alex as she watched Earth below us. I imagined that neither of us had ever expected to see Earth like this in anything other than a picture on the internet, so I understood the emotion going through her.

Alex finally realized I was staring at her. She took a deep breath and held it as she looked into my eyes and I looked into hers. Her eyes were still glossy from the tears built up in them, but they only made her look even more beautiful. I realized then that I didn't care what happened after this moment. As far as I was concerned, I wanted to live in this moment with her forever. I quickly leaned forward, pressing my lips to hers. For a moment, I wasn't sure if I had overstepped myself until she began kissing me back. I moved my body closer to hers and wrapped my arms around her in an effort to merge us together. Her lips tasted of grapes and were so soft to the touch. She increased the pressure of our kiss as both of our desires magnified. As we kissed, I felt her skin brushing me as the softness of the contact threatened to overwhelm me. The heat inside of me built to the point where my very soul wanted to explode. The flame burning brightly in my heart flared up in an effort to incinerate everything around it. Regardless of the raging inferno burning through my veins, I resolved that not even the fires of Hell would distract me from the kiss.

I reluctantly pulled back from Alex, allowing both of us to start breathing again. Her face and cheeks were flushed deep red, as the kiss had caught her by surprise. Her eyes darted back and forth from my eyes to my lips. I saw the engine behind her eyes processing what had just happened. The emotions inside of me were all over the place. I wanted so badly to kiss her again and at the same time wanted to let her make the next move. Her slight hesitation at the beginning of the kiss could have been her surprise or could have been something different, and I didn't want my feelings for her to interfere with the bit of common decency I still had. It was obvious to me that Alex would be unable to deny that she had desired the kiss as much as I did. However, it still concerned me that my actions may have damaged what little friendship we had in place. I needed her to tell me that something more was possible. I wasn't about to destroy what little we had for my own selfish reasons. So, she could take all the time she needed to come to terms with her emotions; she was worth waiting for.

As I looked into her eyes, I noticed that they kept going back and forth between my lips and my eyes and occasionally glanced off to the side. I started to question my earlier wisdom, as she became more agitated the longer that I waited for her to respond. I raised my hand to touch her arm to reassure her that everything was going to be all right…but as my hand approached, she crushed her arm into her side and her other hand clamped down on it to prevent it from being moved. I could tell from her posture that she was getting defensive and her agitation was peaking. I thought back to the moment that I'd kissed her and the reaction she had to it and I just couldn't figure out what was causing her such distress.

I needed her to open up and tell me what to do, so I decided to ask, "Alex?"

Before I could get another word out, she released the arm I was trying to touch and slapped me across the face. I stood there for a moment in shock, stunned by what she had just done. The slap itself was sharp, but didn't really hurt that much; the shock of what she just did confused me. As I looked back at her, I saw she was even more upset. Tears pooled in her eyes and the hand that she slapped me with covered her mouth.

It was difficult to tell if she was still upset about the kiss or for slapping me, but I figured it didn't matter either way. She locked her eyes on me again and I could still see the emotion behind them as she walked past me toward the rest of the group. I didn't even try to stop her to explain what had just happened. I figured it was just best to let it go for the moment. I turned back to face the glass wall, but the view no longer commanded my attention…just the thoughts of a kiss that felt truly wonderful — and then the follow up, well not so much.

"We should be going."

I turned at the Administrator's statement. If he'd noticed what happened between Alex and I, he had the decency to keep it to himself.

Phillip and Simon kept glancing at me. It was clear that they had seen something; I just wasn't sure how much they had seen, not that it really mattered. We all followed the Administrator as he led us to the elevator and returned us to the hangar for the ride back down. I kept looking at Alex to see if I could figure out the problem, but she looked at everything but me.

The shuttle ride back to the island wasn't as thrilling as the ride up was, at least for me. Alex sat next to Simon as we boarded, causing Phillip to swap places and take her old spot. There was still a seat available near her, but I figured I didn't need to push her any further away. I had taken a chance and misinterpreted her feelings towards me. I spent the entire flight down thinking of ways I could get her alone to apologize. When we landed, we walked back to the waterfall oasis we had originally started at. However, we were never alone again. So, I figured the boat ride home would be my next best chance.

As we arrived at the oasis, the tent from earlier was still there and we all crossed over to it. Inside was a prepared meal, which looked to be Greek in nature. I guess one final hot meal would be nice before starting our trip back home, so we sat down and had one final meal together.

As we ate our meal in silence, I shook away my thoughts of Alex off long enough to recap everything I had seen and heard during our visit. The island and the station were not what I had first imagined, a private hideout of some billionaire recluse trying to take over the world.

I looked up at the Administrator as he took a bite out of a gyro he had assembled and asked, "What now?"

The Administrator put down his food and finished chewing, staring at me as he prepared to answer.

"Now, it's time for you all to return to your home and finish school."

I couldn't believe what he just said. I imagined a lot of responses but not that.

"That's it?" I asked. "After all that you have shown us and we're just dismissed?"

The Administrator continued to look at me, as the others stopped eating and listened to what was being said.

"Kyle, I'm sure you each came here with expectations of what you would find. I can only hope that what I have shown you has impressed upon you the importance of what I am trying to help create. But more importantly, I wanted to impress on you all how fragile this way of life is."

He paused for a moment and I thought about what he said, it still felt like at the very least he should invite us to stay...at least give us the choice.

The Administrator leaned forward into the table and gestured at all of us.

"Though I understand that before me are three young men and a young lady capable of embracing this life, I also understand that there are those in the world who care about you and aren't ready to let you go."

I thought of my mom and realized that even if she let me come here, which I doubted, she would be left alone. I looked at the others and I could tell they were thinking the same thing. Alex, of course, still wouldn't look at me.

"What about the others here that have family elsewhere?" I asked.

The Administrator continued without taking much time to think.

"Those here who are your age or younger either arrived after the time of their majority according to their country of origin and they left home, as it were, or they were born to those already here. You see Kyle, as much as I would love you four to join our society, pulling you away from your families would create tremendous amounts of the attention that we are trying to avoid."

I thought about what he was saying. Yeah, if we chose to leave our lives and move here, the Administrator would have the FBI poking their noses in all the wrong places. I thought about all that I had seen and realized that I wouldn't want to risk this world for my own selfish desires. Though I didn't like it, I understood what he was saying. I nodded and the Administrator sat back in his chair.

Simon spoke up during our moment of silence.

"What if we want to come here after high school? How do we get in touch with you?"

As he spoke, I kicked myself for not thinking of that first because it was a very valid question.

The rest of us looked at the Administrator as he responded, "Don't worry, Simon. I will be keeping an eye on all of you. When you step out into the world, I'll be watching. If you are still interested, you are more than welcome to join us."

Simon seemed to relax, as did the rest of us at his statement. Though we couldn't stay for a very good reason, at least the opportunity still existed for us to embrace this world at a later date if we wanted to.

Something dawned on me that I'd wanted to ask him when we first met, but I had gotten sidetracked.

"Administrator, why build this island and the space station and basically create your own world? Why not just try to change the world we already live in?"

The Administrator smiled at the question.

"I'd thought about that when I first considered all of this. I concluded that change is often resisted by society. Most people grow used to the way things are and are uncomfortable with change. Change does eventually come, but the process is normally measured in decades if not longer. I felt it would be easier to create a whole new world than to change the one already made."

As we all finished eating, I realized that it was time for us to get going. The sun was going down and if we sailed through the night, we could be back in Oregon by tomorrow afternoon. So, I stood up from my chair and pushed it back under the table.

"I guess it is time for us to go, then."

The others started getting up and stacked their silverware and napkins onto their plates.

The Administrator interrupted our brief spat of depression.

"Before you go, there is the matter of the game we haven't finished."

I thought about our meeting in this very tent this morning and remembered that the Administrator had tasked each of us with writing one word on a small note card describing ourselves. I pulled the folded-up card out of my pocket as the others did the same, including the Administrator.

He began explaining the purpose of the game.

"Part of my job as Administrator is to search the world for others like myself who can and will embrace this life and help this place grow. Those whom I feel are a danger to this world are kept at an arm's length and guided in different directions. At times I will find one here or there, but they are often few and far between."

I opened my card, flattened it, and laid it on the table in front of the Administrator. The others, including the Administrator, did the same. Simon's paper had the word "Hot" written on it, but it was crossed out for another word. It was a word that matched the rest of the cards displayed before us…"DREAMER."

We looked among our cards, finding it hard to believe that each of us had chosen the same word to describe ourselves.

I looked at the Administrator as he started speaking again.

"I had hoped that you four were like me. What I'd learned about each of you before you came here was that as unique as each of you are, you each possess the same qualities that I look for in others. Those qualities are what create the dreamers in the world, the dreamers that I want in my world."

The Administrator shook hands with each of us and wished us well on our journey home. I couldn't think of anything else to say at that moment or any other question that really needed to be answered right then. So, I walked out of the tent with the others following as I marched up the trail leading to the boat and our trip home. The Administrator didn't follow to see us off. The boat was still where we left it, so we all climbed on board and sailed away from the sunset.

Dreamers

CHAPTER 17 – THE HUNT BEGINS

FBI FIELD OFFICE, PORTLAND, OREGON
AGENT KATHRYN MORGAN

I sat at my desk after returning from my lunch break. I was in my mid-thirties and had been with the FBI for going on ten years. As a female agent, I felt like I had to claw my way up a men's-only club. Regardless, I considered myself an excellent agent and had dozens of major investigations behind me. Standing at 5'2" with chestnut brown hair, I've never really turned heads nor have I ever inspired terror in those I've arrested. But as an investigator, I was always extremely adept at filtering through even minute evidence and finding links where other agents hadn't. Because of this ability, my superiors rewarded me for successes. Well, if you call being transferred to Portland, Oregon a reward, that is. I was transferred to Portland a little over two years ago as a field promotion and was technically second in command of all field agents in a tri-state area. Though the promotion was a step in the right direction, I'd always dreaming of being assigned to the FBI headquarters in Washington DC.

After returning from lunch, I decided to review the criminal file associated with a six-month long investigation involving weapons trafficking. I'd first started the case after a routine customs inspection revealed a container of illegal semi-automatic weapons being smuggled in from overseas through Oregon's ports. The location and those responsible for shipping the contraband hadn't yet been determined, but I felt confident that a break would come soon. Surveillance was already in place on the people receiving the merchandise and now it was only a waiting game until the next shipment arrived. The original shipment was handled badly by the first agent who responded, causing any possible follow up with the shipper or the receiver to be dicey. Because of that, I'd been assigned to the case and had built it from the ground up. A knock came at my door. As I looked up, my boss, Senior Agent Sam Roberts, walked into my office.

I smiled up at him, "Hi, Sam!"

He smiled at me, "How was lunch, Kate?"

I looked at Sam and knew that he hadn't walked in here just to see how my lunch had gone, but figured he was just making small talk to be polite. Sam was in his fifties with graying hair from the stress of the job, but I didn't think that he would ever retire. He was a good field agent who had been with the agency for almost thirty years. He had risen to the Number One spot in the region due to a solid career as a field agent and turned out to be an excellent administrator. He had been offered the opportunity to transfer to DC, but he had turned it down and asked for a quieter post. I wasn't sure if Portland was quieter, considering the amount of work we did here, but it was his choice and he didn't seem to regret it.

I didn't mind humoring him, but I had work to do, so I cut to the chase.

"It was great. What can I do for you?"

Sam looked at the file on my desk.

"Is that the arms trafficking case you're involved with?"

I looked down and back up at Sam. He didn't bother sitting down, for fear of growing roots in anyone's office but his own.

I nodded.

"Yes, it is. I was just reviewing it to make sure I hadn't missed anything."

Sam smiled again.

"I doubt that. You've always been thorough in your investigations."

He fidgeted a little before continuing, "But the reason I came in here was to inform you that I'm transferring the investigation to another agent. I have another job for you."

I stood up, planted my hands on the table, and looked at Sam. I could tell from his expression that he was serious, and I couldn't believe it. In all my years with the FBI, I'd never had an investigation taken away from me. Normally, when an investigation was taken away it was because those above the agent had lost confidence in the agent.

"What's going on? I've been handling this investigation for the past six months and it's close to bearing some results. I don't think this is a good time to transfer it to someone else."

While I spoke, my voice level had risen; I realized I'd started attacking my boss. I took a breath and calmed down, waiting for Sam to respond.

Sam shifted his stance from one leg to another before answering, "I know you've put a lot of legwork into this, Kate. Removing you is not meant to be a punishment, so relax."

I looked down at my desk for a moment and realized that Sam was right; I was overreacting. I sat back down in my chair and tried to relax, though I wasn't sure if I was very convincing.

Sam took that moment to actually sit down in one of the chairs on the other side of my desk, which surprised me.

He continued, "The Director himself contacted me and ordered me to assign my best agent to this new case that he forwarded to my office."

Sam pushed the file he had in his hand across the desk towards me. I closed the trafficking file, pushed it to the side, and opened the new one. The Director of the FBI didn't normally involve himself in cases unless they pertained to national security or were extremely public cases. I opened the file and saw a clipped photo of a skinny young kid with glasses. I flipped the photo up to read the header page, which identified the kid as Simon Weiss.

I looked up at Sam.

"What is this all about?"

It was obvious that Sam he was trying to determine how much to tell me. We'd had a good working relationship in the time I had been here, so hopefully he trusted me.

"I don't really know."

Before I could comment, Sam continued, "The Director didn't give me all the details, Kate. He just stated that this kid was caught hacking into the financial markets. He wants a detailed file built on this kid...family, friends, hobbies...the works. Also, a detailed timeline on what this kid has been doing as far back as you can go."

Sam hadn't told me anything different from what the file would say, either because he didn't trust me with the real reasons or that he didn't know himself.

"Did the Director mention what he was possibly doing in the financial markets? Are we talking economic terrorism or money laundering? What exactly?"

Sam leaned forward and put his hands together like he was praying.

"I'm sorry, Kate, but I really don't know. I spent fifteen minutes on the phone with the Director and was told politely to shut up and not ask so many questions."

I was shocked; the Director didn't normally step on his senior agents like that, especially ones as good as Sam. I could only imagine that his phone call didn't end on any high note.

Sam continued before I could ask anything else, "The Director has taken the gloves off for this one, Kate. He's already spoken with the Justice Department and the Congressional oversight and has been given free rein on this one. Inside of that folder is a signed document federally authorizing you to perform any required surveillance without prior local judicial approval. It will also allow you to detain anyone you choose for questioning to obtain the requested information."

I sat heavily back in my chair, finding it hard to believe what I had just been told. The Patriot Act had allowed a tremendous amount of leeway for investigations into terrorism or anything classified as a threat to national security such as what happened on 9/11. But it also led to an equal amount of human rights abuse and Sam had just told me that I had the authority and responsibility of that Act. Good agents didn't require the use of such Machiavellian methods to achieve their goals. All it took was good, old-fashioned investigation and police work to achieve results.

It was hard to find my voice, but I had to say something, "Sam?"

Sam stood up from his chair and I could tell he was uncomfortable with what he'd just told me.

"Look, Kate, I'm not asking you or ordering you to do anything against your conscience. You're the best investigator I know of. If anyone can get this information without resorting to that letter, then it would be you. But if you think for a moment that you will be unable to perform this assignment, then I need to know now."

I stood up from my desk but found it difficult to find the strength in my legs to hold myself upright, so I leaned against my desk.

"I'll get the job done."

"Pull whatever resources you need to make this happen as fast as possible. I want a detailed report at the end of each week about your progress. If the Director calls again, I want to have something to give him."

I nodded at Sam but he stood there for a second, probably to see if I was serious and okay with this. A few moments later he exited my office and I plopped back down into my chair, causing it to roll a few inches back from my desk.

Dreamers

CHAPTER 18 – SCHOOL'S IN SESSION

OREGON
ALEXI MASTERS

Several weeks after we returned from our adventure, summer vacation ended and our senior year in high school started. My parents were still clueless about my disappearance and hadn't raised any concerns over my closed-off behavior since my return.

After arriving home, I barricaded myself in my room and made the necessary phone call to my best friend Megan to let her know that I had returned. She had covered for me while I was gone, as I'd told my parents I was spending a few days with her on a sleepover. I could imagine the response from my dad if I'd told him I was going off on an illegal cruise with three guys.

I stayed in my room as much as possible for the remaining weeks until school started, brushing up on last year's schoolwork to refresh myself for the coming year. Truthfully, though, I was hiding from Kyle and had been doing so since that fateful kiss at the space station. During the cruise back, the only conversation we had was when we all discussed what we had witnessed and what we planned to do about it.

All of us knew that our initial expectations of finding some sinister empire had been decimated and replaced by a Utopian world that even now seemed like a distant dream. We discussed everything we had seen several times and came to the conclusion that no one outside of us could ever know. Not that anyone would probably believe us, but none of us were willing to risk the possibility of losing the chance of being a part of that future. All throughout the first three years of high school, I'd prepared myself to go off to college and then law school. All of my studying was in preparation for becoming a lawyer to make my father proud. Now, after witnessing this dream world, my future had shattered into a million pieces. Becoming a lawyer just seemed to pale in comparison to what would be possible if I went to work for the Administrator. I didn't doubt for a second that the Administrator would honor his word to us if we asked to join him after high school ended. It scared all of us after coming back and seeing the world with new eyes to know how easy it would be to threaten and possibly destroy what he had created.

The first few weeks back at school were a blur. I attempted to start back where I had left off at the end of last year, but each day was harder and harder to get through. Phillip and Simon walked up to me from time to time to say hi and ask how I was doing. I hadn't visited either of them since we had been back, for fear of running into Kyle. Both of them asked me at separate times to visit, but both times I made excuses. I buried myself in schoolwork and activities. I performed my duties as student body president by helping Megan and my other friends put up banners to welcome returning and new students, but I just felt like a robot going through pre-programmed motions. Megan had noticed right away that I wasn't my normal self. She kept pushing me to tell her what was going on, but

I kept deflecting her questions. I figured I didn't have a lot of time before I would have to tell her something, but I just didn't know what.

Monday morning of a new week had started, and the day was still progressing as monotonously as the previous days and weeks. Megan had gotten fed up with me over the weekend and hadn't called me since we'd last spoken on Saturday morning. She had attempted to pull me out for some shopping, but I had brushed her off without even realizing it. My parents were also noticing that I wasn't myself and without the stress of school starting again to blame it on, they were starting to get nosy.

I decided to stay after school and avoid going home for a little longer. I sat down on the school bleachers and watched the cheerleading team practice and our school football team run drills. I didn't really care about what they were doing. I just wanted to avoid everything and everyone else in my life. But most importantly, I wanted to avoid Kyle. I'm not sure if I could cope with hearing him say my name one more time.

"Alex!"

I sat up straight from my daydreaming and wasn't sure if I'd heard what I'd just heard.

"Alex!"

I turned my head slowly and there was Kyle standing at the end of the bleachers looking at me.

I watched as Kyle started climbing his way towards me. Even after all this time, my body betrayed me in its reaction. God, why did he have to be so freaking gorgeous? Kyle sat down next to me with our arms a few inches from each other and I could feel the electricity passing into me from him being that close. I briefly thought about just running away from him to avoid this encounter, but I knew it would have to happen eventually.

Kyle looked in my eyes as he said, "Alex, I'm sorry."

Emotion surged inside of me at that moment as my body continued betraying me. I choked up at what he had said as tears filled my eyes and I started sniffing to prevent my nose from running.

"For what?" I sobbed, trying unsuccessfully to pull myself together.

I didn't realize how much emotion had built up inside of me over the years and just being near Kyle was like a valve being turned to the on position.

With more sincerity than I had ever heard come from him, he answered, "Alex, I never would have kissed you if I had known it would cause all of this!"

Kyle gestured at me and I realized he was talking about the rut I had been in. I guess even with me avoiding him, he was bound to notice. He thought my emotions were on meltdown because he kissed me. Well, I guess I couldn't deny it was partially due to that. I thought about all the girls he had dated, including Megan, and the pain he had caused them.

I guess now was as good of a time as any, so I whispered, "Why do you hurt people?"

Kyle rocked back in surprise, though I couldn't figure out how that could be a surprise to him. The anger and hatred inside of me that had built up over the last few years made its way to the surface. It gave me the strength to push back everything else and finally confront him about what had been on my mind for years.

I must admit that he did a good job of covering up his past behavior, but it pissed me off that he would act all innocent.

"What? What are you talking about? I never meant to hurt you."

I let out an exasperated noise, "I'm not talking about me. I'm talking about them."

I pointed at the cheerleaders forming a pyramid on the other side of the field.

Kyle looked at them and I saw that the confusion on his face increase. Was he so dense that he couldn't see the hurt he had caused so many girls with his one-week romances? I realized that I would have to spell it out for him, and I figured this was a good moment to give some of his hurt back to him.

I focused on his eyes as I started, to ensure he understood that what I was saying was serious.

"For the past three years, you have gone out with countless girls at this school."

Kyle's left eye scrunched down and the corner of his mouth went up as he shook his head.

"Well, I have spent time with quite a few girls here, but I wouldn't say they were countless."

I wanted to punch him so badly at that moment; I realized that when I'd pushed him into the ocean a few weeks back, I should have gone down into the cabin and backed the boat over him.

I relaxed the fist I had formed with my right hand, as my nails were digging into my hand and it was starting to hurt.

I pointed at him with the index finger of my other hand, "Regardless, you dated them and then you dumped them. Staci, Erica, Bridgette…my list can go on and on."

Kyle kept looking at me with a confused look on his face and I could tell that he just didn't understand or just didn't care about their feelings.

I stood up, as I'd had enough.

"And then you went and hurt Megan. She is my best friend, Kyle, and you hurt her."

Tears were falling down my cheeks and I just couldn't hold it in any longer.

I gritted my teeth together in order to get the rest out without babbling as the tears continued, "And I will not be the next girl you hurt."

Kyle stood up and reached out to touch my arm. I pulled back violently and looked at him with what I could only assume was murder in my eyes.

Kyle fidgeted for a second before responding, "Alex, it wasn't like that."

Kyle looked like he was pleading and I couldn't take it, so I turned around because even the sight of him was making me upset now.

With all the hate I could muster I responded, "I don't care anymore. Stay away from me."

I didn't bother to wait for his answer. I walked back to the school parking lot and, thankfully, Kyle didn't follow me. I cried the entire time I drove home. I replayed my conversation with him over and over in my mind and my emotions became so intense that I couldn't hold it in any longer. I knew without a doubt that I hated Kyle with every fiber of my being for what he had did to those other girls. At the same time, I knew without a doubt that I loved him just as much. The conflict between the two feelings was making me feel sick, to the point of causing chest pains. When I got home, I avoided my parents and locked myself in my room. I was so emotionally exhausted that I crawled into my bed and went to sleep.

The next morning, I woke up as the sun started shining through my window. I thought about what I'd said yesterday and thought about all the crying that I had done. I realized that I'd slept better last night than I had in weeks. I felt rested and, if not happy, at least I wasn't sad. It seemed like I'd found a place of contentment inside of me and that would have to do for now. I got dressed for school and went downstairs to start making up with my family. I had been avoiding them for the past several weeks and it wasn't fair to them or my little sister. As I walked into the kitchen, my mother was cooking on the stove while my little sister sipped orange juice and colored in a book. I smiled and sat down next to her. My sister Emily had recently turned six and was in the first grade. Though they were past simple coloring at that age, Emily never seemed to stop enjoying it.

"Hi, Ems," I said.

Emily looked up at me and smiled as only someone still innocent in the world could.

"Want to help?"

She pushed her coloring book over, so I picked up an orange crayon and joined her.

After arriving back at school, I went to each class and reignited the friendships that I had been ignoring since the beginning of the school year. I didn't see Kyle the first half of the day and I made it to lunch feeling like the day might actually be livable. I still thought about Kyle and the one-sided conversation we'd had yesterday, but it didn't hurt as much anymore. Having a chance to release the pent-up emotions that had been inside of me for what felt like years was a great relief. Megan still wouldn't sit near me at lunchtime, but I actually enjoyed sitting on my own. I took the time to think about all that had happened in my life, including recently; most of it had been good and some of it bad. My self-reflection came to a screeching halt when a girl walked up to my table and sat across from me. I didn't mind sharing, but she didn't have any food for lunch. She was a brunette with straight hair and brown eyes, and I was certain that I knew her from somewhere. Her name was Cary or Carla-something.

I didn't want to appear inhospitable, so I stuck out my hand to shake hers.

"Hi, I'm Alex."

She smirked, "I know who you are, Alex; you're the student body president. I'm Caitlin, but everyone calls me Kat."

She returned my handshake and then put her arms in her lap behind the table.

The moment stretched into awkward and kept going.

"Kat, is there anything I can help you with?"

She took a deep breath and then exhaled.

"I went out with Kyle for a week back in my sophomore year."

I blinked for a second at what she said. There were quite a few girls in this school who could make that claim, so she wasn't that special. I just wondered why she blurted that out as though she had to.

"Okay."

I couldn't keep the sarcasm out of my voice, and I started to get up from the table.

I didn't know where this was going, but I didn't want to deal with it now. I reached for my textbook on the table and just as I did, she grabbed my wrist to try to prevent me from moving.

I saw the determination in her eyes, but I wasn't sure why.

"Please don't go. Please. I just need a few minutes."

I could tell that she felt really uncomfortable talking to me and I felt bad for her, so I sat back down.

"Look, what you did in the past is none of my business."

Kat pulled her arm back, put it in her lap, and looked down.

"That's not what I meant. Let me just rip off the bandage and maybe that will help. Back during the summer vacation between my freshman and sophomore year, my father left us."

I wasn't sure why she needed to tell me this as she continued, "He left me, my mom, and my little brother, apparently to go shack up with some bimbo barely older than me."

I blinked and I saw her fidgeting in her seat, but I still didn't understand why she was telling me this.

"After my dad left, my little brother who was nine at the time became depressed and wouldn't talk to anyone or do anything. He was failing classes and pretty much was angry at the world. I really couldn't blame him. Kyle found out about our situation and offered to come and talk with him. I didn't think it would help very much, but I was willing to try anything, do anything to help my little brother. Kyle went and talked with him while my mom was still at work and it was just me and him at home. After he talked to him for about twenty minutes, he came out and told me that everything was going to be all right. That night, my brother came out of his room after my mom came home and he went up to her..."

Kat started to cry as she explained this to me; I reached across the table and she gave me her hand and we held hands.

"...and he hugged her and he started crying and saying he was sorry. We all cried so much that night. The next day after school Kyle came by again and spent the day with both of us, keeping us moving so we didn't have time to be sad. He came by for almost two weeks straight until he was sure we started to actually live again. He apparently realized he wasn't needed as much, so he only came by every so often after that."

"He helped my family through a rough time and, like I said, I would have done anything for what he did for us. I asked him out on a date, and he agreed."

I choked down the lump in my throat, both from her story and the realization that we had come to this part. I realized that when she said she would do anything, she meant it, and it was starting to make me nauseous.

She smiled as she remembered, "Needless to say, I was surprised when he took me to a retirement home that evening. I didn't really understand why until we entered the activity room and there were a bunch of old people trying to learn how to dance by themselves."

She laughed and wiped at her eyes to clear up the tears from her earlier waterworks.

"You see, none of them really knew how to dance and they were just doing what they could to get by. Kyle knew that I was a dancer from the pictures and trophies I had at my house. He asked me to teach him and them how to dance. I think he just wanted to learn himself, but was too much of a chicken to come out and say it."

I stared at Kat so hard, it felt like my eyes were coming out of my head. What she just told me was just too convincing to be made up, but why had she come here to tell me this at all?

I wanted to know, "So..."

She interrupted before I could continue.

"For a week, I taught Kyle and all those nice people how to dance. I still go back there once a month to give them a class."

She leaned forward across the table, so her face was only about a foot away from mine.

"Kyle helped my brother cope with the loss of our dad by being a big brother to him...and he helped me by showing me that I had worth to someone in this world. Maybe in a small way, but...it was enough. I just thought you should know."

I was speechless and before I could come up with anything else to say, Kat got up and left the lunchroom. I stared at the table with my book still resting on it and then realized that if I didn't get moving, I would be late for class.

I made it to my next class, which happened to be AP Calculus. Our teacher Mr. Hines paired us off to work on the problems together. I was always good with math and didn't have much problem keeping up, but I didn't mind helping out if I could. Considering the conversation I had at lunch, I was willing to do anything to get my mind off of Kyle.

My partner finally scooted over and as she sat down, I looked up. It was Bridgette. She didn't normally partner with me, as I wasn't in her normal circle of friends.

"Bridgette, where did you want to start?" I asked, hoping to occupy my mind with math problems. I knew Bridgette was another one of Kyle's dates; I'd used her as an example when I berated him yesterday.

She looked at me straight away without flinching and whispered, "I want to talk to you about Kyle."

I thought, not again.

That was how the rest of my day went. One girl after another came up to me in my classes or in the hallway, with the last one ambushing me right after school. Each told me about their week with Kyle and how sweet he was. Some told me that he had helped them out in different ways and others he'd just asked for help learning things such as horseback riding, art, meditation, and judo. I knew they were being honest with me, but I tried so hard not to believe them after they had left. But no matter what I said to myself, I couldn't erase the small doubt that these girls had allowed to creep up in me. Had I misinterpreted what Kyle had done all these years? Was he really a decent guy who hadn't deserved me pushing him off of a ship or yelling at him?

Then I remembered Megan. She had told me about the week she had with Kyle. He took her to the dance and then saw her afterwards. The whole situation was starting to confuse me, and I needed to find some way to understand.

After I got home from school, I walked into the kitchen as my mom made a snack for Emily.

"Mom, if it's all right, I'm going to head over to Megan's for a little while."

My mom was always the cool one to my dad's seriousness.

"All right, your dad will be home soon and dinner will be at seven."

I nodded, grabbed a bag of cookies out of the cabinet and went to visit Megan.

Megan lived across the street from me, so we had been friends forever. The way I had been cutting her out of my life for the past month was tantamount to unusual cruelty. I knocked on her door and was both looking forward to seeing her and dreading about what I wanted to talk about. The door flung open quickly and we both said hi to each other, though her greeting sounded a little snotty. I guessed I deserved that.

"Megan, can we talk?"

I held up the bag of cookies before me as a peace offering.

Megan looked at the cookies and then at me for a second and I worried that she would just shut the door because of the way I had been treating her. She opened the door wide and gestured for me to come inside. When I came in, she closed the door and we both went up to her room. We sat down on the carpet in the middle of her room and tore open the cookies.

I pulled one from the package and took a small bite.

"Megan, I wanted to apologize for the way I have been treating you these past few weeks."

My shoulders slumped as I continued, "I was trying to deal with some stuff, and I shouldn't have shut you out. I just didn't know what to do. But you are my best friend and you deserved better, and I'm sorry."

She nodded as she ate her cookie. I waited for her to say something, but she just kept eating until she had finished the cookie.

Megan wiped her fingers on her jeans before speaking, "What you did hurt."

I opened my mouth to apologize again, but she put up her hand to signal me to stop.

"But...I am your best friend and always will be. Just don't let it happen again, okay?"

Tears came out of my eyes.

"Okay."

And then she started to cry. We hugged each other and started to mend the tear that I had created. After a few minutes of crying and holding onto each other, we pulled apart and started laughing. We both reached for another cookie, and she started going off about the last month and what I had missed in gossip and scandals.

I listened attentively as a best friend should until she finally asked what I had been dreading.

"So, what caused you to shut the world out for the past month...to shut me out?"

She stared at me and I loathed answering, but I knew she deserved the truth. I couldn't tell her about the trip I had taken and the world I had experienced, so I decided to focus on something that she would find even more juicy: Kyle.

I told Megan how I'd started to hang out with Kyle and told her about the kiss, but of course I left out the details about where we kissed. She immediately started digging for details, many of which I didn't want to give. I made up plausible alternatives as to where the events had happened. I could tell that she remembered her own experience with Kyle, which was one of the reasons I'd wanted to talk with her; I needed details myself.

I pulled another cookie from the package and took a small bite.

"Megan, I need to know more about what happened between you and Kyle that week you saw each other."

Megan sat back and her posture looked a little defensive.

"I told you already, if you remember."

Megan was trying to leave it at that, but I could tell that she was leaving something out.

"I know you did, but I need to know everything."

She looked at me and I knew she could tell that I wasn't going to leave until she spilled the beans.

"Why?"

I didn't answer right away. She started looking closer at me, making me feel like I was being interrogated. I looked every place I could but directly at her, avoiding her gaze.

She pointed her finger at me accusingly, "You're in love with him!"

She pulled her hand back and covered her mouth in shock.

I mumbled, "Yeah...pretty much."

She started bouncing up and down in excitement as she sat on the floor and I briefly thought she might be having a seizure. I began explaining to her about all the girls who had talked with me today regarding Kyle and what they had said. I explained to her about my blow up with Kyle on the bleachers yesterday afternoon and how he had acted confused. I told her that she was the only person left who had been hurt by him and I needed that justification to keep on hating him. She was apparently the only person who had actually been on a date with him and I needed to know what had happened. She finally calmed down and just kept looking at me.

"When Kyle first asked me out to the dance, I was surprised that he asked me. Honestly, I didn't think I was his type...but I had a crush on him and jumped at the chance."

Megan blushed as she said this, and I felt a little uncomfortable as well, but she continued.

"He was very sweet and gentlemanly as he escorted me to the dance."

She sighed in contentment, "He was a very good dancer, but now I guess we both know why."

I thought back to Kat and what she had taught him.

Megan continued, "The rest of the week we did things like walk in the park, walk downtown, and he even went with me as I shopped for a book."

I shook my head to clear the confusion, "Hold on for a second...so you are saying that during the week you spent with Kyle, you didn't actually go out on a 'date' date with him."

She shook her head with a guilty look plastered on her face.

Then she brightened and interjected, "Well, if you count the prom as a date then we did."

She smiled and seemed satisfied with herself. Wow, I'd had the impression that he had gone out on at least three to four dates with her.

Megan continued where she left off, but I could tell the next part still hurt her a little.

"He came to me at the end of the week to break it off. I think he realized that I wanted to take things further than he was willing to go."

My jaw dropped to the ground.

"Seriously, you had to go there."

She raised both her hands and shrugged.

"Hey, it's not like he isn't a major hottie…which I'm sure even *you* have noticed."

I ran my fingers through my hair in frustration, as I still couldn't figure out why Megan's experience was different from the rest of the girls. From the way she described it, he hadn't just dumped her out of meanness. It was more like he wanted to get out before things got too serious and he didn't think it was working out. But something about that just didn't sit right with me, and it brought up more questions than I had arrived here with. I hugged Megan, invited her over to have dinner with my family, and she agreed to come.

That evening, we hung out in my room and listened to music and talked about school and everything else that we had missed. When I went to bed, I felt better after mending my relationship with Megan…but I still didn't know what to do about

Kyle. It took a long time to get him out of my mind long enough to fall asleep.

Dreamers

CHAPTER 19 – ENEMY AT THE GATES

OREGON
KYLE BISHOP

After being berated and then abandoned by Alex on the school bleachers, I sat where she had to review the brief encounter in my mind. Alex had mentioned that I'd hurt the girls I had spent time with at school as well as her best friend Megan. While it was never my intention to hurt Megan, I had to admit that she might have gotten a little sore with me when I broke it off. My mind kept bringing up images of Alex's face displaying anger and crying while she was accusing me. I thought about when she had pushed me off of the ship for no apparent reason a while back. Then, I thought about how unapproachable she had been over the past few years and how it had gotten progressively worse over time. Was my relationship with those girls what had caused her to be so angry with me? A smile burst on my face for a moment, but I crushed it down quickly as it dawned on me: she was jealous. If she was jealous, that meant she cared about me. The smile reappeared on my face and nothing would remove it. I sat there for the next hour, thinking about how I could repair the damage that was inadvertently caused. I developed a plan to fight to get Alex back, so I spent that night calling some of the girls whose numbers I knew and vowed to hunt down a few more at school the next morning.

The next day at school I ran into two others that I'd been looking for that morning and explained the situation to them. It wasn't easy asking all these girls to divulge sensitive information. I just explained what was going on and asked them to just explain to Alex what had actually happened during our time together. Most of them thought what I was trying to do was sweet. I didn't want to see that look on Alex's face from yesterday afternoon ever again if I could help it. I wanted to spend the rest of my life just ensuring that a smile stayed on her face. That entire day I avoided Alex like the plague; I didn't want to accidentally run into her until she had time to realize the truth. I knew that begging for forgiveness and reiterating that nothing happened would never work, so I hoped this approach would have more success.

After school, Phillip and I drove Simon home. We discussed things that Alex really needed to be in on. I hoped that by tomorrow I would get some type of reaction out of her. If not, then I would have to come up with an even better plan to win her back. After hanging out with Phillip and Simon for a couple of hours, I headed home for the night.

The next day after second period, my patience paid off. As I was pulling books from my locker for class, I heard an angel call out my name behind me. I turned around and there was Alex. She stood near me and I couldn't help but think how beautiful she was today. She smelled of sunflowers and lavender; the combination was intoxicating to me.

Tearing me out of my euphoria, she said, "We need to talk."

I closed my locker door and looked at her for a second. I looked down at her lips then quickly back up to her eyes; I reminded myself to focus on things other than her beauty when she talked to me.

I didn't outright smile, though I definitely wanted to.

"Yes, we do. Meet me after school at Simon's and we can talk there."

I could tell by her reaction that wasn't what she had meant. I figured she wanted time to speak with me alone, and I wanted that as well…but there was something slightly more important that needed to be dealt with first.

Before she could comment, I added, "It's important…please."

I looked at her until she nodded. Then, I walked away…even though I certainly didn't want to. Yes, we had a lot to discuss. I caught up with Phillip and Simon that day and told them that Alex would be over tonight. After school ended, the three of us guys drove over to Simon's house again and waited for Alex to show up.

Simon's room was retro nerd at its best. The centerpiece of the room was his computer system, which took up an entire wall. His walls were covered with *Wired* magazine posters, a picture of Hermione flying on a broomstick from his Harry

Potter fixation, and a bunch of random junk I couldn't even figure the meaning behind. With the exception of his computer, his room looked like he had gone on a garage sale shopping spree. His overhead light was strictly off limits. He utilized only stand-up lamps covered in heavy shades that barely put off enough light to see by. The half dozen lights he had shining throughout his room left shadows on almost every surface.

Phillip and I sat down on a set of bean bags — which aside from a dresser, a computer chair, and a desk — were the only furniture in his room. Simon had converted his closet into a makeshift bed, where he slept a few hours every night.

None of his clothes were hung up. Most of his clothes stayed on his bedroom floor until his mother collected them for washing and put them back in his dresser drawer once a week. At the moment, Simon's computer was putting off a constant buzzing noise that was slightly irritating…but having heard it so much for the past week, I was pretty much used to it. Beyond that, Simon had some modern rock music playing at a pretty high decibel. Normally I would have asked him to shut all that stuff off, but it was on for a reason…a reason I needed to explain to Alex once she showed up.

Simon swiveled in his chair to face me and Phillip, "Any idea what we can do?"

I looked at Simon and then over at Phillip.

Phillip was also looking at me to decide the next course of action. Before I could answer, the doorbell rang and Simon stood up to go answer the door. After about a minute, he walked in with Alex trailing behind him. She looked down at me as she entered the room.

Alex crossed her arms in front of her, but kept her focus on me.

"Kyle, when I said I needed to speak with you…I kind of meant just the two of us."

I looked into Alex's beautiful green eyes and I knew she wanted to speak alone with me, but this was a little more important. I was glad that she'd come; I wasn't completely sure she would actually meet me with such a vague request. I had gambled on her desire to address the issue regarding the other girls in school to draw her here. Apparently, my manipulation had paid off.

I thought about talking with her first, but again reminded myself that why I wanted her here was more important.

"I know you did, but there is something else we need to discuss first."

Alex looked at Phillip, over to Simon, and then back at me.

"And that is?"

I stood up from my bean bag, followed by Phillip. I walked up to Alex and grabbed both of her arms. Fortunately, she didn't flinch or pull away…but I could tell from her expression that she was still weighing her response.

I looked her in the eyes as I asked, "In the past few weeks have you seen anything strange? Anyone following you around or anything like that?"

She looked at me for a second or two, looked over at Simon and Phillip, and then back at me.

"No, is everything ok? And Simon, would you please turn the music and that irritating noise off please? I'm getting a headache."

I shook my head.

"No, he can't. Come here, I want to show you something."

I walked up to one of Simon's windows and slightly pulled aside a piece of his curtain.

"See the van across the street?"

Alex walked up by me and looked through the small sliver of window I offered her.

"You mean the cable van across the street near the junction box?"

I nodded and released the curtain.

"Have you seen any of those around your neighborhood in the last few weeks? Plumbers, delivery trucks, electricians...anything?"

Alex took a moment to think about the question. I knew her analytical mind wouldn't just reflexively answer without reviewing the facts first.

After five seconds or so, she shook her head.

"What's this all about?"

I backed up a step from her, stared at her for a second, and then looked over at Simon and Phillip.

Phillip spoke up, "If she hasn't seen any, then they must not be on to her."

He paused for a second and I shifted my stance out of anger at myself, "...until now!"

I swore out loud at myself for being such an idiot. I walked over to Simon's closet door and punched it out of anger. I had assumed that they were watching her as well and she might not have noticed.

With confusion in her voice Alex asked, "What are you all talking about?"

I turned to face her with guilt and anger on my face.

"We're being watched, Alex. And it's possible that up until the moment you walked through Simon's door it was just us three. Because of my stupid mistake, I might have just put you in danger as well."

Alex walked up to me, grabbing my left arm at the bicep and giving it a slight squeeze of reassurance.

She looked back at Simon and Phillip.

"Tell me everything."

Phillip started explaining while I fumed silently over my ignorance.

"Just after we got back, Kyle and I started to see an increasing number of vans and trucks around us. Due to our past run-in with your father, we have both developed a healthy sense of awareness for our surroundings at almost all times. After we brought it to Simon's attention, he began a search himself…but on a different level."

Simon walked over to his desk and pulled a dish cloth away from a small line of what appeared to be electronic components. Alex started to pick them up and look at them.

Simon continued where Phillip had left off.

"The large one there..." he pointed at a square electronic circuit board that was barely an inch by inch in size "... was the first one I found inside my computer. It's an electronic transmitter that sends any information entered or viewed on a computer to a receiver."

Alex looked at Simon and said, "That doesn't mean the van outside is behind it."

Simon walked a step closer to Alex and picked up the transmitter from the desk as he continued, "The small wire leading from this board is a short-range transmitter...if not to that van or one like it, then it would have to be a house or something really close. I'm talking within a few hundred yards at best."

Alex gestured at the others on the desk, "And these?"

"The others I found wired into fire alarms and vents throughout my house. I'm not sure if I got them all or not...hence the background noise."

Alex stood there in shock for a second, thinking about what we'd said.

She looked at me and asked, "Do you think this is because..."

I moved quickly, placing my hand over her mouth before she could complete the sentence.

She looked at me with her eyes wide at what I had done. I knew the last thing that had touched her soft lips had been gentler than my hand.

I pulled my hand from her mouth and replaced it with a finger in front of her lips to remind her to watch what she said.

"It's possible. But we can't say anything anywhere about that, because we just can't be sure."

I took my finger off her lips and put it back down at my side.

She looked into my eyes, "So, what do we do?"

My eyes glanced down briefly as my mind went through the possible courses of action. Most of them seemed too aggressive and I didn't want to put my friends in harm's way without more facts.

I needed more information before I could do anything, and we had no way to contact the Administrator.

"For now, nothing. Just watch and be careful what you say. We'll wait and let them make the next move. Just continue to act like the normal high school kids that we are. Agreed?"

I waited until they'd all agreed and then figured it was time for us to call it an evening.

Simon saw us to the door and onto the porch. I looked at Alex and asked, "Alex, would you mind giving me a ride home?"

She stopped short and looked up at me in surprise. She looked at Phillip and then back at me before answering, "All right."

She walked over to her car to get it started while I waited behind for a second with Phillip.

"Are you going to be all right?" I asked him.

Phillip nodded.

"I'll be fine; I'll see you at school tomorrow."

Phillip went to his car as I climbed into the passenger seat in Alex's car. After getting in and buckling my seat belt, she backed out of the driveway and started down the road. Using my peripheral vision, I glanced at the cable truck as we drove by…but didn't see anything out of the ordinary except the fact that it shouldn't have been there.

I sighed as I tried to relax some of the tension inside of me.

"I'm sorry about dragging you into this, Alex. If I had known they hadn't been on to you, I would never have let you come here."

I looked over at Alex and she briefly looked at me before returning her attention back to the road.

"Don't be. We're in this together…all of us."

She looked at me as she said the last part, trying to stress her sincerity.

I looked forward.

"You wanted to talk."

I said it as a statement more than a question. I had no idea if we would get another chance, so I figured now was as good a time as any.

Alex glanced at me briefly.

"Yeah, I did. I take it you sent those girls to talk to me today?"

I nodded.

"I figured you wouldn't be very patient with me if I tried to explain. I knew that you were really upset with me yesterday and I didn't want to make things worse. I just didn't want you to keep going on thinking that I was such a jerk."

Alex smiled a little.

"I was leaning more towards asshat, but I guess that will do."

I laughed as Alex continued, "There is still something I don't understand."

I looked at her curiously, "Megan?"

Before I could answer, she continued, "She wasn't like the others and she didn't have anything to teach you. So…why?"

She glanced at me as often as she could while still trying to drive safely.

I sighed again before answering, as what I was about to say wasn't going to be easy for me.

"She did have something to teach me."

I looked at Alex and made sure she looked into my eyes at least two or three times before I finished what I had to say.

"She taught me about you."

Alex gripped the steering wheel a little harder and her skin started to flush.

"Don't get me wrong; Megan is wonderful and great to be around. But in a sense, you were right originally. I did use her and then threw her away. I never meant to cause her any pain. I was trying to be just friends with her…but it didn't exactly work out that way, so I ended it."

Alex started inhaling and exhaling a little louder and I could tell that she was trying to keep her emotions under control. I also realized that we were getting close to my house.

I decided to go ahead and get it all out there.

"When I went out with her, I took what opportunities I had to slip in questions about you. I was trying to learn as much about you as I could without giving away the fact that I was interested in you. I knew that she was your best friend, and I knew if she figured out that I was interested in you that she would tell on me. I guess I was just too much of a coward to approach you directly."

Alex couldn't seem to contain her emotions anymore and started crying. She put her hand up to her nose and mouth as she started hyperventilating.

I couldn't stop though; I had to finish, and I wanted her to know everything.

"I should have had the courage to walk up to you that first day in school and ask you out directly, but I was scared."

The tears were still going down her face as she asked, "Scared of what?"

"I was scared that you would say no, and I didn't want to risk that. As time passed and you started going out with others, I figured you just weren't interested…so I tried to move on. But every time I hung out with someone else, I couldn't stop thinking about you. And the more time passed and the more you seemed to hate me, the easier it was for me to stay away."

I looked at Alex, "I just wanted you to be happy…even if it wasn't with me."

She sobbed into her hand; I hated seeing her cry. I sat back in my seat as she pulled into my driveway and parked behind my mother's car. I waited a few seconds for her to compose herself and remind me of what a horrible person she thought I was. But after about a minute, she started staring out the windshield, so I unbuckled my seatbelt and opened the car door.

"Thanks for the ride, Alex, and let one of us know if you start noticing anything strange."

I looked at her one last time as I pulled myself out of her car and closed the door. I'd started walking up to my house door when I heard Alex calling my name.

I turned around as Alex ran up to me and stopped just in front of me.

"You were right; you should have asked me back then."

She closed the distance between us and pushed her lips to mine.

She wrapped her arms around my neck; I wrapped mine around her shoulder and lower back, holding on to her for dear life. Her lips were as soft as I remembered and tasted just as sweet as that first time. She didn't hold back as she leaned heavily into me and refused to stop. I felt the joy inside of me exploding at that moment and I didn't care who was watching as we embraced there in front of my house.

After what felt like eternity and still nowhere nearly long enough, Alex let go of me and then took a half-step back to start breathing again. Her cheeks were flushed, either from the crying or the kiss. Her beautiful, soft lips were swollen from the kiss and her chest heaved in and out as she tried to get her breathing under control. I was also trying to calm down from the passion of the moment, but part of me demanded that I kiss her again. She licked her lips, and I couldn't help but think about how sexy that made her look.

After a few awkward moments she asked, "Will you sit with me at lunch tomorrow?"

It took me a moment for my brain to realize that she'd asked me a question and was expecting an answer.

"I'd like that."

I smiled so much that I felt the muscles in my face protesting. Alex's smile was dazzling as she took a few steps backwards and turned to get back in her car. No "Goodbye" or "I'll see you soon." We just parted, expecting each other to be there. As I watched her drive away, I couldn't help but feel a loss in my chest at her leaving…but I also felt the heat from the flame she'd started inside me. After I finished reminiscing, I noticed a minivan with oddly strong tint on its windows at the neighbors three doors down. I turned away and went into my house to help my mother with dinner.

CHAPTER 20 – THE TURNING POINT

FBI FIELD OFFICE, PORTLAND, OREGON
AGENT KATHRYN MORGAN

I walked into Sam's office for our weekly debriefing on my assignment. The Director had been pushing him hard for speedy results, but there was only so much that could be done with the limited time I'd been given. Sam was talking on the phone and gestured for me to have a seat. I sat across from him and waited patiently for him to complete his phone call.

"Thank you; thank you. Let me know what you find out. Bye."

Sam hung up the phone and then sat up straighter at his desk.

Dreamers

"I've been reading your reports and then forwarding them to the Director. He wanted me to extend his appreciation for the exceptional work you have been doing."

I looked at Sam and I saw that he was blowing smoke, trying to soften the beaches so to speak. Sam realized I wasn't buying into his bull, so he switched gears.

"What else have you found out this week?"

I sat up straight and told him about the new wrinkle in the investigation. I had added a fourth person into the "conspiracy" circle, a young girl named Alexi Masters. A few nights again, agents had identified her entering the target's house and leaving later with Kyle Bishop. It appeared that he was her boyfriend. I told Sam that I wasn't aware of this development when I'd first added Mr. Bishop to the surveillance.

Sam agreed with me that it was probably a recent turn of events, but it made my investigation just that much bigger.

"Kate, have you had any luck filling in the missing days with Simon Weiss?"

During my investigation, I had identified several days where Mr. Weiss had dropped off the face of the Earth. The tap on his computer allowed us to download enough information to determine that he had reserved a room at a hotel in California during this time. Follow up with agents down there verified that the information was bogus and seemed to be fabricated to cover his tracks for the missing time. After the first day I extended my investigation to include Kyle Bishop and Phillip Jennings, as they appeared to be close friends with the subject. Research into their background had also shown an almost three-day gap at the same time as Mr. Weiss.

We had only begun researching Ms. Masters, which became more difficult once we determined that her father was the local sheriff. Because of that little wrinkle, I was limited in our ability to access the assistance of local law enforcement.

I shook my head.

"No, nothing as of yet. I've begun expanding the investigation into distant family and friends to see if anything turns up, but it's unlikely."

I fidgeted in my seat. I should have done a better job of covering myself, because Sam was as observant as I was.

He caught on to my hesitation immediately.

"Is something wrong with your investigation?"

I wasn't going to lie to Sam, even though it was difficult for me to keep this from him, but I was confident that I could still conduct my investigation.

"A *slight* problem has developed. It's possible that they may be on to us."

Sam's eyebrows rose.

I continued before he could comment, "All of the surveillance devices we put in Mr. Weiss' house have gone offline. His phone tap is still running, as it is going directly through the phone company, but we lost all visual and audio inside his home."

Sam leaned back in his chair and rubbed his mouth and chin with his hand as he thought about what I had said.

"Do you think the investigation has been compromised?"

I thought about his question for a minute. It wasn't the first time that a subject had found, normally by accident, a surveillance device that was planted around them and it probably wouldn't be the last. I figured I still stood a chance to figure out what happened during that missing time, which seemed to be the most important aspect of this investigation.

I still didn't understand the purpose behind the investigation, and I doubted Sam had figured it out either.

"I'm confident I can finish the investigation and get the remaining information that was requested; I just need a little more time. That's all."

I spoke as confidently as I could, but I wasn't entirely sure I had convinced Sam. He nodded.

"All right, I'll pass the information on to the Director this evening. Keep up the good work and let me know if anything else develops."

I got up, returned to my office, and sat down heavily in my chair. I hadn't lied to Sam; I was confident that with enough time, I would get answers. I just hoped that the Director was patient enough to wait. I turned back to the files I had created on each of the four subjects and stacked them neatly, with Simon Weiss' on the top. I packed up a few other items and decided to head home for the evening. Tomorrow I would consider approaching the investigation from a different standpoint and see if it would be more successful.

Later that evening as I stood in front of my microwave in my apartment heating up some chicken casserole leftovers, my cell phone started vibrating. I picked it up off of the kitchen island and realized that the incoming call was from Sam.

"Hey Sam, is everything all right?"

"Kate, bring them in."

I paused for a second, trying to grasp what he was saying.

"Sam, I need more time. Just a little longer and I'm positive we'll have something."

I knew what he was asking and I felt it was a mistake at this juncture of my investigation.

I wanted to plead my case some more, but Sam interrupted me, "The Director has ordered that they be brought in and detained for questioning to determine what happened during those missing days."

I could tell by Sam's tone that he had been left with no choice, but I still felt it was wrong.

"Detain them for what reason, Sam? We could detain Simon Weiss for the hacking, though our evidence is rather thin. The other three haven't broken any laws that I have been able to determine yet."

For the first time since I had known Sam, he got upset.

"Just do it, Kate. That's an order. Or do I need to find someone else to complete your assignment?"

That statement stung and I couldn't help but feel for the first time in my life that I was crossing a line I couldn't step back from.

"No, sir. I'll do it first thing in the morning."

Sam became silent after that; he knew that I wasn't happy about what he ordered me to do because I had called him "sir." Between us, it had always been Sam and Kate. I hung up my cell phone and slammed it onto the kitchen island, not caring if I broke it or not.

I looked at Simon's file next to the phone and opened it up. Paper clipped to the front inside cover was the letter that gave me the authorization to detain or arrest anyone I felt was necessary. I was crossing a line, and I needed a shower to wash off the filth that had started to cling to me. I closed the file and walked out of the kitchen towards the bathroom, not even caring that the microwave had dinged.

Early the next morning, several hours before the sun came up, I contacted all of the agents and teams I had in the area and advised them of the situation. I planned a simultaneous raid on three of the kids' houses. Ms. Masters' house was going to be handled a little more delicately, and I would be directly involved. Her father was the town sheriff, meaning that he was armed, and I preferred not to put my agents at risk of any more harm than was absolutely necessary.

At exactly 7 am, the other three teams broke down the front doors of the houses to which they were assigned. With minimal force, they detained Simon Weiss, Phillip Jennings, and Kyle Bishop. The team leaders called me on my cell, reporting on their successes and that an agent was left behind at each residence to provide the families with the necessary contact information to get a hold of Sam's office in Portland. I figured that they could give him grief, considering how he had planted this mess in my lap.

I walked up to Alexi Masters' house with a junior agent in tow while another agent stood by the car in which we had arrived. When I got to the door, I knocked and waited a few moments for someone to answer. I heard the bolts on the door being unlocked just before the door opened. Before me stood a man I easily identified as William

Masters, Alexi's father and the town sheriff. The fact that he was fully dressed for work with a nametag also made it quite obvious. Mr. Masters was almost six feet tall with short combed-over hair with some slight graying on the edges. His face was weathered from spending so much of his life outdoors and on patrol, but his features were soft and fatherly. His uniform was crisply ironed and his dress shoes were polished to a fine shine, showing that his character demanded perfection.

I pulled out my credentials and held them up to Mr. Masters.

"Mr. Masters, I'm Agent Kathryn Morgan of the Federal Bureau of Investigations."

I could tell that my introduction startled him as a small-town sheriff. I didn't imagine he'd had too much interaction beyond emails and the occasional phone call with the FBI during the course of his duties.

After recovering from the shock he asked, "How can I help you, agent?"

I knew this next part wouldn't go over too well, but it had to be done.

"Is your daughter home, sir? I need to speak with her."

I knew that he'd understand I was asking about his oldest child and not his youngest.

He didn't move from the door and I could tell he was getting defensive from both his posture and the tone that followed.

"What's this all about?"

Just then Alexi Masters passed by on the other side of the door, obviously dressed for school. She saw me talking to her dad, came up to the door, and tried to look at us past the small portion of door that her dad had left available. I looked at her as she came closer.

I figured I still risked a fight, but I kept going.

"Alexi Masters, I'm here to place you under arrest."

I could tell that she was shocked and her father was starting to get mad. He used his right arm to push his daughter behind him. As he did so, I noticed that the agent I'd left at the car was walking a little closer.

Mr. Masters took a half step forward, further blocking the door.

"On what charge?"

I looked at Mr. Masters, "Material Witness Statute, sir."

Mr. Masters' jaw dropped open, as I imagined he wasn't expecting that response…much less the fact I was here to arrest his daughter.

"Witness for what?"

I looked him dead in the eyes.

"I'm sorry, Mr. Masters, but that is classified for the moment."

I stepped closer to Mr. Masters.

"Sir, you need to move out of the way and allow us to do our duty or I will be forced to arrest you for obstruction of a federal investigation."

He looked at me for a minute, probably to determine how serious I was. He then turned around to face his daughter. Mrs. Masters had also come into my view, as she wondered what was going on.

Mr. Masters gave his daughter a hug as he spoke to her.

"Honey, you need to go with these agents until I can figure out what is going on."

After he finished saying this, her mother cried and hugged her as well. Mr. Masters then pulled his wife away and allowed us access to his daughter. I signaled for the other agent to cuff her and she didn't resist when he restrained her.

I looked at Alexi Masters as she was being cuffed. Most criminals I'd put in handcuffs either cried with their head down in shame or became extremely defensive. Alexi Masters did neither. She just looked at me, resigning herself to being arrested. The agent escorted her to the back seat of our car.

Mr. Masters asked, "Where are you taking her?"

"For the moment, she will be detained at our field office in Portland."

I handed over a copy of my card and he jerked it from my hand in anger. I understood his reaction as her father, but I was relieved that as the sheriff he understood the law and didn't complicate the situation further.

I returned to the car and took the back seat with Alexi Masters. The other agent returned to the driver's side and started the car. Alexi Masters looked out the window at her parents. I saw Mr. Masters standing behind his wife with his hands on her shoulders.

As the car started driving away, I expected Alexi Masters to start crying...but she just faced forward and sat back in her seat, as though resigned to her fate. To my surprise, Ms. Masters didn't ask any questions or even speak a word during the drive. When we finally arrived at the field office, we escorted her to a holding cell in the basement and I made sure that she was separated from the others. For the moment, each of them thought that they were the only person being detained and I wanted to keep it that way.

I stopped by Sam's office to update him on the various arrests. I wasn't completely sure where we were going from here, but I figured I would give them a few hours to absorb the reality of their situation before I started pulling them out separately for questioning.

I spent the next couple of hours filling out paperwork on the arrests as well as reviewing the arrest documents that had been completed by the other agents. Nothing was conducted at the agency without an extensive paper trail to fall back on at a later date. I figured that now was a good a time as any to start the interviews, so I got up and straightened up my suit. I picked up the files that I had compiled on each of the kids and walked out of my office to take the elevator to the basement. On my way, I snagged one of the other agents who'd assisted in the arrest to sit with me during the process.

I walked into the detention area and up to the agent who manned the sign in/out desk. I pulled up the clipboard and began filling out the necessary information, figuring that I would start with Simon as he was the primary subject in this case. I handed it back to the desk agent and he reviewed the information I'd signed. He set down the clipboard and stood in front of me, but for some reason he wasn't moving.

He fidgeted a little before speaking.

"I'm sorry, Agent Morgan, but the person you are requesting to see is no longer being detained here."

I looked at the agent like he had lost his mind.

"What do you mean he isn't here? We brought him in here less than three hours ago…him and three others."

I snatched the clipboard off the table to see who'd signed them out and realized that all four had been signed out by Agent Sam Roberts not an hour after they arrived. I glared at the agent and he was smart enough to take a step back from me as I turned around to get back on the elevator. As I got back to the floor on which me and Sam worked, the agent with me split off…obviously smart enough to realize that he didn't want to be anywhere around me for my next conversation.

I was so upset that I opened up Sam's office door and barged in without even asking for permission first. Sam was talking on the phone as I arrived and he didn't look happy with my interruption, but at the moment I really didn't care. He just said "Yes, sir" several times during his call, so I assumed he was on the phone with the Director. He pointed at one of his chairs, but I refused to sit down and just glared at him.

Sam seemed to resign himself to the fact that I wasn't going to sit, so he finished up his conversation and finally hung up.

I didn't give him a chance to breathe.

"What the hell, Sam? Where are they?"

I glared daggers into Sam, and he had the decency to swallow before answering. Sam stood up behind his desk and refused to look at me. Right now, I didn't care if I tanked my career. Everything that happened from the moment I was ordered to do this investigation had gone from bad to outright crap.

He spent a moment shuffling papers on his desk before answering.

"Calm down, Kate. The detainees have been transferred out by order of the Director."

I glared at Sam and wondered if he contained the balls to tell the Director what to go do with himself.

"Where?" I spit out at him.

"Agent Morgan?"

I realized that I had stepped past the limit of our professional boundaries.

I took a moment to calm down, but I still refused to sit down.

"I'm sorry. Where did he take them, Sam?"

After Sam waited a few seconds, so he could rise to the top of our pissing contest, he said "They were flown out to DC after the Director requisitioned a modified transport from the U.S. Marshals Service."

I looked at Sam and couldn't think of any dignified responses to that, so he continued.

"This investigation as far as this office is concerned is over. All documentation that you have on this case is to be turned over to me within the next half hour. Do I make myself clear?"

My teeth grated together in my mouth at what he had just said.

"Sam...sir, this is BS and you know it. What are we going to tell their families when they call in here?"

Sam slammed his palm down onto his table and as loud as both of us were yelling, I was sure everyone outside of the office was steering clear.

"Enough! That has been dealt with and this case is out of our hands. Have one of the agents outside bring me all the files you have on this case and then go home for the day."

I looked at Sam with shock on my face, but it didn't lessen the anger I felt inside. I realized there was nothing I could do short of quitting, and I doubted that would help those kids I'd just helped legally kidnap. I held up the files I had with me and Sam took them out of my hands, never losing eye contact with me.

I yanked open his office door and didn't bother closing it before I left. I walked the short distance to my own office and gestured at the agent who'd originally gone downstairs with me to come into my office. I went to the front of my desk and started yanking open drawers. He stood by the door, refusing to come in any further. Smart agent, I thought. I pulled out everything I had committed to paper or disk and dropped them into the other agent's hands.

"Take them to Agent Roberts," I ordered with no amount of kindness in my voice.

After the agent quickly moved out of my office with the remains of my case, I slammed my office door behind him. I picked up my coffee cup and threw it up against the office wall, shattering it into dozens of pieces and splattering the remains of my coffee all over the place. I swore out loud and walked once around the office to secure my remaining files and desk and collect my coat and wallet. I jerked the door open, letting it slam behind me.

Sam stood at his door and watched me as I walked by. I glared at him. I was pissed at him for putting that mess in my lap in the first place and then yanking it out from under me. I walked down the hall to the elevator. Everyone moved out of my way as I walked by, avoiding my wrath. As the elevator door started to close, I looked at Sam standing at the end of the hallway and we locked eyes.

I muttered, "Darn you."

The doors finally closed, and I went home for the remainder of the day.

I wasn't sure if I would still have a job tomorrow, and I really didn't care. I would worry about that later.

Dreamers

CHAPTER 21 – INTERROGATION

OREGON AND WASHINGTON DC
KYLE BISHOP

Even though I'd expected it to happen, I was still caught by surprise when the FBI showed up at my front door. It would have been nice if they had knocked politely...but instead they smashed the lock and barged in, scaring the life out of my mom just as she was getting ready for work. Though my mother was in shock, she called out for me and wanted to know if I was all right. My anger at the situation was more at the forefront than any other shock I might have felt, as I had figured out what was going on almost immediately.

My mom was held face down onto the kitchen floor until I had been handcuffed and dragged out to the waiting car. As the car began driving away, I looked back through my open front door and noticed that the agent was helping my mother back onto her feet. They apparently had completed their sweep of the house and found no one else of interest. It was a great relief to know that my mother wouldn't be taken into custody. Being arrested would cause her to lose both of her jobs, though I was sure she would throw a fit when they told her why I was arrested.

I didn't know how many hours that three car rides, two cells, and a plane ride took. I was isolated in this concrete-walled room with one door and an obvious two-way mirror. My hands were handcuffed to the back of the metal chair I was sitting in, which was bolted to the floor. Aside from a brief bathroom break in my cell when I arrived at these accommodations, I had been offered nothing to either eat or drink. At least they had taken off the stupid hood that made my nose itch. I looked around the interrogation room, but didn't see anything else. I figured that any cameras were probably filming away right behind the glass window. Since I had time to waste, I began thinking of Phillip, Simon, and Alex. I wasn't sure if they had also been arrested, but I figured it was rather likely. They were probably keeping us all separated, so we couldn't work on a story together. I worried about Simon and Phillip, but I worried about Alex the most. Though I knew she was made of some strong stuff, I wasn't sure how long she would hold out once they started threatening her future. The thought of them upsetting her at all made me angry. I knew Alex was a stickler for the law and if the FBI was smart, they would use that against her conscience. I could only hope that she would hold out, though I wasn't sure what any of us would be holding out for. All the movement and pushing I'd endured seemed rather extreme even for the FBI. I figured that they were playing mind games with me. I decided to sit still and wait.

After what could have been minutes or maybe an hour — it was hard to tell — the door to the room opened and two agents walked in. Each wore a suit, which seemed to be the standard for the FBI nowadays. I saw holster straps inside each of their coats, but didn't see their guns.

The first agent was Caucasian with thinning brown hair and hazel eyes. From my judgment, he was just under six feet tall. This agent looked to be in his early fifties, judging by the wrinkles on his face and the sunspots on his hands. Obviously, this agent spent a great deal of time outdoors…either for work or whatever he chose to do in his off-duty time. He walked with authority as he took his seat on the other side of the table to my left.

The other agent seemed to be a bruiser. He was also Caucasian, but he tested the stitching on his suit with each movement he made. The agent was at least 6'4". He was bald, with a nose that looked like it had been broken a time or two. His blue-gray eyes had a perpetual meanness to them. I suspected he would be the "bad cop" to this other one's "good cop." I decided that the nickname "Muscles" would be appropriate.

The first agent set a file down on the desk, but didn't open it. I looked between the two while a third agent pushed in a cart with a TV on top of it. He pushed it next to the shorter agent and left. The two agents assigned to me both looked as though they were waiting for me to say something, but I was content to stare at one or the other. We glared back and forth at each other. After a few minutes had passed in our pissing contest, the first agent looked down at his file and then back up at me.

"I'm Agent Brandis."

He gestured at Muscles and added, "This is Agent Ganth."

Agent Brandis paused for a moment, probably still waiting for me to freak out.

"You have been placed under arrest and moved to a secure facility until such time as we deem it prudent to transfer you to a federal prison…"

Agent Brandis paused for dramatic effect; too bad it was wasted on me.

"…or, *with your cooperation*, released back into the public."

He waited again to see if I would react in any way, but I just stared at him like I was waiting for a revelation from him. He spoke very calmly, but he either couldn't or didn't hide the undertone of condescension in his voice.

Agent Brandis continued, "Before we begin, is there anything you would like to say?"

He placed his hands on top of the folder, which he still hadn't opened. Muscles still glared at me in an effort to work on his intimidation routine. I figured now was a good time to bring up my concern for my friends, my mom, or ask for a lawyer, but I knew why I was here and what these two goons were after.

The only thing I could come up with was to act unpredictably from what they were expecting.

"No, I'm good, thanks."

Muscles glanced briefly over at Agent Brandis and then went back to his glaring. Agent Brandis hid his thoughts well, as I hadn't seen any change in his facial features from my lackluster statement. He opened the file in front of him and started to slowly go through the pages one at a time like it was a fascinating novel. The scene reminded me of Agent Smith from *The Matrix* and I briefly hoped he would accidently call me Mr. Anderson. Though in this case, neither of the agents wore glasses of any kind.

Agent Brandis interrupted my inner monologue.

"Kyle Bishop."

He said it as if he couldn't believe my mom actually named me that. It was difficult to tell if that was a statement or a question, so I figured I'd continue to wait. He looked as though he was reading one of the pages, but that didn't fool me for a second. I was sure that he'd probably memorized whatever was in that file before he walked in the door. I had to watch myself around him. I could tell that he liked playing mind games. He was probably betting on me to have an emotional outburst, but I planned to disappoint him…though I was tempted to burst into tears and start begging his forgiveness for no apparent reason just to see his reaction. Nah…I decided I would hold off for the moment.

In his typical Matrix-themed interrogation he continued speaking, "Well…hmm…it would seem, Mr. Bishop, that you appear to be a bright student. Solid grades, you participate in activities, and apparently are a bit of a ladies' man."

Agent Brandis' eyebrows raised as though he was surprised.

He looked up at me and then back down at the file as he continued, "You apparently had some minor indiscretions with the law but nothing too major…"

He looked up at me again, "…until now."

I looked at him with all the emotion of watching a boring sitcom on television and I was just waiting for the crickets to chirp in the background. I wondered if it was legal for federal agents to impersonate movie actors and wished they would at least come up with something original. Agent Brandis' lips moved briefly like he wanted to say something else, but he went back to his file. After another minute or two, he closed the file, folded his hands on top of it, and looked at me. If he'd pulled out a tracking device to implant in my navel, I would have been officially done.

Agent Brandis broke from his bad impersonation for a moment and spoke like a normal person.

"Mr. Bishop, this file contains a detailed chronology of your life, as brief as it has been. The reason you are here is to help me determine what is missing and why."

As if on cue, the television next to him lit up and I saw a grainy image of me standing on a dock. I immediately recognized where it was, but I schooled myself not to show any reaction and was confident that I hadn't given anything away. The image started playing with video only, showing the conversation Phillip and I had until Simon joined us. There was a blip in the footage, as though something had gotten edited. Then, I saw us on Phillip's uncle's boat while Alex ran our way.

It was stupid of me not to think that there could have been a camera at the dock. At the time, I hadn't thought to look around the area for any cameras. In my defense though, I hadn't expected to find a whole new world.

After the boat pulled away from the dock, the television shut off. I looked at Agent Brandis as he continued to study me. I just glared back at him with indifference and waited.

Agent Brandis gestured with his hand over his shoulder at the television and said, "A little over a month ago, you and your friends went on a little trip. During that trip you were gone for slightly over three days before you returned home."

Agent Brandis paused again, and I wondered if he was aware of his penchant for pausing as he continued, "Tell us where you were for those three days and I'll see that you are returned home to your mother."

As Agent Brandis brought up my mom, I couldn't crush my desire to punch him in the mouth...but that thought was pointless, considering my hands were still secured.

He demanded, "Now...where exactly did you and your friends go during your trip?"

I answered with the first thing that came to my mind, "We went fishing."

Muscles sat up straighter in his chair, if that was even possible.

"Fishing," Agent Brandis nodded his head as though he actually believed me. "And what did you catch?"

"Fish."

I looked at him like he was stupid and should have already known that answer.

Before he could respond I added, "Except Alex. She cast like a girl, so her pole followed the hook right into the water. Needless to say, she dined on peanut butter crackers for her efforts that entire trip."

I looked over at Muscles since he was content to glare, "Hey, Tinkerbell, would you mind getting me a glass of water? All this talking has made me a little thirsty."

I don't know if it was my statement or my tone, but Muscles slammed his fist into the table. He stood, leaned over and pointed his sausage-sized finger at me.

"Listen, you little smart ass, you had better start cooperating and giving us some answers if you know what is good for you," Muscles snapped.

Could his response have been any more cliché? I mean, what was he going to do? Find me a nice friendly roommate during my stay here or call and tell my mom? Also, he gave me a strong impression of a biker that you'd see at some bar and pray you didn't piss off. I wondered if the FBI was contracting out for Muscles or if he'd changed careers.

I looked at Muscles as he glared at me and the color of his cheeks started turning red. Wow, they were really going for the "good cop, bad cop" routine.

I stated with some sarcasm-laced seriousness, "Have a seat, sweetie. Wait until the grown-ups are done talking before interrupting."

I noticed the color of his skin starting to turn red and purple, but before he could do anything Agent Brandis got him to sit down in his seat like a good girl.

I looked at Agent Brandis and figured this would probably go on forever, but I figured it was a good time for a break. I looked at Muscles as he fumed in his chair and made a kissing motion and sound with my lips at him. He moved incredibly fast for a guy his size as he lurched out of his chair; I saw a big meaty fist heading my way before everything went black.

I awoke a little later with a splitting headache and reluctantly admitted to myself that I didn't see that coming. I sat up slowly and regretted it immediately, as I became nauseous and the pain in my face about made me pass out again. I slowly turned my head to take in my five-star accommodations complete with a steel toilet and sink combo for my sanitary needs and my own private plastic mat to sleep on. Now if only room service would bring me something to eat.

I shook off the intense throbbing in my face and tried to focus more on my room. I shifted over and planted my feet firmly on the ground. I breathed in and out a few times to help focus my vision and then glanced over my cell again. My cell was a six by eight concrete box with the most comfort being provided by my sleeping accommodations. The cell door was a solid metal affair with a small square panel on both the top and the bottom of the door. Both panels had to be opened from the outside for any type of fresh air. The whole place resembled a dungeon, but with better pest control. I looked at the lower panel on the door and noticed a small plastic tray on the floor in front of the door.

I walked over to see what was on the menu today. I picked up a plastic tray, which was a nasty reddish-orange color. In the tray's compartments was a sandwich with American cheese and mystery meat, sliced pineapple that was turning a little brown, and a plastic cup with about two-thirds of it filled with some kind of red juice. All in all, the food still looked better than what they served at school. I shrugged and sat on my bunk. I started absently chewing on my sandwich, which caused me to wince during every bite. Muscles apparently didn't hit like a girl. I looked around for a mirror or a reflective surface to check out the damage…but no options were available, so I returned to enjoying my meal.

All the time I had been herded around, I wasn't sure whether it was night or day at the moment. I had no idea what was up with the FBI these days…but as far as they seemed to be concerned, there was no such thing as legal rights.

After finishing my meal, I tossed my tray over to the front of the cell…causing it to bounce off of the cell door to signal to my host that it could be removed. I lied down and thought about the events up to now and the role the FBI seemed to be playing. Their tactics were a bit more aggressive than I had expected. At worst, I figured they would grill me for information and threaten me with jail or prison considering that I was legally an adult.

I thought about the others, but mostly I thought about Alex. I was sure she was here somewhere and it upset me to know that she was probably getting the same treatment. The thought of someone harming her made me angry, which I used to fuel myself and hold out longer. Eventually they had to give up, especially if they didn't learn anything through all of this. I knew my mom and definitely Alex's family were raising Cain about us being detained and the FBI would be on a tight clock to get results. I had to just hold out as long as I could, so I steeled myself for the coming interrogations.

CHAPTER 22 – A CHANGE IN TEMPO

FBI CUSTODY, UNKNOWN LOCATION
ALEXI MASTERS

It felt like days since I had been brought to this new facility, wherever it was located. I hadn't had a bath since I had been arrested. I was limited to washing myself with cold water from the stupid cell's sink. Though I couldn't exactly look at myself in a mirror, I imagined I looked pretty bad from the lack of bathing combined with the stress of this ordeal. I paced my cell, trying to combat the boredom and attempting to fight off the scenarios that my mind conjured. Since I had arrived here, I had been escorted into a small room several times and questioned about the missing days...which must have been over a month ago now. It surprised me when they showed a dock video of us leaving on Phillip's boat, but it was nice to see Kyle again even if it was just a video image of him. I wondered what Kyle was going through as well as what Phillip and especially Simon had endured. I worried the most about Simon, as I figured he was the most susceptible to coercion. Being underage and not physically imposing like Kyle and Phillip would be a significant disadvantage for him.

I looked around my cell for the millionth time and decided to face the back wall to eliminate distractions. I had to think this through. I knew my cell was solid and most likely soundproof, which I had verified when I screamed my head off the first day I was here with no response. I'd hoped that one of the others would be in a cell or something next to me and I could verify that they were all right. During my interview process, the agents had first threatened me first with tanking my education if I didn't cooperate. The coercion eventually moved up to a prison term. They had correctly guessed that using the law against me would be my greatest weakness and that might have worked before all of this. But after the boat trip to the island, I'd resolved not to say anything regardless of the consequences. The world that the Administrator had created was just too important. Sacrificing what he created to save the future of one person was idiotic and I wasn't about to give it away to save my own skin.

I sighed and thought about my dad, my mom, and my little sister. I'm sure my parents had made some excuse to Emily about my absence, but I knew my parents were probably losing their minds to get me back. I figured if we stood any chance of getting out of this mess it would be with my dad.

My thoughts were interrupted when my cell door was unlocked and opened. I turned around and saw the same two agents, the only two I had seen since my arrest several days ago. Agent Fields, the only female agent of the two, entered my cell first. She looked to be about my height with dark brown hair that seemed rather stringy in places, as it was secured in a bun on the back of her head. She wore a gray two-piece suit with a white blouse underneath and a set of black dress shoes that were decently shined. Agent Fields had attempted the kind motherly routine on me, but something about her just felt off. I glanced beyond her to the other agent, who remained at the cell door. I couldn't remember his name; looking at him always made my skin crawl. He was at least six feet tall with the standard agent's suit and a military haircut. His hair appeared to be blonde, though it was short enough that I questioned my guess. His eyes were what really creeped me out. He stared at me as though he was either undressing me in his mind or determining how much I would scream if I was cut with a knife. I wasn't sure if he was armed with a knife…but if anyone had one, it would definitely be him.

I looked back at Agent Fields as she pulled a pair of handcuffs out from her waistband behind her back and I knew what she expected. I turned back around and placed my hands behind my back while she cuffed me. Then, she grabbed my forearm and escorted me out of the cell and down the hall to the interrogation room. I was surprised when we continued walking past the interrogation room. We didn't stop until we arrived at the next door down, which I assumed was the room on the other side of the glass mirror. My other escort opened the door and smiled at me, causing my skin to crawl as I was led inside. I was right. Inside the room was a video camera set up at the far wall, which aimed at the window and into the interrogation room. The room itself was solid concrete like my cell. Below the two-way mirror was a small table built into the wall, but there were no chairs. However, what was on the other side of the window held my attention.

"Kyle."

I whispered his name loud enough that I was sure my escort had overheard, but I didn't care.

Kyle was sitting down and handcuffed to the metal chair in the interrogation room, but the table and other chairs were no longer there. My heart soared at seeing him there, not realizing how much I had missed him. Agent Fields let go of my arm, so I walked closer to the window to get a better look at Kyle. He seemed to be in good spirits, but I noticed a nasty bruise on the right side of his face just above his mouth and below his eye. The bruise still looked red and purple with a tinge of yellow mixed in, as though it was just starting to heal. His right eye was bloodshot, probably from whatever had hit him.

I looked back at Agent Fields, who seemed to be content to stand there and wait for me to do something. I glanced at the other agent and he had an evil grin on his face, which caused me to turn back to Kyle and look away from him. As I turned back to Kyle, the door on the other side opened up and an agent walked inside. He was huge and bald. Kyle glanced up at him and I heard from a speaker above the window.

"Hey, sweetie. Your boyfriend not coming in?"

My eyes grew big at what Kyle had just said and I briefly considered that he had gone mad.

The last thing he should have been doing was upsetting someone who looked like that. The towering mountain stopped in front of him. Kyle stared up at the agent for what must have been a good minute with neither of them saying anything. I figured he was just there to intimidate him until the other agent Kyle had mentioned arrived.

All of a sudden, Kyle's head jerked back hard and what looked like blood splattered down his face from his nose. I screamed from shock more than anything, as I hadn't even seen what happened. I looked closer at the agent and realized his fists were balled up after just hitting Kyle. I couldn't believe that a federal agent had just hit Kyle. Assaulting a suspect was supposed to be illegal. The agent walked slowly back and forth in front of Kyle, probably deciding where he was going to hit him next.

Being more alert this time, I saw when the agent swung again and hit Kyle with his fist connecting on the left side of Kyle's face. Tears started flowing down my cheeks as I watched Kyle get hit a third time by this monster who was supposed to be in law enforcement. I turned my head back quickly as tears continued to fall down and faced Agent Fields.

I screamed, "Stop this; he's hurting him."

Agent Fields kept a neutral expression on her face and her partner appeared to be enjoying the show, which disgusted me. I could hear through the speaker above the window as each hit impacted on Kyle and the grunt he made. The agent in there didn't seem interested in asking him any questions.

I turned again to Agent Fields, "Please, stop this."

I cried as tears continued down my face and onto my already dirty blouse.

Agent Fields considered this for a moment before responding, "Only you have the power to make this end, Ms. Masters."

She walked up next to me, so I turned to look back at Kyle as he continued to be beaten on the other side of the window.

"All you have to do is tell us about those missing days and all this will end."

I realized at that moment that I was the one being interrogated and Kyle had become the coercive factor. I sobbed and didn't even care; I just didn't want Kyle to be hurt anymore. I thought about the information she was requesting, and I thought about the Administrator and what he was trying to do. I had promised myself that I wouldn't tell them anything when this all began, but I wasn't expecting Kyle to be beaten like some animal in front of me. I looked up at Kyle; there seemed to be a brief pause between each strike. Blood ran down Kyle's face and his right eye was already swollen shut. I looked at his left eye, trying to figure out what to do next. Kyle looked up with his one good eye at the agent who was beating him and I saw the defiance in his face.

I resolved then that I wouldn't say anything, even if I was the one in that chair instead of Kyle. If he could still fight under the abuse he was enduring, then I wasn't going to betray his sacrifice.

I turned to Agent Fields and looked at her dead in the eyes with all the hatred I had for what she was allowing, for the evil in the agent next to her, and for the monster on the other side of the glass.

I stated defiantly, "I have nothing more to say to you."

I saw her eyes twitch slightly at my statement, but I no longer cared. I turned back to look at Kyle and wished that I could transfer what strength I had into him to help him hold out. I heard Agent Fields step back to join her partner while I watched Kyle....the man I loved...get beaten half to death.

Perhaps I'd always known that I was in love with Kyle from that first moment we saw each other. It was the only thing that could have explained the pain I endured over several years thinking that he had treated the other girls in school so poorly. And it was the only way I could understand that when I had betrayed him and turned him in to my father, why it had hurt so badly. Because I loved Kyle, I refused to betray him again. If he was willing to endure the punishment he was receiving, then I also needed to endure it.

After a few more minutes of hits, I was surprised that Kyle hadn't passed out. I prayed that he would pass out, so he wouldn't feel the pain being caused by the agent.

A beeping noise started going off behind me and I also heard it coming through the speaker over my head. I turned back as both agents pulled pagers from their belts. I saw disbelief coming onto their faces.

Agent Fields put her pager back quickly, stepped forward, grabbed my arm, and dragged me to the door. I looked back one last time at Kyle, noticing that the agent inside was also looking at a pager.

Once Agent Fields and I made it back to the hallway, there were red lights flashing everywhere. The lights went out and the entire hallway became deathly black, almost immediately followed by some floodlights around the hallway blinking on.

Agent Fields looked at her partner, "Go see what's going on while I secure the prisoner."

As the creep ran off, Agent Fields quickly escorted me to my cell. Once we arrived at my cell, Agent Fields began removing the handcuffs. I heard the interrogation room door open behind me, so I screamed Kyle's name. Agent Fields pushed me roughly inside, causing me to trip and fall onto the floor of my cell. She slammed the cell door behind me, and I heard the lock set in place. I jumped up, ran to my cell door, and began banging on it with my fist while yelling Kyle's name over and over, hoping that he heard me and knew that he wasn't alone here.

Dreamers

CHAPTER 23 – INVASION

FBI HEADQUARTERS, WASHINGTON DC
AGENT JASON RAMIREZ

I ran down the hall towards the elevator as Agent Fields returned Alexi Masters to her cell. Being physically active, first from a stint in the U.S. Marine Corps and then with active SWAT duty and fieldwork with the FBI, made it effortless for me to move quickly through the building. As I ran down the hallway, I briefly thought about the session that had just ended and the hope that we would be able to push Ms. Masters over the edge.

Agent Fields had adopted a caring approach towards the subject, while I was left with the more aggressive stance. I hated opting for the pervert persona, but this had been the first female I'd helped interrogate. I wasn't completely confident that I could pull anything off, so I had kept my mouth shut and just looked intimidating. By the brief glances from the subject, I would have to say I had been somewhat successful judging by the disgusted looks on her face. My last post before being honorably discharged from the Marines was at Guantanamo Bay, Cuba. While there, I assisted in the detainment and interrogation of terrorists. It wasn't glamorous work, but I had a knack for it and pushing people over the edge had never really bothered me. Additional training provided by the FBI allowed me to approach an interrogation with the classic good cop/bad cop persona often portrayed in television.

My momentum from running down the hall was finally halted as I slammed into the elevator door. I realized that with the power out, the elevators would be useless. I ran back about twenty feet and slammed into the stairwell fire door…the alarm didn't even go off as I barreled through it. I took the stairs two at a time, trying to get up to the tactical room on the ground floor. The Hoover Building was huge and normally had several hundred people in it at any time of the day. Even though it was very early in the morning, the entire building had ongoing operations as well as a full SWAT team on call. I was one of the members of the team, though still junior in my post. The entire team was made up of former military members and had become a solid unit over the past few years. The team consisted of two small seven-man strike teams with one communications specialist; we were always geared for war. The page that we had gotten while we were still in with Ms. Masters was a breach alert that the FBI headquarters was under attack.

The response to such an attack had been drilled into us repeatedly since 9/11. The first seven men to arrive at the armory, regardless of their rank, were to suit up and would be designated as Team One. During an actual attack, Team One would build a defensive screen until more men arrived to create Team Two. Once both teams were in place — and depending on the severity of the threat — the team commanders would either play offense or continue with defense. None of our many practice drills had included a loss of power, but we had been trained in night vision goggles just in case. Fortunately, the floodlights in the building were still functional.

Once I passed the underground parking garage and arrived at the ground floor, I pushed through the stairwell door and entered chaos. Other agents were already running by me, armed with either their field piece or an assault rifle and vest from the armory. I heard gunshots going off in the distance, possibly in another wing. Any clerical or janitorial staff members were to immediately lock themselves down in the nearest room and stay face down on the floor until the all clear signal was given.

I turned right, ran down the hall, and headed left towards the armory. As I got closer, I saw guys in the hallway suiting up. I pushed past them towards an open locker and started to put on all the tactical gear, which included padding from head to toe as well as a Kevlar helmet. Those not part of the SWAT team were limited to just a bulletproof vest and their choice of a semi-automatic weapon or a shotgun. As I put my gear on, I glanced over and saw the first team moving off down the hallway; I realized that the rest of us were playing catch-up.

I looked at the agent next to me, "What is going on? Is this some type of drill?"

The man was arming himself up and loading his assault rifle as he replied, "No, it isn't. The reception doors were apparently breached. We heard calls coming from their hand mikes as well as some shots being fired until everything went silent. We don't know how many are inside or if it's the only breach point. Other agents are heading towards the other access points to secure them."

I paused for a brief second in shock, but then pulled myself together. I wasn't sure who had the balls to invade the FBI, but my thoughts ran back to 9/11 and I figured this had to be a terrorist attack. After I finished putting on the remainder of my gear, I picked up an automatic rifle and loaded it with a fresh clip. Once completed, I turned back to the other agent and lined up behind him as we had been drilled.

I leaned near his shoulder and asked, "Did anyone contact the DC Police about the breach?"

He looked back at me and shook his head.

"I don't know, but the alarms on the front doors should have clued them in before the power went out."

He glanced forward and then back at me adding, "I hope."

Team Two was formed only two minutes after Team One had moved out. I looked down the line and realized that I was fifth in line, which meant I wasn't on communications duty this time. Whoever was last was assigned to monitor and maintain communications during the incident.

The squad leader gestured us forward as we began a brisk jog down the hallway. Other agents moved out of our way as we went by. We ran from the rear section of the building into the courtyard that acted as a break area for the agents on duty when the weather permitted. Because it was still so early in the morning, it was dark outside. As we ran by, I noticed other agents combing the area for any hidden perpetrators. Because it was so dark, with only the glare of floodlights streaming out of office windows, the other agents relied on flashlights to see.

As we arrived at the opposite side of the courtyard, we all pressed ourselves against the wall next to the open door that led to the reception area. I heard a massive amount of gunfire and I prepped myself for the coming battle. By the sounds of things, this was definitely not a drill. The squad leader gestured for us to move. He stormed into the building with his gun ready while the rest of us followed closely behind. The hallway we'd breached into came to a "T" junction at the end of the hall. I saw that the other squad had barricaded the intersection facing both ways down the hall. Continuous fire poured out in both directions at the invaders. Small light blue balls of energy that disappeared into a brief static discharge on impact slammed into the barricade and walls near Team One. As we got closer, the whole squad ducked down while moving to stay behind the makeshift barricade that was in place. I leaned heavily against a desk that had been dragged out into the hallway. On the floor in front of me were two agents from Team One who were out of commission. I didn't notice any blood coming from them, but both appeared to be unconscious. Some of the other agents who weren't on the SWAT detail started to pull the bodies further down the hallway and out of the line of fire.

I peeked up quickly over the desk to identify the targets, but only saw a lot of smoke with those blue balls coming out of it in from the reception area. I knew reception was on the other side of this part of the complex, so the intruders had already made it a third of the way into the building. I looked deeper into the smoke as a blue ball discharged out of thin air, briefly outlining the silhouette of a person behind it and just as quickly disappearing. I blinked for a split second at what I saw, before someone behind me pulled me down as several of the blue balls passed right where I had been. I popped up from my position and put out a quick three-round burst of bullets where I'd last seen the flicker. I got a brief glimpse of the intruder before they disappeared again.

I hunched back down behind the cover, not believing what I'd just witnessed. I realized that the attackers had the ability to stealth themselves. I knew about the stealth fighters used in the Gulf War, but those only reduced their signal enough to avoid being tracked by radar. I had never heard of anything that could go invisible, short of science-fiction.

I listened in as other agents throughout the building began reporting breaches. Our two teams were not enough to stop them all. The other agents were trained in unarmed and armed combat, so they would have to hold out the best they could. The rest of us continued returning fire, but from what I could determine it didn't appear that we had more than one or two on either side of us.

Then, something smacked into the back of my legs just as I was about to fire. I ducked back down quickly and saw my squad leader lying on his back with his head at my feet. I realized he was unconscious and started to look around for a wound, but couldn't find any on him.

I looked at the other squad leader, since he had been here longer.

"What is going on?"

He quickly glanced at me and then at my squad leader before answering, "Whatever the heck they are shooting at us doesn't seem to be slowed down when it hits our body armor. He's unconscious like the others. From what I can tell they aren't shooting to kill, but darned if I know why."

He gestured to one of the plainclothes agents down the hall to come and drag my squad leader away and I returned to the battle.

I started to hear broken radio chatter, which I ignored for the most part until a voice I recognized came online.

"Repeat your last transmission, you were broken up." I yelled into the mike.

The person on the other end sounded like Agent Fields, "I repeat, the holding area has been breached by unknown assailants. One agent is down, and I don't think I can hold out."

Her transmission cut out as I realized that whoever we were fighting here was just a diversion, as they weren't interested in pushing further into the facility. This was a jail break out and they were after the four teenaged detainees.

I looked at the only remaining squad leader and yelled, "This is a diversion. The holding cells are under attack."

The squad leader looked back at me, "What do you mean? Who's being held down there?"

I realized then that he hadn't been briefed about our detainees, but this wasn't my most important concern at the moment. I didn't know how else to respond, so I vaguely explained that four people were being detained and questioned for possible terrorist involvement.

The squad leader assessed the situation as he internally debated the benefits of holding our current ground against losing the valuable detainees whom we had the responsibility to guard. He glanced back at me before speaking again.

"All right, Agent Ramirez, take two men and head to the holding area and secure it. We'll hold out here."

I nodded my head as I gestured for two of the guys in my squad to follow me. We stayed low as we made our way back down the hall and out into the courtyard. As we ran across the courtyard, we kept looking around to make sure that we didn't run into an ambush. I noticed that the area had been cleared and the agents had moved on to either back up Team One or venture deeper into the facility to shore up our defenses there. Just before we made it to the other side of the courtyard, I heard a slight wind sucking noise as though air was being blown through a turbine from behind me. I told the group to hold up for a second as I turned around to see what it was.

The entrance to the reception wing had blown out into the courtyard, with almost a perfect spherical section cut out of the entire building. Some of the agents backing up Team One had blown out of the opening and into the courtyard. Directly overhead, several lights shown down into the courtyard and the surrounding windows. The beams weren't very wide, but they were extremely powerful and lit up the area more than I would have expected. It was still dark beyond the beams, but I figured some form of helicopter was about to land. I hadn't heard anything over the radios stating that we had incoming support via helicopter, so I considered it hostile. I aimed my gun at the lights and opened fire. I couldn't tell if I was hitting anything, but one of the light beams immediately locked onto our position and the three of us started spreading out to take cover.

I hid behind a metal trash can that was hugging a park bench and bolted into concrete. Though the trash can wasn't exactly an armored wall, I figured some cover was better than none. The aircraft was coming down quickly from directly overhead. It was too big to be a helicopter, but I didn't recognize the design. An intense purple light flared on the bottom section of the craft. I figured whatever it was going to do wouldn't be good, as I'd seen enough sci-fi crap this morning to last a lifetime. I picked myself up and screamed into my mike for the other two with me to get out of the area. I had barely made two steps before I heard a discharge behind me. I glanced back quickly and saw some kind of purple light pulse slam into the center of the courtyard. The moment it hit, everything around it blew outward from the shockwave including me and my team. My gun blew from my hands while wrenching the strap from my body as I flew into the air. I noticed that the remaining windows surrounding the courtyard blew into whatever building they were a part of. I was far enough away from the focal point of the blast, but I was still hurled almost twenty feet. My body rolled to an abrupt stop against the wing we had been heading to.

I'd hit the ground hard enough to have the wind knocked out of me; my senses were completely disoriented. I felt the vibration of the craft as it landed in the courtyard. My blurred vision allowed me to make out some kind of ramp being lowered and a couple people in white suits filing out from the aircraft. I did what I could to hold on to consciousness, but I felt myself losing the battle.

The courtyard was completely bathed in light now, and whoever these people were now in charge of the FBI headquarters. One of the intruders walked over to one of my team members who'd landed near me. Then, the intruder made their way over to me. I looked up and couldn't determine if they were male or female with the suit they had on. Being closer allowed me to get a better look at them, even with my blurred vision. The assailant was completely covered from head to toe in some type of white rubberized armor. The head section was oval in shape with two red lights where the eyes would normally be. I couldn't make out any other feature as the intruder lifted up some weird gun with a rather large barrel and pointed it directly at me. I briefly felt bad about letting the agency down, but I imagined it would have taken the entire U.S. Army to stop these guys. The gun fired and the last thing I saw before darkness claimed me was blue light.

CHAPTER 24 – RESCUE

FBI HEADQUARTERS, WASHINGTON DC
JYNX COLLINS

Our shuttle landed on top of a half-empty parking garage just a few blocks away from our target. We were tasked with a rescue operation. I was the newest member of the team and also the youngest and the shortest as evidenced by some brief teasing. At just under five feet tall, I was often the butt of jokes by the other recruits during training. Those jokes stopped when I started wiping the floor with the rest of the guys during unarmed combat training. Though, I guess it wasn't appropriate to use the term "guys" since two other members on my team were also girls like me. I was born on the island sixteen years ago. My father was the Head of Security for the entire operation.

I didn't learn until I was older that the life I led on the island wasn't the norm for the rest of the world. My mother had died in childbirth and my father said he'd jumped at the chance to get me out of England. Once we were on the island, I went to school starting at the age of two. After I turned twelve, my schooling was supplemented by brief immersions into various fields to help me determine my true academic interests. Realizing that I didn't have the technical aptitude to excel at science and engineering, I opted to apprentice with security. At sixteen, my formal schooling ended and my in-depth training with the security detail commenced.

For the last seven months I had been through extensive physical and mental training, including hand-to-hand combat, weapons familiarization, and stealth. The area in which someone wanted to serve and the trainer determined the length of training. Specializing in something could take four to ten years to earn a master's level achievement. Those who obtained a master's level were considered leaders in their field...but even then, they were still expected to supplement their work duties with further education or training. I knew it would be a never-ending process. If it wasn't for the relaxed pace of life and the wonderful ball of sand that I called home, I doubt I would have ever made it. My dad Percival Smythe (or "The Butler" as he was called behind his back due to his stiff demeanor) was a tough taskmaster. Because I was raised by him it was easy to adapt to his methods of teaching, but my training was often handled by others who had already completed the security program.

I loved my dad very much. It was a credit to him that he was able to keep up with me at all while I was growing up. It was impossible for me to keep still, and he would forever be sending out security alerts to have them hunt me down. I smiled briefly at the memories.

Dad expected perfection when I performed, and I wasn't about to let him down when he needed me the most.

We had identified that our targets were in danger the moment they had been arrested by the FBI. AMIE put them under close surveillance. All video and audio we could pull out of the ether was ours for the taking. They were tracked from Oregon to Washington DC over a period of several days. According to AMIE, FBI procedure mandated that they be questioned and detained until no longer deemed a threat.

Dad had informed us of their visit to the island and it was surmised that they were being questioned about their time there. During my brief time with security, I had learned that outside government agencies were closing in on the Administrator and this was to be expected. We had all hoped the kids would just be questioned and released after a few days, but it didn't work out that way. I wasn't sure why I thought of them as kids, considering that three of the four were older than me. But everyone else in security called them the kids, so it had stuck for now.

AMIE had entered the FBI database and determined that the agents were authorized to use any methods necessary to obtain the data the Director considered vital to national security. Video feed we had received of the cute sandy-haired boy named Kyle getting beaten by some gorilla was the final straw.

So, my dad had gotten approval from the Administrator almost immediately to extract them forcefully from the U.S. Government. I imagined this would light us up quite nicely with the rest of the world, but I left that problem to the Administrator to deal with.

This is how I found myself at an aged parking garage that overlooked the U.S. Capitol. Many of the buildings in my viewpoint were old, but impressive. They were a far cry from the shabbiness of the structure on which we were perched or those that immediately surrounded us. Even the FBI headquarters was a rundown building from what I could see, but it was still imposing.

The shuttle took off just after we exited. It would move to a safe altitude and wait for the signal to commence the extraction. During the planning stage, someone suggested that we land directly in the FBI compound's courtyard until the area could be more secured. Though we knew from scans that there were several hundred people inside, we discarded that idea because a direct assault from the top would expose us to too many unknowns.

My suit was the result of molecular engineering research that had been completed over a decade ago. Since then, the ops suit had been refined and upgraded. It was exclusively used by the security arm that spanned the entire operation, both on the island and above. Considering my size,

I would have appreciated some super strength or speed from the suit...but its benefits were not that good. The suit was form built for each individual and only worked for the person for whom it was created. The inside was completely self-contained, with isolated oxygen and waste recycling abilities. Knowing that I had the ability to drink processed sweat and waste wasn't the highlight that I enjoyed most about it, so I avoided ingesting anything at all costs. The suit's skin was a nano-crystal polymer, much like that of a chameleon, allowing the suit to mimic its background. The suit wasn't perfect, and an operative could be compromised if your opponent knew what to look for. The skin was also hardened and tested against modern, commonly used weapons...or so I had been told. I did know that our own weapons required multiple shots in order to incapacitate the wearer. Because of this and the non-lethal function of or weapons, our training exercises were always live fire and full contact.

The helmet provided a neutral view of the environment and filtered out light and shadows, leaving just the solid parts. Because of this, I could see clearly in any environment and any form of flash bang or stun device would be ineffective. Also, the helmet had a small visual display that was set up either on the right or left side of the helmet as determined by the operator to show whatever visual image that was downloaded into it. Since I had been assigned to the primary extraction team, we would have a direct visual link transmitted from the team going in the front doors that were creating the distraction. This information was helpful as it allowed us real time awareness of the distractions effectiveness and whether or not our own plans needed to change to compensate for any unexpected variables. Whichever side didn't contain the video image was reserved for a floor plan of the facility and thumbnail pictures of our targets. I had no idea who the four kids were, but I figured it was pretty bad if the U.S. Government was arresting kids these days. Since the kids had visited the island, they were considered under our protection until told otherwise.

Our ground team was composed of twelve operators ranging from age sixteen to twenty-three. My father was waiting in the shuttle and would provide support for the extraction. We wore our suits and were cloaked from the surrounding environment. Our team leader signaled us forward vocally through the communications channels inside our headsets. Each operator had the ability to communicate with the shuttle and the island if necessary, but those features wouldn't be needed for this rescue. Once we got closer to our target, we all split up. Two headed to the front doors. Four separated into two two-man groups that would breach the facility from Tenth and E streets respectively. The six who remained would breach the parking garage below the street and then split up again. At that time, two would secure the parking garage and help clear a path to the courtyard where our final extraction would take place. That left just four of us to rescue the kids.

The other five and I remained on Ninth Street within a few feet of the building and out of the way of traffic. Our assault would be executed last. The two operators at the front door had the honor of drawing as much attention as possible away from the rest of the building and hopefully thinning out the detention area. We didn't think that any of the FBI agents would willingly shoot their suspects...but after witnessing the beating of the blonde-haired boy, we decided not to take any unnecessary risks.

I heard a loud explosion near the front of the building. From my internal camera view, I saw the two operators rushing through the broken glass and crumbled bricks into the reception area. The front breach was made as loudly as feasible to enhance the distraction, so directional explosives were used. I saw a few lights going on in the building across from us, probably from any security or janitorial staff members who were still on duty. I would say we had been heard.

I focused on my internal camera view and saw agents shooting in the direction of the two operators. Those engaging the operators were being picked off one after the other without much pause. The stealth ability of the suits was downgraded in that environment with all the rubble and smoke blowing around, but still offered them some protection. After the reception area had been cleared, the operator I was monitoring split off from his partner and turned right into the complex. The ground floor in that section was rectangular, meeting up about thirty feet in at a T-junction leading out to the courtyard. The operators had been instructed to keep all the attention in that section for as long as possible and prevent anyone from coming up from behind. We expected the local cops to respond, but had planned to be out of the facility either before or just after they arrived. The operator's camera showed him clearing each room he passed, ensuring that no hostile people would be left behind him. Those in front of him who had jumped out in the hallway or leaned outside an office door were quickly neutralized. I switched my video over to the other operator and verified that he was progressing at the same pace.

I hated waiting, knowing that the other two were taking fire, but the mission required us all to do our part…which had been drilled into me from Day One. I sat there and monitored the forward team while occasionally glancing around the street I was on for any unexpected aggressors. The camera I was monitoring showed the operator cresting the last corner of the rectangle to gain a visual on the T-junction. What I saw was almost laughable. The agents had hastily constructed a barricade on either side of the T-junction, supposedly to prevent any further progress into the facility. From the feed, it appeared that the response team was more heavily geared than the normal agents I had already seen. There were about a half dozen directly inside the barricade, dressed head to toe in black body armor of some sort. I didn't know the specifications of that armor, but I questioned whether it would hold out as well as mine did. The operators just shifted up and down the corridor, occasionally ducking into one of the offices, but that appeared to be unnecessary. The armor we wore seemed to be sufficient to hold off the weapons the agents had used. The operator was only moving around to either prevent themselves from being focused on or to make it look like there were more than just two.

After another minute, we all received a signal from the forward operators stating that the resident response team had just been reinforced. I wasn't in charge, but I hoped that meant it was time for us to get started. My current team leader instructed two others to set up the breach. Apparently, it was time to go. I felt the adrenaline inside me build up and my hands shook a little from it. I wasn't afraid and had complete confidence in the suit I was wearing as well as in the others around me. This was just the first active operation I was a part of, and I didn't want to screw it up. I was greatly surprised when I had been assigned to the team, considering I was one of the newest trainees. I was advised by our team leader that he, not my father, had chosen the team. My father had faith in the people he trained and those he placed in charge. Apparently, that faith extended to me...which I couldn't help but appreciate.

As commanded by our current leader, the six of us moved forward. Another operator and I each grabbed a foot-long cylinder that we had brought along. We walked into the road and separated ourselves about six feet apart. Once I was in position, I jabbed the metal pylon hard into the concrete of the road to ignite the firing bolts in the pylon. The pressure of the bolts firing secured the pylon about four inches into the ground. Immediately on top of the cylinder, a red strobe light started going off. Since we were breaching the underground garage, a hole needed to be made in the middle of Ninth Street to gain access. The strobe lights were warnings to any cars or pedestrians that something was wrong. As dark as it was out here, an accident could happen if someone wasn't paying attention and it wasn't our goal to fatally harm anyone. The other operator planted his pylon just as the remaining four operators came forward. They formed a four-person grid with a person at each corner. All four of them placed a smaller cylinder at each of the corners. Once they were all in place, we waited about ten seconds for a green light to appear on top of each cylinder. Once the lights turned solid green, that confirmed a connection had been made and there wasn't anybody occupying the space in the garage directly below us.

As all four cylinders lit up green, a high-pitched whine came through my audio pickup. Then, the square asphalt section we had outlined dropped down into the underground garage below. Between here and the garage below, I saw a four-foot gap of concrete and earth as well as the rubble on the ground about three stories down. We had been trained on how to approach this. So, a moment after that road disappeared, I jumped into the hole that had been left behind. The shock absorbers built into my boots cushioned the impact of the fall and I crouched just as I hit the ground to help balance me. Once down, I immediately scanned the area for any targets, but didn't find anyone in this section of the parking garage. The next two behind me immediately went their separate ways around the garage, securing our route to the stairwell. The stairwell was directly under the facility, so this was the closest we could get in our breach. Once the remainder of my four-man team was down, we moved as a group straight towards the staircase. According to the floor plan in my helmet display, the stairs led up to the main floor and down to the detention area. The two who were searching the garage would meet up with two others, who would stay to guard access to the stairs once their sweep was completed. When they arrived, those two would go up into the facility and start clearing a path to the courtyard. That left me and my group leader to go downstairs and free the kids from their cells. We started making our way down the stairs, with one of us moving forward at a time. As we reached the next landing, we began spotting each other from floor to floor all the way down.

I arrived at the stairwell door outside of the detention area first and waited there until the leader could join me. He positioned himself to be first into the hallway beyond, so I grabbed a hold of the door handle and prepared to yank it open at his command. Once the command was given, I pulled as hard as I could. He shot through the door with me following right behind him. On the other side, I noticed the elevator that was offline to my left and the corridor to the cells stretching to the right. Realizing that there was no threat in the direction of the elevator, we both turned right and started walking down the hall.

The hallway had several rooms on either side that appeared to be administrative offices, probably for whoever manned this dungeon. We checked each one to ensure they were empty before continuing on. Our search continued until we finally arrived at the detention center door. For security reasons, the door was made of solid metal about an inch thick to prevent escapes. The leader walked up to the door slowly and tested the handle to see if the door would open. By the little movement I saw, that was a big fat "no."

Our team leader swiveled his helmet to look at me and commanded, "Blow it."

I nodded at his command as I swapped places with him and handed him my stun rifle, so I could work with both my hands. I pulled four small cylinders from a leg compartment on my suit and began placing them at the four corners of the door. Once each cylinder was in place, I toggled a small switch on each of them and waited for a small LED on top to light up green. I stepped back slightly, waiting for the sync to complete. My patience was rewarded by an energy field that covered the entire surface of the door on our side. I smiled inside my helmet and then stepped back to reclaim my stun rifle. I aimed my rifle at the door.

Before firing, I thought about something and looked over at the leader.

"What if there is someone on the other side?"

"It can't be helped, and we'll have to take the chance."

I shrugged, looked back at the door and fired. The stun rifle discharged a small sphere of electrical plasma directly at the door. The plasma only held its shape for about two seconds when fired. This allowed enough time for the plasma to hit whatever target at which you were aiming. In the case of a person, the shot caused a massive electrical surge through the body and neural shutdown. Essentially, in less than a second the target would be knocked out cold...but not before enjoying the wonderful feeling of electricity running through their nervous system and the pain that came with it. I had been on the receiving end of the stun rifle many times during training and even the suit I wore would only absorb so much before failing.

An interesting side effect to the weapon was when the electric plasma collided with another electrically charged object. The field that extended across the door was electrically charged. When my bolt hit the field, an instantaneous reaction occurred on a molecular level…causing both the field and any object near it to polarize separately. It was similar to putting two magnets with the same charge together and causing them to repel from each other. In the case of a much larger field like the one I set up on the door, the powerful polarity caused the huge metal door to blow off its frame and launch into the room beyond. The second it took the door to travel from where it was to the wall on the other side of the room allowed me enough time to see someone standing on the other side just before being clipped by the door as it went by. I immediately followed behind the door and into the larger room. The person whom the door had hit was sprawled on the ground off to my right.

I went towards the person and verified that they were still alive, but neutralized.

I heard shots off to my right and felt one impact my shoulder, but the suit absorbed the kinetic energy from the bullet. I saw a female agent braced beyond a doorway yelling for help through her attached microphone. She then turned and went further back down the hallway; I figured that was where the kids were being held. The leader went after her while I stayed behind. All this took less than a second to process as I focused my attention back to my immediate target. As I got closer to the agent who had been hit by the door, I could tell that it was a man…and he was huge. I identified him as the bald agent in the video who'd beaten up the cute sandy-haired boy. The big guy was still getting up after being swiped by the huge metal door, so I couldn't waste any more time with him. I lifted my rifle up and fired a round into his back. Regardless of his size, he was unable to deal with the neural overload caused by the shot and he collapsed into unconsciousness. I walked by him to search the remaining area, but paused briefly to consider shooting him again just to be safe. Nah. Besides I couldn't justify myself beyond the need for wanting a little payback for the boy he had hurt, and I didn't want to be that kind of person.

I continued searching through the rooms in the immediate area and identified two separate interrogation and monitoring rooms, but all were empty. I turned left and headed down the hallway after the leader to assist him if necessary. The hallway only went about six feet before opening up into a small holding area with four cells. The female agent was out cold on the floor and the leader was searching her. After a few seconds, he stood up with a large set of brass keys on a key ring and walked over to the cell doors. He came up to the first door on the left and opened the observation port to look inside. He closed it quickly and moved to the other door. I went back to the entry way into this section and stood guard while he searched for the kids. I glanced back repeatedly and noticed that at the second door he went through the selection of keys until he had the right one to open the cell door. He opened the cell door wide and on the other side I saw the tall Asian kid from my photo looking out. The look on his face seemed rather bewildered. I realized he couldn't see us, and the door had just magically opened for him.

I transmitted to the leader, "Our cloak is on, and he can't see us."

"De-cloak!" he ordered.

I accessed my visual controls inside my helmet and shut down my suit's stealth ability.

Once we became visible, the kid in the cell jumped back slightly in surprise. The leader advised the kid that we were sent by the Administrator and that he needed to come with us. To his credit, the kid need much convincing to come out of his cell. Getting a closer look at him, I thought he was cute as well. The Asian kid stood near me at the request of the leader as he continued on to the next cell. It also must have been empty or at the very least did not contain one of our targets, as he moved to the last one in this section. Our luck held out for a second time, as the leader opened that cell to reveal a young kid with glasses and I positively identified him as one of our targets. Wow, he was cute too in a nerdish sort of way. But considering my dad, who was I to complain? Once the second kid with glasses was out of his cell, the Asian kid rushed over to him and enveloped him in a bear hug. It looked like they were both happy to see each other and I assumed that they were probably prevented from interacting with each other while staying here. Neither looked like they were in bad condition, but the clothes they wore were just plain nasty and I was thankful I couldn't smell anything through my suit.

The leader gestured for me to keep searching, so I went back down the short hall and passed through the interrogation section into the next area. Apparently, this was a mirror opposite of the other holding area. Again, I saw four cell doors. There were no other agents waiting to ambush us in this section, so I figured we had cleared them out of the area. I didn't bother going up to the doors to look inside to locate the remaining two kids on our list, as the observation ports were too high off the ground for me to see into. Again, I hated being so short...but I buried the thought and returned to guarding the entryway. The leader came into the area, followed by both of the kids we had already found. Starting on his left, he started looking through the observation port on the first door he came to. He was apparently satisfied with what was in there, gestured for the Asian kid to open the door and handed him the key ring. As the kid fumbled with the keys, he moved to the next cell and then on to the next one. Apparently, neither contained the remaining targets. The leader went to the last cell and seemed to have found one of our final targets.

I glanced over at the first cell door, which now opened. A pretty blonde girl flew out of the cell and into the Asian kid's arms. After hugging him, she turned to the boy with glasses and hugged him as well. Both seemed happy with finding each other, but the girl still seemed rather upset and started looking around. Seeing me by the entrance and the leader at the other door, the Asian kid quickly explained to her that we were here to rescue them.

The blonde girl moved to the cell next to her, yanked the observation port open, and yelled "Kyle."

I assumed Kyle was the sandy-haired boy. The leader told the girl and the Asian kid that he was over here, and both raced over to the door. The leader backed up to allow them access. The girl looked into the open observation port again. She started crying and urged the Asian kid, whom she called Phillip, to hurry up. Once Phillip had the door unlocked and open, she pushed past him to our last target who was lying crumpled on the cell's bed. Well, what I assumed was our last target. From what I could see of his face from this distance, my identification wasn't a hundred percent. I figured if she identified him, then that was good enough.

The leader stuck his head in the door and told them that we needed to go. He asked Phillip to assist with carrying Kyle. The blonde girl backed up further into the cell to give them access, though she did so reluctantly. Phillip and the leader grabbed our fourth target. Each grabbed an arm and sat him upright in bed. By the movement of his head, I would say that he was either unconscious or too physically weak to move. I was going with the former hypothesis over the latter.

Once they had Kyle sitting upright, both locked wrists underneath him at the seat of his pants and made a makeshift seat with their hands and wrists to balance him on. Both lifted him at the same time and our fourth target was now mobile. Once they all got out into the larger area, the leader instructed me to lead the way to the courtyard.

I looked at the other two kids we had rescued, "Stay between me and him at all times unless I tell you otherwise."

By the reaction the two gave me, I imagine they weren't expecting someone female to be in this suit…but that was immaterial. Once I saw that each understood, I turned my back and started sweeping for any new hostiles in the direction of the staircase.

It took us just over sixty seconds, according to my suit's chronometer, to make it to the stairwell door. Since we were at the lowest level, I no longer had to worry about any hostiles behind me. So, I started to work my way up the multiple flights of stairs. I notified the operatives we'd left to secure the stairs above us that we were on our way up with four non-combatants in tow.

They acknowledged my communications and I switched channels.

"Shuttle, we have the targets in custody and are enroute to our evacuation site."

I wasn't allowed to directly command the shuttle to land, as my dad was in charge of the overall mission and was monitoring all of the operators at one time. We met up with the operative on guard in the stairwell who offered to take the place of Phillip and the leader in supporting the target, but both declined. Over the radio, I heard my dad command all operators to start moving towards the courtyard and disable all hostiles. Both stairwell guards immediately started up the stairs at a brisk pace, with the remainder of us following behind. Once we made it to the ground floor level, we saw that the door into the building was already open with one of our guards standing just beyond it.

Once we crossed the threshold into a long hallway, he advised us to stay put because the way up ahead was still not clear. I nodded as he moved off to my left and stood guard, facing the direction of the corridor that we needed to go down. I moved to the right a few feet down the corridor to guard against anyone coming from that direction. I glanced behind me just as the leader and Phillip placed Kyle on the ground and took a brief rest. The leader knelt and faced left towards our exit, as the other three kids attended to their friend. I turned back down the corridor, which was littered with unconscious agents and walls riddled with holes; I doubted that anything would come my way. I focused on the video feed from the forward operatives inside my helmet and noticed that the operative I was monitoring had pulled a large white sphere the size of a cantaloupe out of his backpack.

The operative grabbed the top and bottom half of the orb in a palm grip and twisted hard. The whole sphere parted about one inch, showing a red pulsing light that circled around it. Once the orb opened, the agents behind the barricade pointed at the operative. I remembered that the orb required a burst of energy to activate and accept the programming from the operative's suit. That energy requirement drained the suit enough that the stealth field would no longer function until the suit had time to recharge. The agents behind the barricade opened fire on the operative, but he ignored them as all his attention was on the orb. The operative at the other end of the hall also uncloaked and started methodically targeting the agents, taking them out one by one. Since a diversion was no longer required, the operatives were now allowed to better control their shots and start actively disabling agents. The other operative could have remained in stealth, but I could tell it was their intention to help draw some of the fire away from the operative with the sphere in his hands. After two more agents behind the barricade went down, the operative I was monitoring twisted the orb and closed it up...and the entire orb turned red.

The operative released the orb and it hovered for a brief second before it started floating down the corridor towards the barricade and rose closer to the ceiling. The agents noticed it immediately, but only a few shot at it as they appeared to be unsure of its nature. The other operative stopped shooting as well, for fear of damaging the orb. When the orb reached the center of the barrier, it stopped and pulsed a bright red light faster and faster. Whoever was in charge of the agents must have realized that they were about to have a bad day and ordered his men to flee. Those who were still mobile sprang up from the barricade, firing off one last time. Then, they rushed down to the only available exit they had into the courtyard.

The pulsing sequence took less than five seconds to complete. The section of the building that the operative faced disintegrated outwards. The farther away from the orb, the larger the pieces that survived...but they were still propelled by the momentum of the flash. In training we had been introduced to the orb and I knew that its construction allowed for specific programming in its detonation. That programming included what types of materials to destroy. Biological material such as a human being or a desk plant and anything close to it could be removed from its programming as a viable target for the orb as long as it was programmed correctly, which I figured it had been.

The blast disintegrated the building and office materials, creating a perfect sphere of destruction. Anything biological within a fifteen-foot radius such as the downed agents below the orb would simply fall to the next available surface below them. Any agent outside the blast and within a twenty-five- foot radius would be impacted by the physical blast and propelled away with the rest of the debris into walls or whatever else was in their way. The orb had the potential to cause serious injuries, but was non-lethal for the most part.

Going by the visual display, the operative on the other side of the hallway had braced himself for the blast and hadn't fallen back. The operative I was monitoring had probably done the same, but both began moving across the hole they had created while debris from overhead continued falling down around them.

"Shuttle incoming; prepare for evacuation," I heard my dad state in my helmet, so I turned towards the group.

The leader and Phillip were already picking up Kyle, so I looked at the operative beyond them.

"Is the way clear?" I asked.

"Yes, it is."

This operative led the way, so I took up the rear guard and made sure that our targets stayed between me and him as the leader helped secure the center. After we worked our way down the hallways, we finally made it out into the courtyard. As the last person through the door, I was the last to notice that our shuttle was parked in the middle of the courtyard. The shuttle's ramp was facing us and we all hustled over to it so we could get our targets on board. I slowed my pace as I approached another operative who stood over a downed agent. Though our suits didn't display any rank or insignia, my display did paint an outline over the operative in front of me identifying him as Command. I realized that it was my father and he'd just neutralized the agent on the ground in front of him. He looked up at me as I approached.

"Get on board. Now."

The other agents in the building had converged at various times on the courtyard. Once we were all aboard, the pilot didn't wait for us to secure ourselves before taking off and getting some distance between us and the FBI.

This shuttle was designed specifically for security, so all the seats were against the sides of the shuttle. I sat down in one with my rifle in my lap and looked at the three kids in the center of the shuttle tending to their unconscious friend. One of the operatives knelt next to them and began scanning the sandy-haired boy to assess his medical condition. Our shuttle would be back at the island in less than an hour and it was his job to make sure the boy's life wasn't at further risk.

After a few minutes, the operative advised the other kids that their friend would be all right and he would get full medical care once we returned to the island. The other operatives tried to relax. The adrenaline we'd all felt was burning off and I couldn't help but feel tired after the ordeal. The boy with glasses sat next to me and stared at everything, including me. I faced forward and sent the command in my helmet to release. The nano-filaments around my neck and on the back of my head parted, allowing me to pull the helmet forward and off my head.

As I sat straight again, I felt my black hair fluff out a little. I wore my hair spiked off to the left and right side of my head and face. The spikes only extended a few inches, as I kept my hair short to more easily manage. I ran my hand through my hair to make sure everything was still in place and was thankful that the suit kept me well-ventilated; otherwise, this stuff would be pasted to my scalp. After lowering my arm, I noticed the boy next to me staring at me.

"Yes?" I asked in my soft, doll-like voice.

My eyebrows raised, waiting for him to say something. He stumbled a bit and pointed at me and then at my hair as I considered that he may have accidentally swallowed his tongue during his ordeal.

I glared at him, "Spit it out!"

I figured he was about to say something stupid like, "Hey, you're a girl" or something else I would have to hit him for. I wasn't teased much anymore for my size or my voice because everyone knew that I wouldn't hesitate to knock them out…not to mention that any teasing would offend my dad.

The boy responded so quietly that I doubted anyone else inside the shuttle heard.

"You're very pretty."

For a moment I was shocked by what he'd said, and I wasn't sure if I'd heard him correctly. I felt heat building up in my cheeks at his comment. I looked closer at him than I had before, beyond his weird glasses and into his eyes. All the time I had lived on the island, a boy had never paid me a compliment; my dad just didn't count. After a minute or two of consideration, I decided that my first assessment had been correct: he was cute.

"Thank you," I whispered back at him and then faced forward.

During the rest of flight back to the island, we both glanced at each other from time to time.

CHAPTER 25 – A NEW BEGINNING

PACIFIC OCEAN
KYLE BISHOP

As I opened my eyes, I saw the ceiling of a dimly lit room. I blinked a few times to clear my head and tried to think back to the last thing I remembered. Oh, yes, Muscles and I were getting acquainted. I figured that I'd finally passed out from the beating and they were allowing me to rest and heal up before Round Two. I was kind of surprised about the last session, as Muscles hadn't asked me any questions. No matter what I came up with, I just couldn't seem to figure out the purpose of it beyond torturing me to soften me up for a future interrogation. I blinked a few more times and licked my lips, as my mouth tasted rather dry. I tried to sit up, but my body seemed to be held in place and I couldn't move anything.

I scratched out a very faint "Hello," hoping someone would hear me.

Wherever I was, it wasn't my cell...as the ceiling wasn't made from concrete, but it was pure white from what I could make out in the low light. After another minute I saw a small shadow move at the edge of my peripheral vision, so I tried to call out again. Though I was able to speak louder, my query was still rather soft.

A lady leaned over me and smiled. I blinked again and tried to focus on her. She looked to be in her thirties with dark brown hair and soft brown eyes. She had a very kind look to her that would probably have made me relax if I had been capable of doing so.

"How are you feeling, Kyle?"

Her voice was soft and reassuring as she spoke.

I focused on speaking as clearly as possible, but it still came out scratchy.

"Where am I and who are you?"

She smiled even more before responding, "I'm Dr. Christina Evans and you're in Medical at the moment."

She started running an object back and forth across my head and face, and I saw a flat red beam shining out of it as it crossed over my eyes.

She put her device away and then leaned over me again.

"What's the last thing you remember?"

I thought back to Muscles, "I got hit by a truck...repeatedly."

She laughed softly at my joke.

"Well, since your run-in with traffic, the Administrator had you and your friends rescued."

I stared at her, finding what she said to be unbelievable...considering that I'd been recently detained by the FBI and secured who knows where.

My eyes wandered as I thought about this, but then they snapped back to her.

"Not to sound rude, but why should I believe anything you say?"

The doctor smiled even more, "I guess the Administrator was right to place his trust in you, Kyle."

She reached over and touched something attached to the bed on which I was lying.

I felt the restraints across my body dissipate as she said, "Don't take my word for it."

She put her hand behind my head, grabbed my arm and helped me sit up. As I sat up, my head swam for a second and my vision blurred. The doctor pushed a cup into my hand and I started drinking, not caring what it was. The cup apparently contained water and I drained it.

I gave myself a moment to focus again and suddenly noticed Alex across the room sleeping on a couch. Her hair cascaded down her shoulder and onto the front of her neck while her chest rose and fell with each breath. She looked like an angel sleeping there. I remembered the first time I saw her with her eyes closed when she lying under the sun on the boat we had taken to the island.

The doctor leaned towards me and spoke softly, "She has been here since you first arrived."

The doctor smiled and added, "She refused to leave your side until you were awake."

My heart soared knowing that Alex cared about me so much.

"Can you help me up, please?"

The doctor appeared to debate my request for a brief second, but helped me stand. Once I was vertical, I released my grip on her arm and tested my balance. I still felt incredibly weak, but I also felt like I was on the mend. I gazed at Alex's sleeping face again. I slowly walked towards her, taking one step at a time, until I stood in front of the couch. I grabbed the arm of the couch near Alex's head and used it for support as I lowered myself to my knees. Every movement was a reminder of the soreness I felt all over my body, including my bones. I watched Alex's eyelashes twitch as her eyes pressed against her lids while they moved from a dream. The skin of her cheekbones was so smooth that for a brief moment, I couldn't imagine that she was anything other than an angel sent from God.

I heard the doctor behind me walking away and I was grateful for the privacy. My gaze wandered further down Alex's beautiful face as I took in each soft angle. I remembered the first day that I saw her so many years ago and the connection we'd shared even back then. My mind sped forward through our time at school and the brief times I had seen her again. I remembered the wonderful moments I'd had with her as well as the more aggressive times that often followed. I couldn't imagine loving, cherishing, holding, fighting against, and being a part of anyone else. I didn't want to imagine a moment without those feelings, without her in my life...forever.

My gaze wandered back down Alex's face to her lips, and I remembered the perfect kiss we'd shared at the space station, only for it to be crushed by the pigheadedness of the woman lying before me. A big smile spread across my face at that memory and I didn't care that it hurt so much to smile. I looked at her again, at her beautiful soft lips. Now would be the perfect time for another one of those moments. I started to lean forward over her. As my lips neared hers, I paused. My mind drifted back to when she'd hit me after that first kiss and when she'd pushed me off the boat on purpose. I knew that if I kissed her again, I would have to be willing to accept the consequences of my actions.

My eyes shifted to hers, and I saw that she was still asleep and dreaming. The smile returned to my face as I realized that if Alex hit me again, it would be so worth it. I closed the distance between our lips and lightly pressed my lips to hers, slowly increasing the pressure from one second to the next. After a moment, I felt her tense before me and her eyes popped open.

I pulled away from Alex's soft, sweet lips far enough so that I could look into her eyes. Her mouth opened up slightly enough that I knew she wanted to say something. I quickly placed my index finger over her lips and she paused. We stared into each other's eyes for what felt like eternity.

I glanced briefly away from her to think about what I wanted to say and then my gaze snapped back to hers.

"I don't know what the future holds for either of us," I murmured.

She looked like she wanted to respond, but my finger still guarded her lips as I continued.

"Where we will go or what we will do. But I can't imagine a future without you there next to me."

I looked at her lips, breaking our eye contact for a brief moment. Then, my gaze returned to her eyes.

"I know...I know I've made some mistakes with us. I've hurt someone you care about deeply. I can only ask your forgiveness. And hope that one day you can forgive me. And that perhaps, you could come to love me as much as I have loved you from the very first moment that I saw you."

Alex's eyes started watering. What I was saying was upsetting her again and I felt the pain inside of me because of it. My finger still pressed into her soft lips, I looked deeper into her eyes and tried to convey to her from the emotion displayed in my face and the sincerity of my voice that everything I said and would say was absolutely true.

I swallowed my fear before continuing, "I want you... I..."

My voice broke, but I forced it down and started again.

"You take all the time you need, and if the day should ever come where you can forgive me, I will still be here. I will be here as your friend..."

I looked away from her as I finished, "...and perhaps one day, we can be something more."

I released my finger from her lips.

"I will always love you, Alexi Masters...and I don't think my heart could ever love another as much as I love you."

I gazed into her beautiful green eyes, which were filled with the fire and determination that I had fallen in love with. Her eyes scanned my face for several moments. Waiting for her to speak was getting more and more uncomfortable. I grabbed the headrest again to pull myself up. Her arm shot out as she grabbed the medical gown I wore and yanked me down, causing my knees to bang into the floor. The moment I impacted, a really painful jolt went through my body from my toes to my head; I thought for a moment I would black out. I fought to stay conscious as Alex pulled my face closer to hers.

Her lips twitched briefly, "Sorry."

I smiled at her and felt warmth growing inside me, "I'll live."

We gazed into each other's eyes a little longer before she spoke again.

"I wasn't sure...that..."

She seemed to be fighting to figure out what she wanted to say.

"...I had feelings for you. For a long time, I had difficulty looking beyond the anger and the hurt I felt whenever I saw you."

I paused for a second and realized this wasn't going as I had hoped it would. I internally sighed, knowing what was coming and was content to just be her friend if she'd let me.

Alex glanced down briefly and then back up again at my face.

"What I feel for you...confuses me. When I first saw you, I thought it was love at first sight...but as time went on, the hurt began to grow inside me. I couldn't believe that we could ever have anything...better...between us like... friendship."

When she spoke that last word, she at least did it with kindness in her voice...which meant perhaps the future could be changed between us.

"When you were in that chair being beaten by that agent..."

I stiffened a little, realizing she had witnessed that and wishing she hadn't.

"...I cried on the other side of that window. But I cried, not just because I had to watch you get hurt."

I tried to understand what she saying, but I couldn't.

She grasped both sides of my face with the palms of her hands and forced me to stare in her eyes as she continued, "I cried because I was afraid. I was afraid that I would never get the chance to tell you how much I love you."

The last words she spoke were so soft, I wasn't sure if I had heard her correctly. My heart started pounding so fast in response and it seemed convinced that we hadn't imagined it. Not letting go of my face, she pulled me down to her and urgently pressed her lips to mine. I leaned some of my weight into her to help support me as we kissed. I couldn't imagine anything but her at that moment. The kiss we shared now was more profound than those that came before it. At that moment, we both knew without doubt that we loved each other. Without breaking our kiss, I pulled myself across her body to lie on the couch with her. After a while, my nausea returned and I felt myself drifting into the darkness again.

I whispered as Alex rested her head against my chest, "Please don't leave me."

The darkness started closing around my vision and everything became hazy and shadowed. Just before oblivion finally claimed me, I could have sworn she replied, "Never!"

###

Two days later, after I had finally healed enough to move around freely, the Administrator's Head of Security Percival Smythe visited me. The Administrator wanted me to come to Sol Station to discuss some things. I figured he wanted to talk about what had happened. At the very least I owed him a thank you for rescuing us, especially Alex.

I smiled about the change in our behavior towards each other. We were still learning what it was like to be in love and we couldn't seem to stand being away from each other for more than a few hours at a time. After talking with the others, they helped me piece together what had happened while I was sleeping.

I figured the FBI wouldn't stop pursuing us, especially now that they had been hurt by the Administrator. Also, I couldn't help but feel responsible putting all of this in danger. So, I boarded a shuttle by myself to fly up to Sol Station to speak with the Administrator.

When I arrived, one of the station's residents told me to go to the greenhouse. They walked off, expecting that I would know the way. I did know the way, but I was humbled by the trust they'd placed in me by allowing me to wander freely throughout the station. I took the elevator to the station's greenhouse and walked onto the pathway surrounded by green plants. I didn't see the Administrator so I began walking along the path, figuring he was probably in the secluded area with the nice view. As I crested around the wall of foliage, I saw the Administrator standing close to the huge window with the blue Earth shining below him. I walked up to his right side and took a moment to enjoy the view. Earth was so beautiful from up here that it was hard to imagine it wasn't just as wonderful on the surface.

I looked at the Administrator before commenting, "Administrator, I want to apologize to you."

"For what?"

The Administrator's expression appeared calm, which surprised me because I'd expected him to look confused or even angry.

I looked directly at him as I answered, "Because of me and my meddling, I've put you and all you have dreamed of at risk."

The Administrator smiled and slightly shook his head before he responded, "You didn't put us at any more risk than we already were."

He turned back to face Earth and continued, "If not the FBI, then some other federal agency in any number of countries would have been the first. We've been aware that our operations have started to become more visible and the time for hiding is coming to an end."

The Administrator turned back to face me and added, "If anything, it is my fault because I lacked faith in humanity as a whole. I hid all of this because I did not feel that they were ready for it and may never be."

I considered what he said and realized that he was right. Humanity couldn't be trusted right now, as my experience with the FBI had proven. But I imagined that there were others out there like me, Alex, Phillip and Simon who could be called upon to join us.

I looked up at the Administrator, "What happens now?"

The Administrator continued smiling and glanced slightly past my right shoulder before he answered, "For now, I have a job for you."

He turned his gaze back to me and remarked, "If you have the courage to embrace it."

He looked beyond me, so I turned to see what he was looking at. I saw a spaceship approaching that appeared to be about six hundred feet long. The front nose was curved downward similar to an eagle's beak, but tapered off at the end. The belly of the spaceship extended a little lower than the rest of the craft and a bit out on each side of the main body. The ship appeared peppered with rugged-looking electronic components as well as what looked like observation and apartment windows. The tail of the spaceship flared behind the rest of the craft and was trailed by several long, soft blue cones of energy that burned and pushed the ship forward.

"Unbelievable," I muttered.

The Administrator looked at the ship passing by and said with a smile, "Welcome to my world!"

Dreamers

CHAPTER 26 – CHECKMATE

WHITE HOUSE, WASHINGTON DC (AROUND 9:30 AM ON THE MORNING OF THE ATTACK) AGENT CHRISTOPHER LENNOX, DIRECTOR OF THE FBI

As I was being escorted to the Oval Office to speak with the President of the United States, I couldn't help but admire the history around me. I had taken this walk through the White House many times since I had been appointed as the Director of the FBI. I had recently celebrated my fifty-fourth birthday at home in Virginia with my wife, my kids, and my grandkids. I looked in the mirror and realized that public service takes its toll, as the gray hair on my head now outnumbered the dark hair that remained. I had been with the FBI for over thirty years and figured that the position of Director was an adequate stepping-stone until I ascended to the office that I was approaching.

The case my agents had stumbled across grew quickly as more and more evidence became available. The complexity and size of this operation was staggering, as was the threat to the safety of the country as far as I was concerned. But more importantly, I saw it as an opportunity to step out into the public eye in a big way and help me when I ran for President in a few years.

The Secret Service agents who were escorting me to see the President paused outside the closed door to the Oval Office and waited. I knew that my request to see the President had been abrupt and I'd been fit in to his schedule as best he could. A receptionist advised me that the President's meeting was wrapping up and that I could go inside in just a moment. I nodded at her, and she returned to her duties. I had briefed the President when this case started. As it continued to grow, the President's interest built with it. The detainment of the four kids from some small town in Oregon was the break we'd needed. Questioning them didn't lead to any information, which surprised me and forced me to consider the devotion or fanaticism this phantom organization was building. The agent next to me listened to his ear mike. Then, he opened the door for me.

As I walked into the Oval Office, the other people the President had been with exited through the other access door. The President stood behind his desk organizing some papers from his meeting. President George Ferguson had started his first term just under two years ago. Perhaps I could prevent a second. I buried that thought as I studied the man in charge of the nation and felt a little disappointed. President Ferguson had won the election on the simple fact that his opponents weren't much better options for the American people, and he was seen as the lesser of all the evils. As an independent nominee, the President was a neutral entity for voters. He had grown up as a farm boy and progressed into law as he had gotten older.

At sixty-one years of age, the President was surprisingly in great condition; unfortunate for me. His tenure so far had included the passage of several agricultural and energy reforms, as he pushed to get the nation's consumers to convert to electric or alternate fuel-sourced vehicles. Beyond his pet projects, the President had proven malleable to my suggestions and had encouraged and authorized me to pursue this investigation at my discretion.

I spotted the Secretary of Defense General Victor Hurley leaving and I signaled for him to remain if he could. The President looked up at me for my boldness and I saw the questions in his eyes.

"Mr. President, if you don't mind, I would like Victor to stay. What I have to tell you will concern him as well."

Victor paused on his way back to the room and awaited the President's decision.

The President asked me, "Is this about that investigation you were conducting?"

I knew the President was referring to *the* investigation so I answered, "Yes, Mr. President. The situation has become more difficult."

I wasn't sure difficult was the most accurate word, but I didn't want to scare the President. He nodded for Victor to stay.

"Tell Victor about the investigation while I go refresh myself," the President said.

A couple minutes later, the President returned and gestured for us to sit in the couches in front of his desk.

He looked at Victor, "All caught up?"

Victor nodded at the President, who looked at me and demanded, "So, what's this all about? I had to clear an important meeting with the Ambassador of China, so this better be good."

I placed a folder on the coffee table before me, but left it closed as I replied, "Mr. President, at 0214 hours, local time, the headquarters of the FBI was attacked."

Both the President and Victor looked stunned by my statement.

"And why am I not hearing about this until now?", the President asked.

Director Lennox coughed into his hand briefly before answering, "My apologies Mr. President. Due to the severity of the damage imposed and the disruption in communication, it took some time to develop a clear picture of events. I felt it necessary to hold off notification until we could asses the complete picture behind the attack."

I pressed ahead hoping the President would drop the issue of timeliness adding, "We believe the attack was carried out by at least a dozen individuals, all wearing some form of advanced body armor and weaponry."

The President appeared angry. Good, I wanted him angry.

"Does anyone else know about this?" the President demanded.

I figured he wouldn't like what I had to say next, but it was his job to deal with the people...for now.

"Only a few at the moment, but several explosions caused irreparable damage to the building and the response by the local police was noticed. Right now, reporters are surrounding the building and I expect it will be on the morning news pretty soon."

The President blinked as he considered this information.

Victor leaned forward and asked, "Were there any casualties?"

The President quickly looked up at me, as he hadn't gotten around to that question yet.

I looked at Victor before responding, "Thankfully, there were no fatalities during the incident…but we have a lot of wounded, some in serious condition."

The President forced himself to swallow before speaking, "How many?"

I didn't answer right away. The next part was the worst of it and even with the facts, I had to be convincing to push him in the right direction.

"How many?" he growled at me.

Despite his many flaws, the President was definitely a patriot.

I suppressed a smile as I answered, "Our final count put the wounded at two hundred and eighteen agents."

I could tell that piece of information shocked them both, so I pressed forward, "Mr. President, twelve individuals attacked a federal building just down the street from here and disabled over two hundred of my agents and almost destroyed the building in the process."

I shifted a bit closer to the President, "Twelve, Mr. President, without a single casualty on their side that we know about."

The President sat back in his chair and I could tell that the information was sinking in. Much like the attacks of 9/11, the news of this event had to be received with the same desire for justice if not vengeance

Victor spoke up again, "Any idea as to why they attacked your office?"

"Our agents were attempting to protect several witnesses that came forward regarding the investigation. During the assault, they were kidnapped from our custody."

The President stood up at that moment and both of us followed suit.

"Are you telling me that this organization or whatever you call it has kidnapped American citizens?" the President snapped.

I put a chastised look of guilt on my face to give him the impression of remorse for my failure.

I looked at Victor and then back at the President before answering, "That's exactly what I'm saying, Mr. President."

The President walked away from us and went behind his desk to look out the window.

He turned around and faced us both as we approached his desk, "Then, the gloves are off."

He looked at Victor, "I want you to coordinate between the FBI and the other intelligence agencies and start gathering everything you can about this organization and the location of our people. Task whatever military resources you need to achieve that goal and make it a priority."

Victor nodded, "Yes, Mr. President."

The President turned back to face me. I couldn't have been happier over this turn of events; I'd turned a catastrophe into a very big hand up in replacing this buffoon. A few press releases and the sympathy of the American people would help elect me to this very room in two years' time.

The President put his hands on his desk and leaned over before asking, "Can you find them?"

I buried my thoughts and looked directly at the President of the United States before confidently answering, "Mr. President, I think I've figured out where they are."

###

Also by Neutralus

Dreamers' War – Dreamers Series Book 2

About the Author

You don't need to know about the author.

The story is what matters.

You should fall in love with the book, the story, the characters.

Who I am, should not matter.

That is exactly why I chose a *nom de plume* and a publisher that respects my right to privacy.

Other than the fact that I enjoy writing, here's what I'm willing to share since my publisher said I had to share five things.

1. I value my privacy highly!
2. I am married.
3. We have a rescue cat.
4. I was in the Navy.
5. I write but I still have a "day job."

Learn more online at:

www.authorneutralus.com